Invasive Species

I0667342

Author's Forward

I'd like to take a moment to frame this book and give the unwary reader an opportunity to know what they're getting in to. If you are already familiar with what this book contains, or you are of that special adventurous breed, feel free to skip forward to Chapter 1. If you have stumbled across this text and have no prior knowledge of what it contains, then please take a moment to read this forward. I'd rather you make an informed decision about reading (and paying for) this book than receive a slew of criticisms about how this story is "too weird for me." This book will be too weird for some people. That is OK.

This book is born out of my own personal desire. I have been frustrated in the past by the nature of the rarer fetishes. Namely, as fetishes get more unusual, and their audiences grow smaller, the average quality of material involving that fetish decreases. Of course, this is to be expected. Successful erotica producers know how to target the bigger audiences, and it's usually not worth their time to produce content for tiny fractions of their consumer base. This simple fact of nature and economics is, however inevitable, super frustrating.

So from that aggravation, I began writing a series of short stories with the intent of bringing a high-quality polished product to some of the lesser-represented fetishes. That isn't to say that there isn't already some great stuff out there that covers this same material. And that isn't to say that this is the single highest quality work. I won't claim that this is perfect, but I will contend that the average quality of erotica involving these fetishes has increased with the publication of this book. I don't pat myself on the back very often, but I have put a significant amount of work into this, and I hope it shows.

What exactly does this book contain? Of course, telling you what to expect involves spoiling it. So here is my official warning: the rest of this forward contains spoilers regarding the nature of the acts contained within this book. If you don't want to know, then skip forward to Chapter 1.

I have outlined the contents of each individual chapter in another section, titled, "Chapter Summaries." There is also a quick synopsis of each chapter, so that if you want to skip a section you may read the summary and dive right back in wherever you want. I will briefly explain in this forward the bulk of things that appear repeatedly and most notably throughout this book.

Probably the most significant thing to note is that this book contains primarily anthropomorphic characters. Yes, this is furry porn. The reason for this is two-fold: first, people who enjoy anthropomorphic erotica are generally more receptive to all of the other things found in this story, and second, furry characters are more interesting in this context. Particularly, it allows for bodies of all shapes and sizes. Characters in this book have equipment between their legs closely representative of their animal counterparts.

Tentacles, slime, and transformation are the most ubiquitous themes, and appear in nearly every chapter. In some cases these transformations take the form of two creatures merging in some way, and in other cases they involve one creature drastically changing shape. One of the more unique versions of this is known as "cock transformation," and is what it sounds like. One person is transformed into the penis of another person.

Fetishes along the lines of consumption appear in several chapters. These are generally referred to collectively as "vore," and come in many

4

different flavors. When one person eats another, it's referred to as "vore" or "oral vore;" when the consumption occurs phallically it's called "cock vore," anally it's "anal vore," and so on in every conceivable manner with the curious exception of vaginal vore which is generally referred to as "unbirth." Further, oral vore is typically split into "hard" and "soft" which is an indicator of whether or not blood and gore is involved. Most vore also addresses what happens to the recipient afterwards, whether it be a more traditional digestion or a non-lethal substitute. This book contains soft oral vore, cock vore, and unbirth. The vore results in "cum digestion," which is where the recipient is transformed into semen.

Hypnosis, mind-link, shared consciousness and other similar themes of unconscious control appear in nearly every chapter. This typically takes the form of the eponymous creature coercing other characters to do its bidding. For more thoughts on this subject in particular, see the "A Note on Consent" below. Additionally, different characters will at times "communicate" their physical sensations or desires to each other, typically through physical contact or after having been consumed in some manner.

The main character is transformed into a "hermaphrodite" a short way into the story. I put "hermaphrodite" in quotes because in reality she is transformed into the erotic idealization of hermaphroditism, which doesn't actually exist in the real world. But that's OK, because the other things in this book don't exist either. You may or may not be familiar with the terms "futa" or "futanari," which are different words for basically the same thing.

There are many instances of varying severities of penile urethral penetration in this book, also known as "sounding." These penetrations can range from something the size of a pencil to an entire person. This is a fetish that I particularly enjoy, so it makes an appearance at basically every opportunity.

Copious amounts of semen, pre cum, slime, drool and the like appear in numerous instances. This book is, in fact, quite wet. Along these same lines there are also many cases of swelling, bulging and inflation.

If I were to note the sexual preference of this book, I would have to say that there is none. Every character in this book is pan-sexual to the point of it being its own fetish. There are some scenes that you might characterize as "gay" or "straight," but only when you take that scene on its own. This story takes place in that special fantasy fetish land where literally everyone is turned on by literally everyone, and just about every combination of male/female/herm scene appears at one point or another.

That covers the vast majority of things that occur in this book that could potentially disturb an unwary reader. Additionally, there are a number of things that don't occur in this book. There is no scat, urine, vomit, blood or gore. There is also no death. Literally everyone in this book makes it out alive, even if I haven't specifically addressed their final fate by the conclusion.

A Note on Consent

There is one aspect of this book that I feel I must address in particular. Most of the acts in this book involve at least one person falling victim to some combination of hypnosis or chemical coercion which puts them in an unresisting state. I think there is a tendency in various erotica communities to dismiss these sorts of situations with labels such as "semi-willing." The fact of the matter is that a lot of the scenes in this book are not strictly consensual.

I would not be surprised if there are people who are fine with every aspect of this book except for that. If that is the one thing that you can't handle, I won't think less of you for it. It's something that I go back and forth on, myself. But I think it's much better to be aware of the nature of a book like this than to try to white-wash and dismiss this vital aspect of the story. With that in mind I think that we must call this book what it is: a rape fantasy.

However, in naming the beast we can now confront it. There is a lot of discussion in all parts of human discourse about rape fantasies, and there's probably little chance on me saying anything new on the subject here. I will simply say that I do not think that the mere existence of rape fantasies is innately bad. And even as I say that, I realize that that is still a somewhat controversial thing to say in some people's minds. But I think that most people hesitate to agree with that sentiment because we have a hard time separating "rape" from "rape fantasy."

Here is how I currently think about the issue. Rape, in the real world, is not a sex act. It is an act of violence. I am nowhere near the first person to say this. We, as humans, as walking sacks of hormones and insecurities, have the ability to incorporate acts of violence into our sexual fantasies. Let me re-iterate that: the violence is co-opted by the sex act, and in the process is no longer violence. We see this all the time in less drastic instances. Whips, floggers, knives, restraints, and the like are all successfully used in the bedroom in a healthy manner. The key to these situations is consent. If a person consents to be subjected to an act of violence, then that violence is subsumed into the sex act. Likewise, a person can consent to be subjected to the violence of rape, and that violence then becomes a part of the fantasy.

But of course, now you're asking where the consent is in this book. How can this be a rape fantasy if no one is consenting? Isn't that just rape? In fact, the person consenting to the rape fantasy is the reader. You, now having been informed about the true nature of this work, can decide from a position of power whether or not you would like to be subjected to it. If you decide to continue reading, then the violence of this story will be co-opted by the sex act that you perform on yourself. That's really what is happening when you read this. The act of reading erotica is a sex act performed on oneself, whether or not you actually touch yourself or bring yourself to orgasm. If you consent to perform this sex act on yourself, then nothing violent has actually happened.

This argument will not change the mind of a lot of people, and that's perfectly fine. If you aren't aroused by rape fantasies, then you shouldn't read them. Whether or not you are does not speak to your character. Most people are not turned on by literally everything. I just wish to explicitly state that it should be possible to defend the existence of rape fantasies without being interpreted as defending rape.

Also, if you have been subjected to sexual violence, please do not feel guilty if you enjoy rape fantasies. You are far from alone. Additionally, if you are burdened by something that you have experienced in the past, be it anything from sexual trauma to physical violence to food poisoning, please reach out to someone who cares about you. There are support groups for just about everything these days, and there's no reason for you to suffer in silence.

I realize that this is a bit more of an academic forward than you may have anticipated, but I honestly felt it necessary. With that out of the way, let's get to the porn.

Chapter summaries

These are all spoilers. If you don't want to read spoilers, skip to Chapter 1.

Chapter 1

Kett witnesses a strange occurrence at the local well. A small creature made entirely of dark slime overtakes three guards, merges two of them into a single transformed beast and drives it to take the third orally and anally. All three guards are then carried into the depths of the well.

M/M/M

Human, Canine

Knot, transformation, tentacles, shape-shifting, voyeurism, bound, double penetration, urethral penetration, public

Chapter 2

Kett returns to the well the next day, not entirely believing what she saw previously. While retrieving water, the creature strikes again, forcing a handful of citizens to merge and mate before pulling them into the well. The creature then talks to Kett and explains that it has been driven from its native lands deep underground, and needs to form a symbiotic relationship with many creatures in order to survive. It offers to transform Kett as part of this symbiotic relationship, so that she can retrieve more citizens, and she agrees.

M/M/M/F/F

Leopardess, Human, Lion, Fox, Canine

Knot, transformation, tentacles, public, double penetration, bound

Chapter 3

Kett is transformed by the creature, and is given some of the creature's ability to transform herself and others. Kett's new body has a penis in addition to everything she had before, as well as several tentacles. The creature helps Kett get acquainted with her new body by using the transformed guards, still trapped in the well. Given the task to seek out new symbiotes, Kett scouts the nearby area and finds her friend Alan, and lures him to a nearby rooftop. There, she uses her new equipment to take Alan anally, and in the process transforms him into her cock.

M/H

Fox, Husky

Multiple cocks, double penetration, tentacles, transformation, cock transformation, urethral insertion, knot

Chapter 4

Kett meets a mouse named Léo, who is a house servant for the noble house Hykan. She borrows him from his labor master, a croc named Carra, and takes him to Alan's house. There, she rides him, and then takes him into her transformed cock and melts him into her cum.

M/H

Fox, Mouse

Cock vore, cum digestion, massive cock, tentacles

Chapter 5

Kett returns to the well to deposit Alan and Léo. With the help of the creature, a transformed denizen of the well brings Kett to orgasm and re-forms Léo. The creature then forces Léo down onto Kett's oversized cock, until Kett orgasms out Alan as well. Alan is transformed and given tentacles similar to Kett. Then, Kett and Léo both penetrate Alan anally.

H/M, H/M/M

Fox, Husky, Mouse

Massive cock, transformation, tentacles, constriction, living cock-sleeve, double penetration, knot

Chapter 6

Léo informs Kett and Alan that the noble house Hykan is hosting an orgy in a few days. Kett decides that they should infiltrate the house so that they can crash the party. The creature implants a seed inside Léo, which has the side effect of giving him a tentacle cock, and Alan and Kett amuse themselves while they watch. After the seed is implanted, Léo and Alan both take Kett together.

H/M/M

Fox, Husky, Mouse

Transformation, tentacles, tentacle cock, urethral insertion, oviposition, double penetration, breath play, knot

Chapter 7

The trio break into the kitchens of the great house, where there is a small well. Léo takes his former labor master, Carra, and implants the seed within her. Alan and Kett keep watch and take a female antelope and male horse, respectively. Kett is transformed into the horse's cock, and the antelope is taken into the transformed manhood. The crocodile descends into the well.

M/F, H/M, M/M/F

Fox, Husky, Mouse, Crocodile, Horse, Antelope

Cock transformation, cock vore, cum digestion, oviposition, transformation, tentacles, urethral insertion, knot

12

Chapter 8

Kett remains in the body of Marshal, the horse, as his transformed cock. Ell, the antelope, is dissolved inside him. Kett forces Marshal into a state of constant arousal for a couple of days until the party comes around. The party begins, and marshal uses a pair of servants as a living sleeve for his transformed cock. Kett and Ell are orgasmed from the horse, and Ell is given a transformation similar to Alan's.

M/F/F

Horse, Rabbit, Cat

Massive cock, Living cock-sleeve, transformation, orgasm denial

Chapter 9

Léo is approached by a badger noblewoman and her twin otter servants. The three play with his tentacle cock before the badger rides him. Léo eats and drinks, finding that he can transform it into seed, and inflates the badger's belly with his cum.

Mouse, Badger, Otter

M/M/M/F

Tentacle cock, cum inflation, double penetration

Chapter 10

Alan approaches the master and mistress of the house, in the center of the room. Haxiten, the master, takes a mantis woman from behind. Drenirya, the mistress, and Zelia, their bodyguard, call Alan forward and the three climb up onto the mantis' back. Zelia shoves her pseudo-cock down Alan's throat, and Alan retaliates with his tentacles, penetrating her. Drenirya rides Alan and coaxes Zelia not to orgasm. Alan orgasms first, so Drenirya lets Zelia take Alan's throat to completion.

M/F/F

Husky, Hyena, Gecko, Leopard, Mantis

Psuedo-penis, feet, tentacles, denial, voyeurism, knot

Chapter 11

The massive transformed crocodile maw bursts up through the floor in the middle of the room, immediately taking the mantis down into its gullet. Drenirya, Zelia and Alan go into the mouth, and are pulled underground. Ell takes Haxiten, and with the creature's help he is forced inside her.

M/F

Leopard, Antelope

Unbirth, tentacles, transformation, bulge, oral vore, breath play, denial, tease, ruined orgasm, urethral penetration

Chapter 12

Léo eats the badger, with the help of the otter twins. Afterwards, they all descend into the crocodile maw.

F/M/M/M

Mouse, Badger, Otter

Oral vore, bulge, cum digestion

Chapter 13

Kett goes around the room and entertains herself. She finds two female servants suspended from the ceiling, and binds two male servants to them. Then, she forces a buck servant to transform his grizzly master into his cock. Kett then joins a blow-bang circle with a cat in the middle and encourages everyone with her tentacles, before bringing the buck over and forcing the cat onto the transformed cock. The buck orgasms and inflates the cat, and then Kett feeds the cat to the crocodile. Kett then rides a series of servants and nobles, feeding them to the crocodile as she sees fit. Afterwards, Kett descends into the maw herself.

M/M/F/F, H/M/M, F/H/M/M/M/M

Fox, Bear, Deer, Wolf, Dog, Cat, Human, Rabbit, Horse, Otter, Mouse, Panther

Bound, tentacles, transformation, cock transformation, double penetration, massive cock, cum inflation, urethral penetration, living cock-sleeve, knot, oral vore

Chapter 14

Underground, everyone pulled into the crocodile's mouth is deposited into an ooze-covered chamber. The cat is transformed into a massive cock, and deposits her load onto Drenirya and Zelia as they are enclosed in a pod of ooze. Ell is bound to the ground and filled by several tentacles, and then re-births Haxiten with Kett's help. Alan straddles the panther and he is dissolved into Alan, then Alan penetrates Marshal's cock and deposits the panther. The otters service Léo until he orgasms, covering the twins and dissolving them. When they reform, the badger has been transformed and given a penis in place of her vagina, while the otters have been given vice versa. The four of them have their way with each other. Haxiten has been transformed, given a vagina, and Kett makes use of it.

M/M, M/M/M, H/F, F/F, M/H/H/H, H/H

Husky, Mouse, Fox, Leopard, Antelope, Horse, Otter, Badger, Cat, Gecko, Hyena,

Transformation, tentacles, urethral insertion, cum digestion, rebirth, bound, bulge

Chapter 1

Solit Town used to be a perfectly normal town with perfectly normal people of perfectly normal varieties. Of course, nobody in particular viewed themselves to be "perfectly normal," but that was mainly because these perfectly normal people were perfectly normal in their disinclination to adventure further abroad than their distaste for strange accents permitted. Solit Town was named Solit Town of course back when it was most literally a town, sporting a perfectly normal population of only a couple hundred or so. Now, however, the perfectly normal town has grown at a perfectly normal pace and has become a perfectly normal city. The fact that this perfectly normal city disguises itself as a perfectly normal town is, in fact, perfectly normal.

Of course, nobody reads stories about perfectly normal people or perfectly normal cities, so by simple virtue of the fact that this narrative is being relayed to you it would be perfectly normal to assume that this perfectly normal city purporting to be a perfectly normal town reached a point where it was not, as the citizens might try to explain contrarily, perfectly normal. The aforementioned assumption, as you might have guessed, is entirely correct. However, simply stating that the city of Solit Town fell under a perfectly not-normal blight wherein a semi-sentient organism of dubious origin took up residence in the aquifer beneath a well somewhere between the center and the outskirts of town would be breaking some perfectly reasonable codes of narrative conveyance, so this story must take a slight, albeit brief, detour to center itself upon the focus of the story: a woman named Kett.

It must first be understood that Kett was, without a doubt, a perfectly normal fox person. It must also be understood that perfectly normal fox people are perfectly normal. In the city of Solit Town, it is perfectly normal to see perfectly normal fox people alongside perfectly normal dog people alongside perfectly normal badger people alongside otters alongside cats alongside perfectly normal people people. One might be inclined to expect to see all of the perfectly normal species and sub-species represented among the population of the city of Solit Town, and one would see what was expected in the vast majority of cases. A notable exception, of course, is the stark lack of perfectly normal dragon people, who not only do not exist as a matter of principle, but also stay away from towns and cities and people that can be described as "perfectly normal" because the intelligence inherent in dragon people informs them of how these places usually conclude their pitiful little existences. Aside from the low representation of the dragonkin demographic, however, most species and sub-species were present in relative abundance.

Kett walked on two legs and had two arms and two breasts and one vagina as one might expect, as she was indeed perfectly normal. She lived in a perfectly normal house made of wood planks covered in a natural sand-colored plaster that made a collection of houses look like a structure of rough stone had been pushed up from underneath the ground. Not many people particularly enjoyed the rather bland appearance of their housing developments, but the earthen walls kept the dwellings cool; it is important to remember that the city of Solit Town rests on an arid and desolate collection of hills, overshadowed on one side by some shallow mountains and overlooking a vast desert. The air was typically dry and the heat was typically high, therefore most citizens made frequent trips to one of the several nearby wells dug deep enough to tap into the vast aquifer beneath the city. Inhabitants of the city were usually equipped with large buckets or jars or jugs with which they brought water back to their dwelling, whereupon they stored it in a trough or underground cell for daily use. The trip to the well was a daily occurrence necessary for survival in the city of Solit Town, so it was particularly unusual for Kett to entirely forget to traverse the wide streets and, well after sundown, happen upon the realization that she had no water.

Not wanting to go the entire night without water, and being thirsty as she was, Kett decided to make the trip while the matter was still fresh in her mind. She walked briskly through the crisp desert air, detecting the faint scent of cactus blossoms on the breeze, and strolled into the small plaza featuring her local well. Upon approaching the clearing, she heard some terse whispers tossed out at the night. Male voices snapped at each other in confusion and Kett slid into the clearing to inspect the matter. Three city watchmen, a canine person and two humans, had gathered around the well, weapons drawn. While it was unclear what the focus of their attention was, Kett could tell from the posture and tone of the guards that there was some perceived hostility in the vicinity of the well.

Kett walked cautiously along the outside of the plaza and crouched behind a bench in order to inspect the cause of the confusion. She did not have to walk much further, however, before it was apparent that there was a small squirming object at the feet of the guards, wriggling and writhing against the masonry of the well.

"Should we kill it?" the guards asked themselves.

"What the hell is it?"

"Does it matter? It obviously has an air of malevolence."

"I'm not sure it has an air of anything other than grossness."

"Maybe you should ask its name."

"I think I'm good. Just stab it already and be done with it."

Before the guards could decide on a concrete course of action, however, the dark writhing mass shot a thin strand of itself toward the feet of one of the human guards. The substance was viscous and damp but had surprising strength, as the guard would attest upon seeing multiple tendrils lash out and fasten themselves to the shins and ankles of his chain-mail armor. He felt the metal constrict against his flesh and cried out with a hint of concern for his own wellbeing as the coiled strands of the creature thickened and gained a considerable hold on his lower legs.

The other two guards stood, slightly dumbfounded, "What should we do?"

"Get this thing off me!" was the predictable response. Slashing downward awkwardly, the constricted conscript attempted to free his legs from the tightening grasp. A slice at the strands of mucus-covered slime detached him from the main body of wriggling mass, but the coils around his legs simply coalesced and bound his shins in place. The squeezing of the tendrils proved too much, and the guard's feet were pulled together with considerable force.

The remaining chunk of the creature seemed unaffected by the attack and turned its attention to the other two guards. Several long writhing tentacles flung out in an arcing motion, landing on the shoulders and chests of the other two watchmen. The gooey substance quickly found its way into all of the intricate creases, cracks and crevices of their armor and gained a solid hold on their bodies. An intense pressure pulled at the two guards, encouraging their bodies to bend down toward the ground. They struggled valiantly, keeping their knees and legs stiff, but the creature fastened itself to their chest-plates and grew around their bodies, sending tendrils into the cracks of the well and into the ground, pulling down with an unexpectedly solid force.

Swiping, clawing, grasping, and ultimately failing to make any effective resistance against the pull of the creature, the two guards fell face-first into the hardened earth beside the well. The first guard, seeing their collapse, attempted to shuffle to their aid but instead lost what was left of his balance and fell onto his back. Constricting tentacles of viscous slime wound their way around the chests of the two guards attached to the creature, and the main body of the creature slid toward their heads. The canine guard could only struggle and watch as the slime met with his companion's skull and began to engulf it. Tendrils worked their way under their armor and could now be felt squirming between flesh and clothing. As the main body of the creature slid its slick surface slowly down the face of the human guard, a handful of small tentacles shot out and attached themselves to the head of the nearby canine guard. The creature wrapped thickening tentacles of slime around the human's entire head, pulling the two guards closer together. Soon both guards were both facing the center mass of the organism, and the ball of writhing slime worked to wrap itself around both of their heads.

The guards felt the cool wet ooze slide across their faces and upper neck and cover their airways. However, instead of suffocating and struggling against the mass of slime, the two guards experienced a growing euphoria not entirely dissimilar to painkilling medicine. They slowly realized that they were face to face within the body of the blob, but they didn't find any incredibly compelling reason to care. The creature tightened its grip against their heads and squeezed their faces together as the appendages attached to their chests and torsos, growing and working their way over their muscled flesh.

The first human soldier, who had fallen onto his back, would have been watching this process in abject horror, but he was having issues of his own. While he was in fact detached from the main body of the creature, the severed slime still managed to give him quite a bit of trouble. The tendrils seemed to grow and twist their way up his calves, always making sure to keep his legs firmly locked together and immobile until the mass of slime rested squarely over his pelvis. He sat up and attempted to claw at the substance and remove it from his person, but the goo stiffened and held tight against his armor, fastened all the way around his hips. Fruitlessly the guard struggled while the ooze seeped in through the cracks in his armor, seeking bare flesh and finding it relatively quickly. The dark slime writhed and contorted; the soldier felt a wave of relaxation course through his body as the cool substance embraced the bare hips beneath his armor. He had to stop and catch his breath as the goo found its way through the cracks, and soon much of it disappeared from sight, squeezing against his toned muscles and running along his inner thighs, unimpeded by clothing and chain.

Meanwhile, the other two guards felt a similar wave of pleasure emanating from their chests and heads as the creature pulled their entire bodies together. Their struggles lessened as the waves of euphoria grew in intensity and their heads swam in pleasure. The consciousness of the two guards began to blur and fade in a heavy haze as their skulls softened and slowly gave in to the pressure of the slime squeezing from all directions. Their faces pressed against each other in a tight embrace, bending and deforming into each other, melding together like they were themselves made of the pliable goo that gripped them. The bodies of the two guards passed into each other, the slime constricting tighter and tighter to make the two bodies function as one. As the consciousness of the guards faded into a deep pleasure, their bodies were pulled together, armor and all, across the hardened ground into the creature's enveloping embrace.

The first soldier was not faring much better as the slime found its way to the front of his hips. Slowly the slime squeezed from all directions and expanded, putting stress on the buckles and snaps that kept the guard's armor on. With a gasp and a moan the guard's belt unsnapped and fell to the ground, revealing the flimsy clothing underneath. The ooze writhed and shredded the garments, exposing the soldier's hips to the night air. Slowly and intentionally, the slime squeezed his pelvis and rear as it closed in around the base of his stiffening cock. Already succumbing to the increasing pleasure of the creature's enchanting touch, the guard moaned aloud as the substance tightened around his rod, holding it upright, sliding slowly, excruciatingly slowly, up the shaft of his cock as it stiffened and elongated until finally he arched his back in pleasure and the cool wet slime enveloped his entire penis. A firm tendril wrapped underneath his scrotum and stiffened, holding his balls tight in their place as the ooze writhed up and down along his shaft. The guard's breath staggered as another wave of delicious pleasure washed through his entire body and the slime slid a thin tendril down into the tight hole atop his throbbing cock.

Minds swimming in semi-conscious pleasure, the two conjoined guards felt their bodies melt as the creature pressed their heads and chests together. Warmth pulsing through their core, armor and clothing falling to the ground, the two men felt only each other's mind, lust and desire filling their shared thoughts. Their vision faded while the creature pulled their bodies close, gripping their hips and legs, pressing tight against their flesh until the dividing line between their muscles disappeared. The slime receded from their merged head and legs and instead pooled around their chest, revealing a single, large, humanoid figure. The two guards fused to create a tall, muscular creature covered in a dark fur. The beast was nearly eight feet tall, immensely muscular, and had an elongated wolf-like snout on his fur-covered head, strips and patches of the dark goo pulsing and coursing over his taut body. This new creature drooled and panted in constant pleasure and desire, hunched over with long arms dragging along the ground. Two large throbbing cocks protruded from the creature's pelvis, the upper appearing to be that of a canine, the lower more human. The beast was driven entirely be pleasure, trembling and breathing heavily as it stared at the human guard writhing and moaning on the ground.

The creature shambled toward the figure of the guard, cocks erect and drooling, long spindles of clear fluid running down their shafts and dripping off their heavy ball sacks. As the guard on the ground felt wave after wave of euphoric pleasure course through his veins, he hardly noticed as this new creation approached and reached out with a long muscular arm and gripped the top of his head with a gigantic clawed hand. The guard moaned in surprise, but his brain was swimming in the deepest waters of pleasure, hardly reacting when the creature forced the human's open and panting mouth onto the throbbing dog cock.

Holding the guard's head down against his hip, the creature howled in gratuitous pleasure as he pushed his hips forward, his human cock dripping freely below the guard's chin. As the guard felt the hot flesh inside his mouth throb and pulse, the ooze embracing his own member only hardened its grip and thickened the tendril that had shot down inside his shaft. He felt the tentacle widen and stretch his cock from the inside, running down to the base and into his body where it expanded and pushed further. The human's body hung from the creature's grip, half-limp in mad pleasure, hardly noticing as the creature rocked his hips forward and back, moaning as the guard's lips slid over the hot flesh and back again.

The guard felt the ooze around his ass squirm and shift, but before he could register a change the creature pulled his head free of the hard dog shaft and grabbed him by the neck with long sinewy fingers. Dragging the guard by the neck and throwing him against the side of the well, the creature grabbed his ass and pushed his stomach against the stone lip, pulling his hindquarters into the air. As the ooze around the guard's cock continued to squeeze and massage him into submission, the creature behind him grabbed the upper canine cock and pushed it against the guard's asshole. The slickness of the creature's drooling pre-cum covered the guard's tight entrance; the creature slammed his throbbing red meat into the guard in one single motion, instantly sliding the slowly-swelling knot in past the guard's asshole.

Screaming incoherently in pleasure and pain, the guard struggled to breathe as he felt the hot thick cock penetrate him. The creature's lower cock rubbed up against the underside of the human's hard shaft, and the dark slime stuck to his pelvis crept down to envelope the beast's thick rod as well, squeezing the two rods together. The creature grabbed the guard's hips roughly and fucked his ass with a baying howl and the sound of wet slapping flesh. The knot slid in and out, stretching the guard's hole as the bulb expanded to more than twice the thickness of the red cock shaft. Collapsing against the edge of the well and panting heavily as his ass was filled again and again, the guard gasped as he felt the ooze continue to stretch the inside of his cock until it burned and stung. The ooze squeezed the creature's lower cock against the human's so that as the creature fucked his ass, his lower cock slid up and down along the underside the human's. Enthralled by the pleasurable effects of the ooze, the human couldn't feel any one particular sexual feeling. Instead, his entire being was consumed with the unceasing and all-encompassing pleasure of the slime's embrace.

The pair of human cocks ground against each other as the ooze pulled them together, tighter and tighter until the hard flesh softened and the dividing line between their shafts disappeared. Ramming his dog cock in to the hilt as the knot swelled to its full thickness, the creature raked his claws against the guard's hips as their human members fused along their entire length. With a dull throb throughout his entire body the guard could feel the desire and lust pouring from the beast. Nerves and blood vessels and flesh combined and both the guard and the creature flexed and clenched their cocks as waves of pleasure ran through their hot veins. The ooze clung to their shafts and stretched up over the slowly merging tip and formed a semi-transparent bubble. Soon, both the creature and the guard howled in the pleasure of combined release, pumping thick hot cum from their throbbing cocks. Their members merged and grew together, creating a massive cock nearly a foot long as cum coursed from their two separate holes simultaneously. The two jets of cum squirted into the semi-transparent bubble formed by the goo, slowly inflating the little pouch with their combined seed until the ooze stretched thin and bobbed heavily from the tip of their shaft. Both the creature and the guard clenched and moaned loudly, more cum shooting into the guard's ass, until they both relaxed slightly and their movement came to a near standstill, their merging complete.

Then, as quickly as the entire scene began, oozing tendrils sprang out from the transformed creature and lifted the pile of trembling pleasure up and over the side of the well. The whole mass of flesh and slime tumbled over the stony lip, and Kett heard only a distant splash a moment later.

Chapter 2

Kett stumbled back to her house in a daze, blinking heavily and rubbing her eyes. She assumed that the heat of the day had gotten to her, and that the episode she witnessed must have been a hallucination. But the next day, curiosity got the better of her, and she decided to return to the well and inspect the area for any sign of the previous night's struggle. She ventured back out to the nearby well, water jar in hand, in the midday sun. The plaza was bustling with the normal activities of the local populous, so it was rather hard to discretely determine if her memory served correctly, but she did manage to casually approach the well like she would on any other day. There was a short line of people waiting for access to the water source, so Kett simply stood in line and looked around the plaza. Nobody seemed distraught; nobody was talking about anything particularly scandalous; no guards or officials could be seen. Soon she was at the well, and Kett took the opportunity to cautiously peer over the stone ledge into the dark abyss. Nothing seemed out of the ordinary. It must have all been a dream. A hallucination.

But as Kett lowered the bucket to retrieve her water, the leopard woman in line behind her shrieked in horror. Something wet and slimy had grasped her ankle, she claimed, but as everyone looked around the culprit was nowhere to be found. Kett looked closely at the ground, fearing the worst, but only found some strange trails and disturbances left in the sandy dust on the baked earth. Turning around to face the well Kett looked closely at the masonry, but the cracks between the stones were too dark to see into. Cautiously, she continued to lower the bucket toward the bottom of the well until she heard the familiar splash and the rope went slack. Slowly turning the crank and looking around the plaza with a suspicious eye, Kett drew the bucket up until it had reached the top. She swept her eyes around the full perimeter once more, checking for any irregularities before turning toward the bucket.

Before Kett could begin pouring the water into her clay jar, a dark blur rushed past her face and toward the leopard behind her. Shrieks and yells filled the air as a mass of black slime clutched to the woman's face, and Kett snapped her gaze back to see the tendrils wrap around the back of the leopard's head. The woman struggled and stumbled, tearing at her face to remove the unwelcome organism, but to no avail. As the populous of the plaza witnessed the creature constricting and covering the woman's head, yells of terror filled the air and all but a few fled the scene. Those few who remained stood around the leopard, yelling at each other and her in order to plan a rescue attempt. The ooze soon covered the leopard's entire head, and little tendrils crawled down her neck and over her back, chest and shoulders, underneath her clothing.

Meanwhile, Kett stood in shock by the well, clutching to the bucket and watching in disbelief as the previous night's events replayed in her mind. Either her hallucinations were incredibly consistent, or there was something foreign living at the bottom of the well. But even as Kett knew what was going to happen to the women and the handful of would-be rescuers, she could not find the courage to so much as move from her position. Frozen in awe and horror, Kett watched as a large male lion grabbed the ooze on the back of the leopard's head and pulled, only to find his hand stuck to the growing mass.

The ooze crawled up the lion's arm and across his chest as it continued to seep down the leopard's torso. A white-furred canine grabbed onto the lion's chest and a fox grabbed onto the leopard's chest in an attempt to separate the pair, but soon all four were stuck together by the hungering creature. The final would-be savior, a small human female, attempted to back away from the amalgamate but a thick tentacle shot out and wrapped around her ankle, pulling her to the ground and dragging her toward the handful of struggling, yelling, quivering people.

Soon their screams died down, and Kett realized that they must be feeling the same kind of pleasure she saw the guards experience the previous night. The ooze pulled the five creatures together and covered their bodies, crawling under their clothing and clutching their flesh. Their struggling slowed and their clothing fell off, piece by piece, shredded by the writhing motions of the strong tendrils of slime. The male lion found himself pulled up close behind the female leopard, his chest pressed firmly against her back, and the male fox was pulled against her front, chest to chest. The ooze slid cool tentacles down over their midsections, over their thighs, and around the two males' ball sacks, squeezing firmly until their cocks slid slowly out of their sheaths. The tendrils constricted and pulled, guiding the two cocks into the leopard's asshole and pussy, the three moaning loudly as they joined. The male canine behind the lion was likewise drawn in, and his throbbing red cock slid up and stiffened while the black tendrils guided it to the lion's tailhole, plunging it deep inside in a single swift motion.

The human woman lay on the ground, several tentacles wriggling over her body. While the slime held her torso tight, oozy tendrils found their way to the woman's holes, sliding slowly into her tight pussy and asshole. She moaned loudly as she let the moisture of the tentacles cool her skin in the hot noon sun, feeling the thickness of the ooze stiffen inside her and pulse rhythmically, pressing firm against her clit as she gyrated her hips against the creature's grasp. Slowly, the tentacles thickened and dragged her along the ground, closer to the mound of moaning and gasping. The human female was drawn upright and pressed against the enraptured leopard, the two entangling themselves in a passionate embrace, the leopard's breath hot and raspy as she clenched and quivered on the fox and lion cocks buried inside her. As the human female dug her fingers into the back fur of the leopard, her fingertips pushed into the pliable skin and penetrated the leopard's flesh. The cool and inviting ooze drew the human to push in further, burying her hands and arms into the leopard's back, clinging close as they kissed.

As the two women embraced, the tentacles forced the fox to pull his throbbing and twitching cock from the leopard. He could only pant and watch in clouded ecstasy as the two women kissed so hard that their heads melded together, their tongues dancing against each other's before their lips fused and sealed their moans behind skin and flesh. The tentacles drew their hips together, encouraging the human and leopard to press against each other in their heated embrace. Their hips ground, tighter and tighter, until their pelvises merged and their clits squeezed against each other and they became a single unified body of flesh.

Once the two women were conjoined, the tendrils around the fox yanked and plunged his twitching cock deep into the human's yearning ass, immediately hilting himself and sliding his pulsing knot into her tight hole. The fox and the lion moaned as they felt each other's cocks through the merged bodies, sliding through the hot flesh with a quickening rhythm, but the lion soon grunted as the canine's knot was pulled roughly from his ass by strong slime. The canine was dragged down to his back and along the ground until he was beneath the merged women, their pussies merged to create a single tight passage. Moaning as a tentacle grabbed him by the hips, the canine could only watch as he was lifted up and his cock guided into the dripping pussy, sliding in between the two throbbing cocks crammed into the merged women's asses, finally arching his back and pushing his knot into the searing-hot flesh and forcing a loud moan from the two women. The fox and the lion groaned loudly as the dog knot pressed against their own cocks, squeezing their throbbing members inside the women's tight holes.

Kett watched as the conjoined victims ground their hips against one another, moaning loudly into the midday sun. The ooze covered their bodies until the entire ensemble was a single jet-black mass of moaning and fucking. Each of the men and women bucked their hips against each other, the three stiff cocks pulsing and throbbing as they slammed into the conjoined women's holes. Forced into a wild frenzy by the delirious touch of the slime, the hapless citizens moaned and cried out, bodies tensing against the creature's strong grip. In a single moment the three men groaned and flexed their muscles, burying themselves in the tight flesh as they came, hot seed pumping into the merged holes. The women moaned against each other's transformed faces, rocking their hips forward and back against the three stiff members hilted inside their bodies, squeezing their holes against the hard shafts as the merged pair orgasmed together with the men trapped in the creature's embrace.

All five citizens remained attached and buried within each other as several long dark tentacles spread out from their feet, sliding along the ground so that the entire mass crept toward the well. Kett could only stare as they moaned at each other, and the tendrils guided their bodies up and over the side of the well before crawling slowly down the stone walls toward the bottom.

Soon the plaza was silent and empty except for Kett, who stood frozen in the same position, holding tightly to the water-filled bucket. She could hear moaning in the depths below her. The fox looked down into the abyss, but was suddenly greeted by the face of the human female who had just been dragged into the well. The woman was returned to her former state, un-merged from the leopard, as if the entire scene beforehand never even happened. She was supported by a single thick tentacle, dark ooze covering most of her body except her chest and face which were crossed with several dark lines of slime embedded into her skin. The woman opened her mouth, and a voice followed, but the voice did not belong to the woman, and her mouth did not move in accordance to what she was saying. The voice was loud and booming, and pronounced each word heavily and distinctly, as if they were not its own.

"You are not afraid."

Kett looked around behind her. "What the hell—."

"Maybe you are a little afraid."

Eyes wide, "I'd say so, yeah."

"You are not as afraid as the others."

"What's going on?"

"You are just the right amount of afraid."

"Alright, I get it, what the hell are you?"

The creature made the woman reach out her hand toward Kett, "Touch me and all will be known."

"I'm—not—so—sure."

"Take my hand and we will commune and I will make known to you from where I have come."

"Commune? Is that what that was?"

"Take my hand and we—."

"Fine! Fine, sheesh." Kett reached out and paused, then slowly touched her fingertip to the ooze covering the woman's hand.

Her eyed dilated. She felt a consciousness inside her, something probing her thoughts, wrapping soft tendrils around the edges of her mind. There were no words, only ideas. Ideals. In a single instant she simply knew that the ooze, the black mass at the bottom of the well, was a creature born deep within the hidden reaches of the planet. It was a rare breed of symbiote who could only survive and grow by absorbing other life forms. Specifically, the organism had a great need for the particular mix of nutrients and chemicals produced during the act of lovemaking. The creature had captured the guards from the night before, and the more recent citizens, and melded them into its own body. This melding process was unique in that it created a permanent physical and psychological bond between the two parties but also preserved a modicum of individuality on the part of the host. The ooze creature provided the many hosts with unending pleasure, both physical and mental, and the creature frequently stimulated the hosts into orgasm so that it may survive.

This particular creature had found its way to the surface from the bottom of the well, fleeing the changing world underneath and fearing for its safety in the realm it came from. Kett was filled with a sense of benevolence as the creature probed her mind. She knew that it desired to survive here, and in order to do that it must, in part, protect the welfare of the people nearby. But at the same time, it must also consume a fair amount of people in order to grow and survive. Willing additions to the symbiotic family, as it was called, were far more beneficial than unwilling prisoners, as the willful would find themselves more aroused and could give more of the fluids the creature needed.

As the creature was mostly unable to move from the area around the well, and could only catch new hosts on its own if they ventured very close, the creature needed an outside agent to bring in new members. Kett could see that the creature intended for her to be that outside agent.

Her head swam as the creature poured knowledge into her mind, and she lost her vision and sense of time. She felt alone in a non-space, floating amid nothingness, but feeling an immense pleasure. She knew she was under the effects of the creature, but it showed her how it was able to transform flesh at will, and how she would be given the same ability. It showed her how she would be transformed, and she liked what she saw. She didn't have a chance to disagree, nor did she particularly want to.

Some of her vision returned and she could see the human girl in front of her again. Kett stepped up onto the side of the well and into the woman's arms, and felt an instant rush of pleasure as the ooze of the creature touched her body. The human woman embraced her, and turned her so that Kett's back was pressed against the woman's smooth chest. Her clothes were torn off and the ooze crawled up her feet and ankles, spreading them at a wide angle. The ooze took a hold of her wrists and bound them to the wrists of the woman, pulling them both out straight. Kett's vision darkened again, and she felt herself consumed by an all-encompasing pleasure as tendrils crawled from the human woman's chest, around Kett's sides and over her torso, thin lines wrapping up under her firm breasts and squeezing, then curving around over the top to just barely touch her nipples. More tendrils crawled up her neck and over her face, and even more spun up her shins and thighs.

She began to drift in and out of consciousness as she felt a thick tentacle slide up between her legs. It was slick and hard, and pushed slowly at her tight tailhole. It slid in slowly, filling her as she had only felt a few times before, and numbing the area as it crawled deeper inside her. Then, beneath her, an offshoot of the slime grew forward, another tendril rubbing up over her wet pussy lips. It hardened and pressed firmly against her clit, sliding down over her pussy until it found her wet entrance and pushed up inside her. She inhaled deeply as it filled her, feeling it press inside her against the tendril in her ass. The two tentacles only slid in, further and further, until she thought she was as full as she could ever be, and then they only continued sliding into her wanting body.

Again the slime beneath her grew forward, another appendage reaching up over her clit, pressing firmly against her pelvis. The thick tentacle slid up her belly until it reached her bellybutton, and then separated from her torso, attached only at her clit. This ooze grew in thickness and hardened until it was a stiff rod standing almost straight up from her pelvis, massaging her clit underneath with powerful waves of pleasure. The tentacle throbbed and pulsed, digging into the flesh above her clit, molding it. Suddenly Kett felt as if the tentacle was a part of her body, and she could feel her pulse racing inside of it. She tensed every muscle in her body, clenching and arching her back as the ooze grew veins and contours down the sides. Kett could feel a burning inside her pelvis and bucked against the tentacles buried deep inside her ass and pussy, yearning for release but unable to reach a final climax. She twitched her whole body involuntarily, clenching muscles in her pelvis she didn't know she had, squeezing and finally screaming in pleasure as a single powerful wave ripped through her entire body, her back arching as a channel shot through the center of the tentacle above her pelvis and a thick jet of cum pulsed out. Kett could only look down in amazement as the tentacle twitched and spasmed, sending hot cum high into the air. Her vision faded as her blood pulsed in her head, body clenching from head to toe. Soon the ooze wrapped around her entire body, pulling her down into the depths of the well in order to complete her transformation.

Chapter 3

Kett's eyes parted slowly among subdued moans and gasps. Her head still swimming in euphoria, she slowly realized that she was engulfed in a warm darkness. Flesh pulsing with a dozen heartbeats, Kett attempted to move her body but found herself constricted, bound in the fetal position within a thin but tough membrane. A voice, that newly familiar voice, informed her that her transformation was nearly complete, and that she should not struggle. And Kett knew, subconsciously or not, that she need not worry. The membrane opened near her head, and slid down her face and body. Several strong tentacles supported her weight, and her eyes adjusted to the darkness.

She was at the bottom of the well, held just above the surface of the water. As she gazed upon her surroundings, she realized that the handful of guards and citizens pulled down into the depths lined the rough stone walls, hanging from the slime in various positions. She noticed that the creature from the deep had made a few new additions to its collection, a full dozen people now bound within the lower reaches of the well, grinding and gyrating against grasping tendrils. The pinprick of light, far above, was nearly blotted out by the dense web of tentacles.

Her gaze then fell to her own body. Kett's vision in the dark seemed improved, but she still had a hard time discerning exactly what she had become. Running her fingertips over her chest she felt her familiar fur, soft and well-kept, but with the addition of centimeter-thin strands of dense slime embedded into her skin, pulled taut over her chest and extremities, perfectly symmetrical, outlining her existing curves. Her hands found her way to her breasts, which had grown slightly, but not overly so, and then her neck, muscular and thin, with fixed tendons of the black ooze running up her face.

Feeling down, over her tight stomach, her hands trembled as she searched for her new appendage. Quivering and rigid, her cock felt hot and alien. It resembled a male fox's manhood, red and tender, complete with a thick bulb at the base, but with the addition of a pair of black tendrils running down the sides, fixed to the yearning flesh. She ran her paw down the length, feeling every inch of her new meat, squeezing hard and clenching her ass cheeks as the intensity of the pleasure surprised her. Sliding her opposite paw down below the base of her cock, Kett felt the familiar twinge of excitement as her finger brushed against her clit. Fingers inching downward, parting her tender lips, the fox pushed a finger into the dripping wetness between her legs. Sudden waves of pleasure coursing through her body caused her to grip her thick cock even harder, squeezing and rubbing her palm over the swelled knot and shaft.

The tentacles supporting her body shifted, and she felt the approval of the creature. It desired to know which, of the captured souls bound to it, she wanted to stimulate her. Head ablaze with passion, her memory flashed back to the first night she saw the creature, and remembered what had happened to the three guards. Immediately her thoughts shot to that gigantic red dog cock, and the long human cock beneath it. No sooner thought than done, the creature lifted her to the wall where the amalgamated creature was suspended. Fixed tight against the wall in a web of dark slime, the creature hung in its final form, merged with the third guard. As Kett watched, the creature squirmed and rustled as the abdomen of the transformed beast shifted. The dog cock, still embedded deep inside the human guard, pressed through the skin and ooze until it was exposed to the cool damp air of the well. Flesh shifting and melding,

Kett found herself staring at the massive dog shaft, twitching expectantly above the large human cock.

Letting the strong grip of the creature turn her around in the cool air, Kett pressed herself against what was left of the guard's chest, feeling the warmth of the two thick rods between her legs. She reached down and stroked the thick dog cock against her own, covering her paw and throbbing flesh with thick pre cum. Moans and grunts filled the echoing well as she bent and guided the tapered tip of the dog cock to her tailhole, pushing back against it, and feeling it slide, slowly, filling her ass with a throbbing heat. She forced herself down until she felt the knot against her clenched asshole, and slid back up, grabbing the human member and positioning it against her wet pussy entrance.

As she pushed back down to engulf the twin shafts, the creature behind her lurched forward and grabbed Kett with four hands, two grabbing her breasts and squeezing while the other two grabbing her cock. Kett clenched and moaned in pleasure, arching her back and pressing her hips down against the guard's, hilting the two massive rods inside her as strong fingers and claws gripped her flesh. A hand grasping her cock slid down below her knot, squeezing the base of her red flesh and pushing her forward, then pulling back, sliding Kett's hips up and down the twin shafts as the other hand stroked the hot length of her own member. Her eyes rolled back and her long muzzle lay open and panting, her head slack against her shoulder as the creature's grip dragged her up and down the length of the two cocks, feeling her flesh kneaded and groped by vice-like fingers, and soon she felt the pressure of climax build up inside her.

Kett's vision faded in passion and pleasure as her body shot thick streams of cum from her throbbing cock, and her pussy and ass clenched against the fullness of the flesh inside her, twitching and pulsing until the guard groaned and climaxed as well, filling her holes with a heat that ran deep into her core. The creature gripped Kett and pulled her down roughly, slamming her against the swollen canine knot and forcing her tailhole wide, pressing relentlessly until the thick bulb of flesh popped into the fox's clenching hole. She shook and groaned, feeling the fluids as they were absorbed into her body, filling her with energy and passion. The cum shot deep inside her and coursed through her veins, flowing through her body, and then in turn shot back out through her own cock, thick and hot, into the depths of the well.

As the pulsing waves of pleasure subsided, the grip of strong tentacles wound around the fox's body and pulled her from the transformed beast's embrace. Once her vision returned and the heat faded from her face, Kett found herself rising slowly up the height of the well. Gentle tentacles pushed her body up to the surface, the pinprick of light growing until her eyes squinted in the afternoon sun. The voice communicated that Kett must now begin her work, and bring back as much of the life-giving nutrients as she could.

Her paws spreading under her weight as she was left alone on the surface, Kett inspected her body in greater detail. Her fur had darkened, ever so slightly, from the warmth of burning kerosene to the color of clouded, ancient amber. She also found a set of fleshy nubs hidden beneath her fur, just above her tail, and two similar nubs on the underside of each wrist. After concentrating on them for a moment, Kett found that they were actually tentacles of her own, fully retracted into her flesh, but capable of growing at a moment's notice into fully-prehensile tendrils of slick ooze.

Kett searched the well's plaza for signs of life, but found only the hot wind. It appeared to Kett's keen mind that the city of Solit Town had declared this particular plaza off-limits to the normal citizenry, as the wells were typically crowded at this point in the day. This was, of course, entirely predictable, and was in fact anticipated by the creature lurking deep in the well. So Kett, still feeling somewhat timid in her new role, decided it was in her best interests to venture beyond the simple plaza, and mingle amongst her neighbors as casually as she could.

Of course, this would only be made more difficult by the fact that she was entirely naked.

But Kett was determined to follow through with her mission. She knew the entire city couldn't be evacuated; it was merely a matter of finding the activity. Kett clambered up to the rooftops of the simple earthen huts and crawled on all fours from roof to roof, peering cautiously over the edge until she approached another plaza. Sure enough, the streets were as active as ever, filled with the millings and socializings customary for city-dwellers. Kett held close to the edge of the roof, gazing onto the crowd, searching without knowing quite what to search for.

As luck would have it, a familiar acquaintance of Kett's passed by not far from her perch. A lean male black and white husky, with muscular limbs and a taut body, strode through the open square. Kett had always looked upon the canine with that faint but ever-present feeling of desire, yet had never actually pursued anything more serious than platonic interaction. The two were friendly enough, and both seemed in a perpetual state of solitude, but the presence of some unspoken and unexplored distance reinforced any barriers constructed through their years of friendship.

However, even as Kett rolled these thoughts through her mind, she looked upon the husky in a new light. She felt herself moisten at the sight of his familiar face, and she noticed the presence of a deep yearning within her core. A hunger that she knew could only be satiated by him.

There was still, of course, the problem of her nudity, and her desire to keep suspicions low. So, instead of running out into the plaza, Kett raised her head over the side of the roof and shouted his name.

"Alan!"

No response.

"Alan! Alan!"

He paused, and an ear quirked in her direction.

"Alan!"

Turning his head toward her, but looking through the crowd at eye-level, Alan failed to spot her. Kett raised her hand above her head and waved quickly, dropping back down before she drew any unwanted attention, and Alan finally noticed the vulpine face atop the building. He squinted curiously, wondering what would possess his friend to be on a roof in the first place, but as she seemed to be calling him over, he decided to approach her and inquire directly.

Finding a ladder in the nearby alley, Alan hoisted himself to the roof only to find Kett hiding behind a conveniently placed barrel.

"What on earth are you doing up here?" His voice carried equal parts amusement and concern.

Kett did her best to hide her naked body from his curious eyes. "I seem to be in a bit of a spot. I need some clothes."

Alan raised an eyebrow. "What's all this about? Don't you have clothes at your place?"

"I can't get back to my place."

A pause. "Ohhh. You're over by the quarantine? I completely forgot you were so close to all that. Are you ok?" Alan attempted an approach to see if Kett was injured, or in need of assistance, but she simply strafed around the barrel to avoid his gaze.

"I'm fine! I'm fine. Can we go to your place? I just need some clothes."

"Are you sure? What happened to your clothes? Does this have anything to do with whatever's going on over there?"

"Um. Kind of?"

"You're acting so strange. Are you sure you're ok?" Alan drew closer, this time hopping around to catch a glimpse of Kett's body, only catching a brief glance of her naked side. "You look...different. What's that in your fur?"

Kett blushed, and knew it would be nearly impossible to get anywhere without Alan seeing her new form, but she feared his reaction. Her transformation was, after all, relatively severe, and she was afraid of the shock it might induce in someone who had known her for many years. But even as she thought this over, Alan drew close again, this time slower, until he was standing over her crouching form, a look of tenderness entering his eyes. "What's happened to you..."

Alan reached out to help Kett up, and she took his hand without a second thought. She stood slowly, and Alan looked into her eyes, gazing at the subtle changes in her face before his expression glazed slightly. He felt a rush of warmth flow through his body from his hand, and his head felt a little lighter. Kett looked back into Alan's eyes and started to realize that her touch had the same effect on people as the goo itself. She hesitated for a brief moment, wondering if she should leave her friend alone, but then the husky brought his other paw up to clasp over her own, and she felt her own rush of lightness. The two drew together atop the roof, staring into each other's hazy eyes, simply wondering why they hadn't spent more time in such close proximity.

Kett's chest pressed against his, her breasts warm against his clothed torso. Soon Kett's malehood responded to the soft touch of Alan's pants, and emerged slowly from her sheath. Alan brought a paw down to Kett's hips and pulled her firmly against him, and he couldn't help but notice her stiffening cock between their bodies—and she couldn't help but notice his. In the back of Alan's mind he knew this was strange. In fact, he had seen Kett naked a few times before, if only in adolescence, and remembered clearly her lack of this particular anatomy. But the back of Alan's mind grew smaller and smaller as soothing waves washed over his brain, and he simply brought his hand down to grasp the base of Kett's thickening shaft.

Embracing each other, the two parted their lips and panted slightly, Kett's hot breath breaking over Alan's hard chest as he looked down at her. She brought her paw down and pressed her palm against the throbbing bulge in his pants, grinding up and down slightly to elicit gentle moans. Alan wrapped his paw around Kett's cock and ran it slowly up toward the tip, awash in a sea of confusion and pleasure. Kett moaned and undid Alan's belt, quickly letting his pants fall to his feet and revealing his pulsing red cock, a thin strand of pre cum already running down the length.

Alan breathed heavily, "What was it you wanted again?"

Kett traced her hand up his chest, grabbing his cloth shirt and ripping it off in a single swift motion, letting her paw press against his soft chest fur. "You." Their muzzles embraced with the ferocity that comes only with wanting a physical union for several years. Their hands pressed against each other, his grasping her breasts, hers clutching his cock as their panting and moaning filled their ears.

A devilish grin crept across Kett's panting maw, and she grew curious as to the functionality of her new tentacle appendages. Flexing unused muscles, Kett forced the two tentacles out from the wrist that clutched tight to Alan's dripping cock. The feeling was unusual to her, but her mind hardly registered the oddity as the prehensile ooze wrapped around Alan's swollen member. He gasped at the new sensation, curious as to its nature but too enraptured by the pleasure to investigate. Kett knew she was pushing all the right buttons, and the ooze wound up the length of Alan's cock until a single thin strand remained poised at the tender hole atop the pulsing meat.

Kett broke the kiss and bit down on Alan's shoulder as the ooze pushed down on Alan's cockhole, sending a thin strand of cool, moist ooze down through the core of his shaft. Alan gasped and his eyes blurred, pleasure and warmth flowing freely from his groin as the tendril bored down through the length of his cock, reaching the base and thickening slowly. He felt his rod swell and stretch from the inside, pulsing and throbbing as the ooze's touch warmed his mind to a soft mush. Alan's maw lay open and panting, unable to form anything close to a coherent thought, when Kett let the small tentacle separate from her wrist and wrap down the length of Alan's cock as it pushed deeper inside.

As Kett's cock grew and twitched, she grabbed Alan's fur and spun him around roughly, showing a strength that neither knew she had. She pressed the husky down against the barrel, bending him over at the waist and holding him by the hips. Bringing her own hips against his, she let her hot swollen member rest between Alan's toned ass cheeks. Alan's only response was a rough pant as he ground his ass against her, already burning with desire.

Kett grabbed her member with one hand and carefully guided the tip to Alan's virgin hole. Pre cum dripped and smeared against the tight entrance, bringing a warm sensation that relaxed Alan to the very core. Slowly, Kett clenched her ass and pushed forward, parting Alan's hole forcefully but tenderly, gripping his hips and pulling as she closed her eyes in the subtle euphoria of feeling her brand new cock plunge deep into the enveloping warmth, held tight by Alan's clenching muscles. Alan gripped the barrel, digging his claws into the wood as he felt himself fill in a way he had never experienced, panting heavily in what should have been pain but only registered as warmth and pleasure. Kett hilted herself within her life-long friend, pressing the growing bulb of her knot against his stretched entrance, head thrown back in pleasure, letting Alan clench and flex his tailhole and squeeze the base of her shaft firmly.

The ooze squirmed and swelled as it slid down into Alan's cock, slithering into his ballsack. Alan gouged deep scratches into the barrel, feeling every movement of the ooze inside him. The portion of the tentacle that remained wrapped around the outside of his rod grew and spread to fully cover the upper half of his member, forming a seal and a pocket which began collecting Alan's pre cum as it drooled from his widening hole.

Alan finally started to relax his muscles and breathe slower as the waves of warmth washed over his mind and body. Kett panted with desire, looking down and gazing at her own cock buried within Alan's ass with fascination. She tilted her hips and drew her cock out slightly, eliciting another loud moan from Alan before pushing it laboriously back in. Again a devilish grin slid across Kett's face as the four tentacles the small of her back grew and wound out toward Alan. Two tendrils grabbed the inside of the canine's hips, pulling him close to Kett, while the remaining two reached down and wrapped around Alan's ankles, holding them spread wide. Kett let the tentacles hold Alan's hips, sliding her cock in and out of his clutching tailhole as she let her paws roam over her own body. She pulled her claws through the fur on her chest, running her hand over her face and throwing her head back and closing her eyes as she plunged in and out of Alan's smoldering hole.

Kett's thrusts grew more and more violent, pushing up against his ass and calves, slapping her balls against his, bucking as hard as she could bear without splintering the barrel beneath her drooling counterpart. The thick knot pressed against Alan's tight entrance with each intense stroke, stretching the canine wider as Kett slammed deep into his tight hole. As her pounding continued, and her throbbing red cock plunged deep into Alan's ass, Kett's hips and thighs started to stick to Alan's flesh like hot tar. Each time Kett drew away, her skin stretched away from Alan like taffy, each stroke thickening her flesh's hold until she found it difficult to pull away more than a few inches. She looked down and her hips were almost directly above Alan's ass, their pelvises merged tightly together, along with their thighs. Their lower legs remained separate, splitting just below the knee, but Kett's tentacles held Alan's ankles tight against her own.

Kett panted and flexed her cock. She could feel that her thick rod was still separate from Alan's ass, and rocked her hips gently to move inside him. But as her mind cleared ever so slightly, she realized that she could feel a great deal of what Alan felt. She concentrated, and felt the tentacle wiggling and flexing inside Alan's shaft.

Alan was not thinking quite so clearly. He felt his consciousness widen, and his swollen thoughts of pleasure merge with those of Kett, though he was not capable of realizing exactly what was happening. Instead, Alan could only focus on the burning pleasure buried deep inside both his asshole and cock. His claws continued to scratch subconsciously at the barrel, slowly and without genuine effort, until Alan realized that his paws were beginning to shorten. Trying to focus, but finding only the blinding pleasure, Alan watched helplessly as his hands shrank and drew into his wrists like a deflating balloon.

Somewhere within his sea of thoughts, Alan realized that his balls were getting somewhat heavier. He felt blood rushing through his entire body with a force he had never experienced before. His body grew hot, hotter than from arousal alone, as his blood pulsed toward his groin and away again. Alan felt himself weaken and collapsed fully against the barrel, unable to move his limbs. His arms deflated and drew closer to his shoulders, hot blood pulsing toward his hips as his ballsack stretched under newfound weight.

Alan could feel his spine soften, if only vaguely. The canine's face flushed with heat, and he couldn't help but open his jaw and pant heavily. Warm drool flowed freely from his mouth, dripping off his tongue and between his sharp teeth. Once his arms receded fully, his shoulders drew in closer to his core. His balls had grown so full and heavy that he felt them swinging gently between his spread legs, bumping against his and Kett's merged thighs. He moaned and noticed his drool tasted sweet, thickening slightly and pooling on the roof beside the barrel.

Kett knew exactly what she was doing, even if she didn't fully understand how. Feeling the canine's flesh soften, she pushed her hips forward, slowly forcing her thick knot against his stretched hole. With unrelenting pressure, Kett ground her hips forward until her pulsing bulb slid past Alan's helpless entrance, his squeezing muscles pulling her forward until she was buried fully within his hot flesh. Alan groaned, his jaw hanging open and drool flooding from his mouth uncontrollably. Kett ground her hips against Alan's, her knot rocking forward and back against his clenching entrance until she felt his flesh close in tight around her member. The warmth of Alan's body flowed through her, up into her hips and torso, as the defining features of her pulsing red shaft disappeared. She could feel Alan's blood running through her veins, hot and sweet. She no longer felt her cock inside Alan's ass, but instead felt Alan's entire body. Reaching down with her free hands, Kett ran flat palms over Alan's back and shivered at the intense pleasure.

Alan's entire figure slimmed, slowly, from shoulders to hips. Kett ran her hands up and down Alan's back, moaning with the same pleasure she found in stroking her new cock for the first time just hours before. Alan could only lap hungrily at the pre cum flowing from his own mouth as he felt every inch of his body grow more and more sensitive, teeth and tongue receding and lips pursing slowly. The fur above Alan's lower torso drew into his skin, revealing pink throbbing flesh underneath.

The slow transformation sped up as it drew to a conclusion. Alan felt as though he were hyperventilating as he panted forcibly through the firm rounded hole that used to be his mouth. He felt his entire body flex and fill with warmth, as though it were a single muscle. With each flexing of his body, he felt himself rise up vertically. His head rounded and smoothed until his nose and eyes closed completely, only his drooling mouth remaining. Alan could feel his balls, heavy and massive, swinging between Kett's legs, nearly touching the ground.

Kett ran her hands up and down Alan's tender body, marveling as it responded by hardening and flexing. She no longer had a definable cock, but flexing those muscles pushed spurts of pre cum out Alan's mouth and down the length of his smooth round chest as he rose vertically. Kett wrapped her arms around the girth of Alan's torso, pulling him close to her body, and rubbing her arms up and down his underside.

Alan felt his mind waver as his entire body flexed, and flexed, and flexed. The sweet taste of Kett's pre cum filled his senses as he felt familiar pulses of tension flow from where his waist used to be up through his head. Each pulse forced air from his mouth, only to have it rush back in when his muscles temporarily relaxed. The pulses grew in intensity and frequency, encompassing every inch of his rock-hard body until finally, suddenly, Alan felt a rush of thick, hot seed well up from deep inside his swollen balls, boring a path straight up through his torso and neck, finally flowing in a single jet of heavy cum from his open mouth.

Kett nearly screamed as she orgasmed, sending cum high up into the air through Alan's entire body. Clutching his body tight, quivering and shaking as she felt stream after stream of cum flow through the bulging shaft along Alan's underside, Kett nearly blacked out where she stood. Pulse after pulse of hot cum flowed from Alan's mouth, covering the roof and sliding down Alan's transformed body, dripping from his sack.

After several moments of standing motionless, Alan's body began to soften. Blood flowed from his body and into Kett's as he bent forward involuntarily. He shortened and shrank, receding down to Kett's hips where black and white fur remained. Slowly, the thick shaft drew into the furred sheath, shrinking until only the oversized bulge of husky fur was visible above the massive swollen ballsack.

Kett finally opened her eyes to inspect herself. Her own cock was gone, replaced by the giant sheath attached to her lower belly. Letting her mind quiet and relax, she could hear the subtle and distant thoughts of Alan, deep inside her. He didn't think in words, but only feelings and emotions. As he lay resting within Kett's groin, Alan thought of pleasure and lust. He seemed to be replaying the previous events in his mind, arousing himself within the confines of Kett's new monochrome sheath.

She smiled and licked her lips, and regretted that she would have to separate from Alan and give him to the creature beneath the well. She very much enjoyed all the possibilities of having a cock, especially one of this size. Kett turned to venture back toward the well, but only took two and a half steps before pausing.

After all, the creature never said she must return after each individual catch.

Chapter 4

Slowly, it dawned on Kett that her previous orgasmic scream might have drawn a little unwanted attention. After all, she couldn't truly remember just how loud she was, seeing as how she just experienced the most intense orgasm of her life. Kett crouched down, just in case anyone was looking up at the rooftops, and noticed that thick puddles of cum covered most of the area around her.

As blood and hormones settled back down into a state more closely resembling sane, Kett remembered that her entire purpose out away from the well was to collect orgasmic juices and other organic matter. It would be a waste to just leave all that cum on the rooftop, she thought.

Not entirely sure how to correct the situation, Kett reached out and let some of her wrist tentacles extend toward a pool of seed. The tips of the tentacles simply popped off, landing in the thick juices, and absorbed the fluid. The bit of goo swelled as the fluid was sucked in, and the growing ball rolled around the rooftop seeking out the nutrients. Before long, a sack of cum-filled goo rolled back to Kett, about the size of a beach ball. The fox reached down to it, letting her wrist tentacles extend toward the goo, and the cum flowed through a channel in the tentacle into Kett's body.

She felt the warm fluid pulse through her veins, tasted the salty seed in her mouth, and felt it pool and drain into her balls. As the orb of cum drained and finally disappeared, Kett's ball-sack grew heavier. Her testicles were still separate from Alan's massive pair, but now Kett's were rivaling his in size. Instead of walking around with two cumbersome pairs clacking against each other, Kett opted to merge the two sets, forming a single pair, each about two feet wide, covered in Alan's black and white fur.

The taste of the absorbed seed lingering in her mouth, and Kett felt Alan's primitive consciousness stirring toward arousal. Realizing that it wouldn't be long before the massive cock that used to be Alan was unbearably stiff, and thus movement through the city nearly impossible, Kett decided to start searching for her next subject.

Alan's clothes remained tossed around nearby, so Kett donned the over-sized and uncharacteristically masculine attire and descended down toward the streets. Luckily the pants were loose enough that the oversized testicles and sheath barely showed through the excess material, and didn't look too suspicious. She wasn't entirely sure what to look for, however. Hanging around at a street corner, propositioning herself to strangers crossed her mind, but that would be unusual this early in the afternoon, and would draw too much unwanted attention. She thought about waiting until another acquaintance happened to pass by, but that could take hours.

Making her way through the crowded plaza, Kett spotted a small, effeminate male mouse near the well, attempting to fill four large jars with water. His white fur was clothed in the colors of one of the Greathouses, clearly marking his status as a house slave for a noble family. Of course, Kett could also conclude that the mouse was a new servant, as attempting to bring four jars of water that big through town is nearly impossible without assistance, and is usually a mistake made only once. Sure enough, once all four jars were filled with water, the mouse attempted to wrap his arms around them and lift, without much success.

Kett moved in quickly, pushing past the socializings and minglings of townsfolk, approaching the young mouse, "Would you like some help?"

The poor mouse nearly dropped all four jars as he jumped, startled. "Uh, um, no I think I can—." One of the middle jars slid and popped out of his grasp, and Kett reacted quickly in order to catch the container before it hit the ground, or even spilled any water.

"You were saying?" Kett smiled and held the jar firm, watching the mouse continue to squirm and struggle to keep a hold of the remaining three. "Let me help you carry these back. There aren't many people that can carry four at a time, and all of them have arms twice as long as yours."

The mouse sighed and set the third jar down, thinking. "Are you a free laborer? I don't have anything to pay you with, but maybe my master will give you a few coins for helping me."

"That will be fine. I'm sure your master would rather have the water and jars back intact, anyway." Kett picked up the jar from the ground, hoisting the two full jars with surprising ease, "Lead the way."

Kett followed the servant mouse through a part of the city she'd seldom seen. The noble houses were massive complexes, full city blocks towering over the huts and common houses around them, built of baked brick and cut stone. The mouse walked in silence, rushing through the crowds with the urgency of a servant unsure of how much grace to expect from his master.

Upon reaching their destination, the mouse led Kett to a smaller building near the back the Hykan estate. The door flung open before the mouse could reach the threshold, and a large crocodile stood blocking the doorway. "Léo! Where the sand devil have you been!"

Léo nearly dropped both his jars out of fright, "Sorry! Terribly sorry!"

The croc scowled at Kett, "And who is this?"

"She offered to help me!"

"Is that right?" The croc stomped over to Kett, snatched the jars of water from her grasp, and stomped back into the building as Léo scampered back inside and the door slammed shut.

Kett stood outside, listening to muffled shouts and apologies, wondering how she thought she was going to make this work. But, she was rather fond of the mouse already, and decided Léo would be of much better use serving her master, not his.

Gathering herself, Kett approached the door and knocked loudly a few times. The crocodile appeared in the doorway in an instant, snarling, "*What?*"

Straining to smile, "Are you Léo's labor master?"

"If Léo can be called a slave then I can be called his master. *What* do you *want?*"

"Do you hire him out at all?"

The croc shifted, sizing Kett up. "We let some of the more senior servants take day jobs, but Léo hasn't earned that privilege yet."

"I am interested in Léo specifically."

"Why should I rent him? And why would you want him?"

Kett smirked, "Mostly I'm interested in his young body. You must admit he has quite the attractive figure compared to what you'd find among other servants."

"Hah! I should've known. So you followed him all the way back here just to plough 'im? Fine, fuck little Léo until he's learned his place, but his rate will be double."

Kett fished around in Alan's pants, searching for what cash Alan had on him. She found a handful of coins in one pocket, and glanced down to find their denomination much larger than she would have expected. Thinking upon it, Kett remembered that Alan was a banker, and quite successful at that. Kett produced two large silver coins and offered them to the croc.

The master croc, in turn, snatched both coins and disappeared behind a slammed-shut door, returning not a moment later to hurl the mouse servant onto the ground beside Kett, "He's back by sundown," and slammed the door shut again.

Léo looked up from the dusty ground, finding Kett standing above. He quickly sprang himself into a bowing position, waiting for Kett to make a move.

"There's no need for that." Kett smiled as the mouse stood. Léo was only about six inches shorter than Kett, but his build was slight and feminine. His clothes hung loosely, probably made for a larger servant before him. Just staring at Léo's soft features stirred Kett's blood, her balls shifting in anticipation. Patting her pants again, she found that Alan's house key was on-hand, and Kett knew Alan's house to be not too far from their location. "Follow me."

Quarry in tow, Kett led the small mouse to Alan's residence, holding the door open for Léo and entering behind him. The mouse stood at attention, head bowed, "What would you have me do?"

Kett hadn't ever bought a servant before, or even a prostitute, so the question felt a little strange, but she felt an illicit thrill from the promise that the mouse would do whatever she desired. When she thought of what she had in mind, however, her breathing shortened a little. She led her servant to Alan's bedroom, and locked the door. "Disrobe."

The mouse bowed his head low, blushing profusely, shifting nervously. Kett could see his apprehension, but could also see hints of arousal. Léo cautiously unbuttoned his shirt, laying it on the bed to reveal his satin chest fur. Unbuckling his belt, he glanced up at Kett, making sure she hadn't changed her mind, but only found an approving grin on the face of his temporary master. Léo slid his pants down, exposing his slender legs, tight ass, and growing manhood. He stood back at attention, head bowed, and waited for further instructions as his shaft grew more erect with each passing moment.

"Now disrobe me."

Léo swallowed hard, taking a hesitant step forward, trying not to make eye contact with Kett. He reached up and undid the clasps of Kett's shirt, noticing the dirt on the otherwise fine material. He parted the shirt and tried not to stare at Kett's breasts, large and inviting, with the alien lines of slick slime winding over her torso. He blinked a couple times as Kett slid the shirt down off her arms, and Léo fumbled with her belt. Finally he unbuckled the strap, and the loose pants fell to the floor without much resistance.

Finding it hard not to stare at the unexpected anatomy below Kett's waist, Léo stood back at attention. Kett's sheath, nearly a foot and a half wide, stirred as the pink tip of her massive cock slid upwards a few inches. She debated for a few seconds on what move she wanted to make, but with every passing moment her desire for the lithe mouse body grew, to the point where she simply grabbed the small creature and tossed him backward on the lush bed, pouncing his prone body immediately after.

Pinning Léo to the billowy comforter on Alan's bed, Kett ground her hips against the swelling manhood beneath her hips. Léo's surprised expression quickly melted to pleasure as pulses of warmth radiated from where Kett held his wrists. He swallowed hard, eyes losing focus for moments at a time as his cock grew to its full length, his racing heartbeat visible in the twitches of his rigid shaft.

Kett slid her dripping pussy up and down along Léo's shaft as she watched his eyes glaze over, finally releasing his wrists as she was confident he now lacked the desire to flee. She rose up on her knees before finding the rigid mouse cock, guiding it to her waiting hole, and sliding down, exquisitely slow, down to hilt the shaft in her warm pussy. Léo let out the tiniest of squeaks as Kett settled herself on his meat, grinding against his hips and watching the small mouse boy melt in pleasure. Kett sat upright on her prey, grasping her breasts and running her fingers through her fur as her giant shaft slid out of her sheath.

The red flesh that was once Alan grew and flexed, pulsing out from Kett's body and hanging horizontally under its own weight. Kett could hear Alan's psuedo-thoughts from within her, craving more and more arousal, growing in intensity and volume as blood filled the giant husky cock. Léo's eyes remained closed in pleasure as Kett gyrated against his buried manhood, and he did not notice the growing flesh until it was so heavy that it fell and rested against the mouse's chest, the tip of the red dog cock only inches from his face. When Léo finally opened his eyes, he was greeted by the sight of Kett's gigantic member drooling a thick drop of pre onto his neck, the scent filling the air and driving him into a deeper fog, pierced only by the intense pleasure of Kett squeezing his manhood within her feminine folds.

Kett moaned and clenched her cock muscles, forcing her shaft to rise a foot off Léo's chest and come back down again, letting the mouse feel the full weight and warmth of the impossible organ. She raised her hips slightly, drawing Léo's rod out of her wet pussy before sliding back down in long, intentional movements. Léo squeaked, barely audible through his silent gasps, and Kett drew up and down along his hard cock in faster movements. With each stroke, Kett's giant shaft flexed up and slapped down onto Léo's body, arousing her further. Léo reached up and wrapped his arms around the head of the blazing hot cock, holding it tight against his plush white fur as Kett fucked with greater intensity. The hole atop Kett's rod flared and widened as she flexed and clenched, throwing her head back as she slammed down on the hard mouse shaft, gouging deep claw marks in her own breasts and chest.

Léo bucked his hips upward and let out a long, quiet squeak as he came forcefully into Kett's pussy. Kett felt the seed within her, tasting it in her mouth, and groaned softly to herself as her body absorbed the mouse's fluids, sucking his shaft dry as Léo remained frozen in delirious pleasure. Kett smirked as she admired her now fully erect dog cock, nearly the full size of Alan himself, the two large lobes of Alan's knot showing their initial growth from the base of the flesh. She remained clenched around Léo for quite some time, waiting for some of the fog to clear from the mouse's mind, but she knew that her pet would only return part-way from his distance as the chemicals from her touch still coursed through his veins.

Kett dismounted the mouse, licking her lips as she tasted the last bit of Léo's juices, and leant up against the headboard of Alan's bed, sitting upright. After a moment the panting mouse opened his eyes and looked up at Kett, at first shocked by the sight of her massive cock standing straight up, reaching above her head in her current position. A single stream of pre cum crawled down Kett's massive shaft, sending shivers down her spine. She smiled down at the mouse, and beckoned him up. The mouse obeyed, cautiously, but still felt the daze of pleasure in his mind. He sat on his knees, between Kett's spread legs, staring at her pulsing flesh.

Taking his hands into her own, Kett let her touch warm his blood and sooth his mind, watching as the mouse relaxed even through his intimidation, and his limp member began pulsing back to life once again. Kett took his hands and raised them up toward the tip of her shaft, placing his hands against her cockhole. The mouse rose on his knees to accommodate her, unaware of her intent. He felt her slide his small hands into her hole, and felt the slick warmth of the inside of her shaft.

Kett swallowed nervously, not sure what to expect from her servant as she put his hands down her cumhole. The immediate pleasure was new and strange to Kett, feeling the slight stretch of her cock from the inside as the mouse's hands were enveloped up to the wrist. Kett's mouth parted as she panted greedily, pushed onward by the voice of Alan inside her, craving more, wanting the mouse boy inside them both.

She clenched and released her grip on Léo's wrists, letting her cock squeeze and hold his paws in place. Her shaft tilted downward toward the mouse as he pulled his hands back toward himself in fogged confusion, the head of Kett's massive rod at the mouse's chest level. Kett squeezed and clenched, pulling on the hands clasped tight within her hole, sliding them slowly deeper. With her rod lowered toward the mouse, Kett could see Léo's face as she pulled him into her wanting entrance. Léo swallowed nervously, gazing in disbelief as he found no strength to pull back against the sucking motion. He felt dizzy as his arms slid in past the elbow, his own cock now hard again without his knowing why.

Kett reached a hand out and extended the tentacles from her wrist, lashing her slimy appendages around the mouse's neck. She moaned aloud as she pulled Léo toward herself with her hand, sinking his arms into her cock halfway up his biceps in a single motion. She forced Léo's head low against his arms as she pulled with solid force. Kett moaned aloud in pleasure as she drew Léo's head against her cockhole, pulling hard until his head forced its way into her flesh, stretching her hole wide. Immediately she moved her tentacles down to Léo's shoulders and upper back, sending out the tentacles from her other hand as well and pulling in a single swift motion to force the mouse's slender shoulders into her dripping shaft, screaming in pleasure and knocking her head back against the headboard.

She felt the mouse squirming and struggling inside her rigid cock, trying to pull out of the suffocating warmth to no avail. Kett was hoping her servant would go willingly, and enjoy his travel, but perhaps he was simply afraid of his final fate. She pulled her rod upright, flinging the mouse upside down, legs flailing above the oversized member. Kett flung out her tentacles and lashed around the base of Léo's rigid cock, wrapping around his lithe hips. She pulled and rotated the mouse within her hole, sending intense waves of pleasure through her body as the soft fur rubbed against the inside of her flesh, stretching her in new directions. With Léo's cock facing her, Kett wrapped her tentacles around his balls and shaft, coiling around his hips and tail and pulling downward.

In a single, slow, laborious motion, Kett pulled the mouse downwards, sliding his entire torso into her cock, feeling the soft white fur and muscled body stretch her hot flesh as a wave of pre cum flowed up and around the mouse's body, spilling out and down the swollen shaft. His slender body disappeared into her meat, a prominent mouse-shaped bulge along the underside of her red cock. She pulled and panted until the mouse was engulfed up to his hips, the base of his member pressed up against the tip of hers, clasped within Kett's slimy tentacles.

Kett drew her cock closer to herself, pulling on Léo's hips until his twitching rod was within range of her mouth. She reached up and wrapped her muzzle around the mouse's shaft, sucking hard and letting her tongue run over the hot flesh. She wrapped her tentacles around the mouse's hips and found his tiny asshole, pressing against the entrance with her slime-covered tentacles. Kett felt Léo stiffen and clench within her cock, his lean muscles alert to her invasion. She pressed the slick tendril firmly, unrelenting until his tailhole finally gave way to her touch, sending her thick tentacle into his hot entrance.

Sucking hard on his cock, Kett probed the mouse boy's ass, thickening her tentacles and flexing them in and out, bucking up against his prostate. She shaped her tongue into a slim tendril of slime, shooting it down into Léo's own cockhole. Léo's hips bucked and squirmed from the sudden invading pleasure, moans muffled by Kett's prison of flesh. Kett's tongue probed inward, curling up inside his body and flexing, widening and stretching his entire cock so that he might feel her same pleasure, forcing two, then three tentacles into his tight ass until he finally exploded in her mouth, shooting hot cum around her tongue and down her throat.

Léo's body went limp, muscles relaxing and legs hanging from the top of Kett's cock, parted. Kett greedily swallowed the mouse's cum and grabbed his ankles with her tentacles, pulling him down the rest of the way. Savoring the taste of the mouse's cum, eyes fluttering as she slid the limp and willing mouse body down her cockhole, Kett leaned back against the headboard and watched with satisfaction as Léo disappeared into her massive rod, groaning to herself in dazed pleasure.

As the mouse's feet disappeared, Kett felt Léo's hands curling inside her and descending into her ball sack. Clenching her pelvic muscles, Kett slowly forced her quarry into her testicles. She grinned with accomplishment as her sack grew to nearly twice their previous size, now accommodating the mouse's full body.

Léo found himself adrift in a sea of delusion and warmth, unable to form full thoughts in the darkness of Kett's testicles. The scent of cum filled his nostrils, his breath soon drawing short from lack of air in his chamber. Léo felt the slick wetness of the walls around him, and the pool of seed submerging half his body. He could hardly process what had just happened to him, his last actions a blur, but soothing waves of dull pleasure washed over his skin. Running his fingers together, he felt the slick moisture of cum, but as he pressed them together they seemed to get smaller. Léo swallowed and discovered the sensation of fluid running down his throat, the musty sweetness of seed filling his mouth. He licked his lips as his tongue started to shrink, slick cum dribbling from the corners of his mouth.

He pressed his hands to his body, attempting to feel what was going on, but only found that his fingers were losing sensation, and his body was softening. His entire body felt slick as cum ran down his face and chest, mingling with what was already pooled in Kett's balls. Léo knew only the sensation of the warm walls closing in around him as he shrank, the level of the seed rising as he dissolved, mind drifting away into an ever further fog until at last Léo existed as nothing more than a slick, salty pool of Kett's cum.

Kett lay motionless as she felt the mouse melt within her, her balls shrinking back down to something closer to their previous size as Léo's consciousness took the same form as Alan's, distant and primitive, but definitely separate from her own. Léo's voice yearned for release, craved to be shot out from Kett's cock in a moment of bliss, and Kett couldn't help but agree. Her body ached for release, but she knew she must wait until she could return to the well, and deposit her two new servants where they would do the most good.

Chapter 5

Returning to the well proved easier than first suspected. Kett rummaged through Alan's closet to find some loose-fitting pants which hid her enlarged maleness so long as nobody looked too closely. Alan's house had a stairwell that exited out onto the roof, so Kett's escape was a simple matter of jumping from building to building until she returned to the familiar abandoned plaza. There were no guards enforcing the quarantine; nobody felt the need to violate the order.

Kett wasted no time in descending into the well, reaching her tendrils out to the stone walls to aid her climb. Upon breeching the lip of the well, feeling the cool damp air against her face, Kett heard the subconscious rumblings of the organism dwelling inside. The slick ooze had crept nearly to the top of the well, bodies and slime crossing in a thick web of pulsing flesh. Kett lowered herself in using her own tentacles, but the creature quickly grabbed her and pulled her into the murky depths. Near the bottom of the well, where the ooze met the water and the subtle moans of a dozen trapped inhabitants filled Kett's ears, the creature's unconscious voice reached out to her mind and simply licked its lips.

Cradled in a solid web of tendrils, slimy cords of ooze crawling over her arms and legs, Kett could already feel the anticipation of release building. She could hear Léo, Alan and the creature crying out for the same thing, to say nothing of what her own body desired. Her clothing was promptly removed by several questing tentacles, exposing her massive sheath to the cool air. Already she could feel her cock drooling a thick gob of pre cum as the giant red tip slid an inch from its sheath. Kett extended her own tentacles, entwining them with the dozens of firm

62

tendrils encircling her body, snaking them out, embracing the creature in every way she could. She arched her back as her slick appendages found some of the nearby denizens of the well, wrapping herself around unseen knotted cocks and pushing into waiting orifices. The creature encouraged her, pushed her on mentally as she pried into a moaning mouth here, a tight asshole there, a drooling pussy, a firm cockhole, and Kett moaned as she felt each and every one as if she were sliding her own cock into the wanting flesh.

Closing her eyes and simply enjoying the unyielding pleasure, Kett arched her back and let the creature probe her body. Tendrils wrapped around her ballsack and tugged down, pulling them taut and stretching them, squeezing and kneading. Soon Kett's giant cock slid, pulsing and dripping, out from her sheath until it lay heavily against her belly and breasts. Lying on her back amid the creature's embrace, her cockhead came up to her chin, leaking pre cum onto her neck and twitching slightly as she pushed her own tentacles deeper into the warm holes provided to her. The voices in her mind and body salivated and ached.

The creature let a pair of larger tentacles wrap around the base of Kett's manhood, squeezing the slight bulge at the bottom and pulling her cock so that it pointed straight up. A section of the wall above her shifted and pulsed, and Kett watched as a feline male was brought out into the open space of the well above her. The cat had obviously been in the creature's grasp for some time, as he had lost many of his features and was penetrated in every way by several pulsing tentacles, but Kett noticed that now his flesh was changing and moving before her eyes. The features of his face receded and his limbs drew into his body, teeth disappearing as his mouth hung open and drooling. With hardly a sound aside from a subtle moan, the feline's mouth widened and his jaw enlarged, his entire head swelling and yawning uncontrollably until he appeared to be nothing more than a gigantic mouth. The orifice merged fully with a thick tentacle and the cat's features faded away so that he now appeared to simply be a tendril of ooze with a giant opening at the end, tongue lolling out to one side.

Slowly, the gaping mouth lowered itself toward Kett's erect cock, parting just enough to let the massive dog shaft slide into the warm maw. Kett moaned aloud as the open tentacle slid down her length, watching as her red flesh disappeared fully into what was moments ago another creature. She could even hear the distant moans of pleasure from the cat as his tongue swept back and forth over her sack. The tentacle bulged and stretched to accept her thickness, the tapered tip plainly visible as the pliable ooze clenched and tightened around the entire length. Every voice in her mind groaned in ecstasy as the maw pulsated and milked her throbbing shaft.

Kett's knot started to swell inside the mouth of the merged tentacle. Thickening and growing as fast as her body could supply blood, her knot stretched the tentacle's mouth to nearly twice its original width. The entrance of the slimy maw was locked in place as the bulge swelled, a deep groan from the cat signaling his pleasure as he rubbed his giant tongue against the underside of Kett's massive member. Soon Kett was squirming and bucking her hips against the tentacle, crying aloud as it milked her, flexing each of her tentacles as they pushed deep inside a dozen blazing sex organs, feeling every hair on her body and inch of slick ooze embracing her flesh as she erupted violently into the wanting maw.

She screamed in pleasure as gallons of seed flew from her red hot shaft, hearing the ecstatic screams of Alan and Léo within her mind. Surge after surge of cum poured from her cock, draining her balls of the lithe mouse boy trapped within. She felt the creature forcibly squeezing her testicles, pushing every last drop of cum from her body as the tentacle inflated, a pocket near the tip of her shaft forming to collect the fluid. The transformed feline maw sucked greedily as Kett drained herself into the clutching depths, pulsing and milking her in desperate need. After minutes of shooting her thick load into the creature, screaming and twisting in pleasure, Kett felt her cock flex and refuse to give another drop. Her mind and vision returning slowly, Kett could feel that little Léo's mind was no longer inside her. Indeed, upon inspecting the inflated bulb within the tentacle, she could see a pool of milky cum faintly visible through the thin translucent membrane.

Léo didn't quite know where he was or what was happening. He did know, however, that he liked it. The first semi-conscious thought he had was to note the heavy salty taste of cum in his mouth. In fact at this point he didn't have a mouth, but his perception returned before fully formed thoughts. His entire body felt like it was submerged in a pool of thick viscous fluid, and the familiar smell of sex filled his senses. He tried opening his eyes but they seemed stuck shut, not having the proper frame of reference to know that he simply didn't have any. But, slowly, the feeling of complete numbness began to coalesce around his torso, a small core of flesh regaining some semblance of sensation, warmth flowing out from his midsection to his neck, his groin, his shoulders. His breathing quickened before he could realize that he had lungs; his mouth hung open and panted before he had a head. The feeling of pulsing warmth and the weight of fluid upon his body focused, slowly changing from broad ubiquitous unconscious pleasure to a small point of actual thought and realization.

In a sudden moment of consciousness Léo's face broke the surface of the pool of cum and gasped for breath, half-formed arms flailing to grasp something, anything in the small smooth chamber of ooze. Delirious with pleasure but finally able to see, Léo opened his eyes and let the heady smell of seed fill his mouth and nose. He slipped and grasped at the slick walls to try and right himself, struggling until he simply sat down against the wall of his chamber and watched in numb fascination as the level of the pool of cum lowered and coalesced onto his body. Léo watched as his fingers reformed on the end of his hand, and soon the mouse was sitting in an empty pod, covered in a thick coating of fluid that slowly soaked into his flesh. Panting, licking his lips, Léo's eyes focused and he realized that his cock was rock hard.

Before Léo could reach down to touch himself, the base of the chamber opened and he slid down the slick tube until he landed on Kett's chest with a thump. Her thick cock, as large as his entire body, still stood straight up directly behind him. Kett and Léo looked at each other, but there was nothing to say. They spent a moment staring at each other, panting, before a devious smile slid across Kett's face. Without having to give a single thought of direction, the creature surrounding them knew Kett's desires. Several tentacles reached out to grab the mouse boy, wrapping around his legs and ankles. Before Léo could think to protest, he was positioned directly above Kett's enormous cock, legs spread at an angle to either side of her pulsing flesh.

The tendrils brought Léo down so that his ass was touching the very tip of Kett's manhood. The tapered point pushed gently at his tight hole as Léo looked down in disbelief, knowing that it couldn't possibly work. Mouth still hung open and panting, he looked to Kett, but she just grinned. The creature's slimy coils drew taut and pulled strongly on Léo's ankles with a firm but not violent pressure. Léo could feel the cock tip, the thickness of his own fist just at the very top, slide back and forth across his slick skin. Soon the tip slid into the shallow divot of Léo's closed entrance, and he could feel spurts of pre cum moistening his hole. As the creature pulled down, slowly, firmly, the pressure built against his clenched opening, prodding and prying, pressing down against the tip of Kett's cock until she slowly, deliberately, flexed her erection and forced the thin tapered tip to pop through Léo's resisting entrance.

Léo cried out in surprise and a twinge of fleeting pain. The two or three inches of flesh inside him were already thicker than anything he'd had before, thicker around than his entire fist. He tilted his head back and closed his eyes, waiting for the shooting pain to subside. To his surprise, the pain disappeared much faster than he expected. In fact, within several seconds of having his hole stretched, he simply wanted more. Léo's own cock pulsed and twitched, a thick bead of pre cum rolling down the length. The tentacles around his legs resumed their firm tugging, and Léo cried out as another inch slid inside his ass.

Kett panted and simply watched in captivated rapture as the tiny mouse slid slowly around her vulpine cock. When Léo had taken four or five inches of her hard flesh, the distortion became clearly visible. Not only had the mouse's hole stretched to accommodate the massiveness of her erection, but his hips were now widening under the force of the intrusion. From her angle she could clearly see that the thickness of Léo's torso was about the same thickness as her shaft. She licked her lips in lust and focused her mind on the creature, feeling where it gripped the mouse and pulling with her own mind, harder than the creature was moments before. The lithe mouse body wriggled and moaned as she pulled hard at his ankles, flexing her rod as his entrance stretched and stretched, eliciting a nearly silent squeak from the mouse as his tight tailhole slid over the subtle flare of her cockhead. As soon as he passed over the thickest part of the flare, Kett bore down hard and slammed the mouse down another two feet, drawing a cry from both of them in unison.

Cum flowed from Léo's hard rod, running down his flesh and dripping off his balls, forced from his body by the invading erection without the release of orgasm. His body bulged up to his collar bone to accommodate the massiveness of Kett's cock. After several moments of blind pleasure, Léo looked down at his body and ran his palms against his belly and chest, noticing that his own flesh was only a thin membrane drawn taut against Kett's meat. He could feel the veins of her thick shaft through his skin. When she flexed, he could feel it swell from the tight ring of muscle at his entrance up to his nipples.

Kett was trapped in bliss as she felt the mouse body squeeze tight against her cock. She maintained the pressure pulling against Léo's ankles absent-mindedly, not even fully aware of her own actions, only feeling the pleasure of stretching Léo's entire body until his firm ass rested at the top of her swollen knot. She was only dimly aware that the subtle tugging would not be enough to force her knot inside, but she kept the firm pressure up until her mind cleared enough to look up and inspect the mouse. She could clearly see her own tapered head bulging and distorting the mouse's throat.

Léo moaned and tilted his head back, just feeling the fullness of his entire body, rubbing his palms up and down his chest and belly, running his fingers through his fur. He could taste Kett's pre cum in his mouth, pooling at the back of his throat. His asshole was now stretched to the size of his chest but he didn't feel any pain, just the supreme satisfaction of being filled to the absolute brim with hot flesh. Léo could feel the broad bulge of Kett's knot pressing against his ass, but it felt too thick to go anywhere. He swallowed and was rewarded with a moan from Kett as his throat tightened in a wave down the head of her cock.

Feeling the hot flesh of the mouse squeeze and pulse around her prick, Kett could only moan in bliss. She writhed and squirmed, still feeling each of her tentacles buried deeper and deeper into holes of every variety. As Kett rocked her hips back and forth, rolling them against the firm grasp of the creature's tendrils, her cock slid up and down, slowly, within Léo's body. He felt his throat snap back to its normal size each time the tapered head drew down to his chest, then stretch back out as Kett pushed her flesh back in.

The sensation of his throat and body stretching, forced apart by the intruding member, only pushed Léo closer and closer to release. He brought one hand down and gripped his hard cock, already slick with his own cum, and stroked his length with long and deliberate movements, using his other hand to massage up and down his torso as the blazing hot meat slid back and forth through his body.

Seeing Léo touch himself, Kett bit her lip in fascinated pleasure and coaxed the creature to bring the mouse down hard against her knot. The tight hole resisted, and the mouse boy threw his head back and moaned as he stroked his cock harder. The creature wrapped a strong cord of slime around Léo's torso, winding up from his waist to his chest, gripping firmly and drawing the living cock sleeve upwards. The mouse's chest collapsed back to its normal shape and size for only a moment before the tendrils slammed him down roughly, forcing Léo's ass to smack against Kett's massive knot. Again, the mouse was slid up two feet, and then slammed back down with a wet slap and screams of bliss from the pair. With each stroke Kett watched as the top half of the mouse popped back to his normal shape then instantly stretched and pulled taught against her cock, taking on the size and shape of her meat. The creature brought the mouse up nearly half the length of Kett's erection and forced him down, again and again, each time the giant knot slamming against the tight ring of muscle, each time pushing just fractions of an inch further.

The mouse could feel his hole stretching and distorting with every slam, reveling in the feeling of Kett's hard flesh impaling his entire body again and again, stroking his own cock as fast as he could. Kett squirmed and writhed as the creature used the mouse's body to fuck her gigantic member, moaning and drooling as Alan's voice screamed for release within her. With each stroke the creature pulled harder, slammed faster, squeezed tighter until the mouse was stroking her cock as fast as he was stroking his own. When Kett felt the pressure build inside her core, that deep tense sensation in her balls, the creature reacted by slamming the mouse down violently and pulling, pulling his legs and torso tight, forcing Kett's knot against the mouse's hole with a rough yank until finally the ball of flesh popped into Léo's ass, stretching his hips and belly to nearly twice their original size and pushing Kett's cock up and out through the mouse's mouth, stretching his lips and jaw to accommodate the tapered head.

Kett screamed in pleasure, and Léo simply moaned, his throat and mouth stretched past the point of being able to make sound. Before either could fully comprehend the sensation, the creature gripped Léo's torso like a vice, squeezing the sleeve of flesh around Kett's cock and ripping the mouse up and back over the knot with an audible popping sound. Léo gasped for air blindly and Kett moaned but the creature instantly brought the mouse down and knotted him again. The thick swell of flesh stretched Léo in every direction, pushing against his own cock from the inside as he gripped it with both hands and stroked himself quickly. Kett watched as the creature forced the mouse up over her knot again, and slammed him down over it, bringing the sleeve of flesh up nearly half the length of her shaft before ramming him down roughly over her entire bulging knot, again and again, forcing the tip of her cock through Léo's throat and mouth with each stroke.

The creature fucked Kett with the mouse sleeve, bringing the tight tube of hot flesh down over the swell of her knot until the pressure grew and culminated inside her, Alan's voice screaming for release inside her mind. With a single motion Léo was slammed down over the entirety of the knot and Kett felt the hot stream of cum shoot through her flesh. Thick ropes of cum shot from Kett's member as it protruded from Léo's upturned mouth, flying up into the air and pouring down over Kett's body and face. Flexing and pulsing her cock muscles, load after load of cum flung into the air, the unbroken stream of gallons of fluid drenching her entire body and filling the damp air with the intense scent of her seed. She opened her mouth and let her juices hit herself in the face, savoring the taste and swallowing greedily as her body dripped and cum ran off her chest and belly.

Kett closed her eyes and let gravity slam her seed against her face, relishing the sensation as she felt her cock start to shrink. She was vaguely aware that her body was dissolving the flesh of her cock and then ejaculating it, though she didn't necessarily care. Bucking her hips and panting violently, soon her member shrank enough that Léo could close his mouth, though the flesh still stretched much of his body. The cum continued to flow out of Kett's cock but now shot against the roof of Léo's mouth, filling his throat faster than he could swallow. Léo felt the hot seed stream down his open throat and pool in his belly atop the massive knot still inside him. He struggled to keep his mouth closed against the force of Kett's ejaculation, but soon her cock had shrunk down past his throat and he simply felt the pulsing rod of flesh pushing out gallons of fluid to fill his stomach.

Léo could feel the cum pooling inside him as his chest returned to its normal size and shape. Soon he could feel the fluid draining away, and slowly realized that his own sack was inflating. The pressure quickly built and Léo shot thick cum out over Kett's chest and breasts. Kett, still amid the bliss of her own orgasm, watched as thick seed poured from her own shrinking cock, filled the mouse and was then immediately shot back out of his cock onto her belly, and this just made her cum harder. The two of them spurted streams of hot cum into and onto each other for several minutes, minds lost in the haze until both their sacks ran dry.

Covered in Kett's cum, Léo leaned forward and put his hands against Kett's belly. The two of them panted silently and looked at each other. Kett's cock had returned to its normal size and shape, though she was still unused to the idea of having one altogether. Léo had likewise returned to his normal lithe mouse shape, licking his lips and swallowing, his mouth tasting of her seed, feeling the now normal fox cock knotted inside his ass, relishing the firm embrace of the tendrils wrapped around his body, not daring to move.

It wasn't long until the pools of cum covering Kett and Léo began to squirm. The fluid drew up and coalesced on Kett's lower chest, running down from the walls above and the water below and gathering into a thickening mound. Kett and Léo watched as the seed piled on top of itself, bulging upwards as the liquid streamed in from every direction. They each licked their lips greedily and let the cum run over their faces, relishing the taste. Soon the mass of fluid took subtle form, the gentle bumps of vertebrae running along the top of the bulge, an arch forming in the middle, the side near Kett's face elongating and splitting open to form a dog's snout. Holes in the growing form grew, then formed the spaces between torso and arms. Slowly the liquid took the definite form of a figure bent over, straddling Kett's chest, the familiar features of the husky solidifying in the face. Soon Alan sat upright, head tilted back and head spinning, cum continually drawing up onto his skin and soaking in to finally reveal his thick fur.

Kett stared at Alan for a long while, gauging his reaction as he panted and his eyes focused. Eventually, Alan looked back at her, but his expression was unreadable. He swallowed hard and licked his lips, looked down at Kett's transformed body, looked at his skin, and noticed the same alien features winding across his flesh. His cock, red and hard and drooling pre cum, had two similar tendrils running up the length. After several long moments, Alan simply leaned down and gripped both of Kett's breasts firmly and dug his claws into her flesh, eliciting a moan from the fox.

The creature, sensing their thoughts, pulled the mouse up off of Kett's cock with a pop, drawing a shudder from the two of them. Alan wasted no time in sliding back over her belly, leaning forward and pushing his ass toward her still erect manhood. Léo reached out and gripped Kett's cock and held it in place, guiding it as Alan slid back and let his tight asshole meet with her tip. Held in place by a pair of small mouse hands, Kett let her member push against Alan's entrance, and bit her lip as it slid into the slick entrance. Alan brought himself down against her knot, pushing against her tits for leverage, moaning as she filled him.

Léo let go of Kett's cock and let the creature raise his body up, pressing his own prick up against Alan's already full hole. Kett and Alan were locked in each other's gaze but each moaned encouragingly. Gripping his cock and sliding the head down between Alan's ass cheeks, then down against Kett's exposed knot, Léo pushed himself up against Alan's hole, pressing firmly until his flesh slid inside. The mouse easily hilted himself in the husky's hole, feeling the tight tunnel of flesh squeeze his shaft hard against the pulsing flesh of Kett's.

The three moaned loudly as Alan rocked his hips forward and back, feeling the twin cocks crammed into his tight tailhole. He gripped Kett's breasts and twisted them slightly, pinching a nipple as he slammed his hips forward and back over their shafts. Léo simply grabbed Kett's thighs and held himself still as Alan fucked them, Kett pushing her hips up to meet Alan's as he pushed back.

Alan, driven more by lust than conscious thought, let his new tendrils of ooze flow out from the small of his back, four tapering lines of slickness reaching around to meet his own filled entrance, pushing inside and twisting around Kett's and Léo's cocks, squeezing them together and wrapping up their lengths, reaching up and pushing into the tips of each of their cocks, two thin tendrils invading them each. Kett and Léo cried out in surprise and pleasure as Alan prodded into their shafts, squeezing and pulsing up and down their lengths as his slid over their flesh.

Kett, momentarily stunned at Alan's actions, simply smiled and brought her hands up and placed them on Alan's thighs. Her tentacles withdrew from their anonymous orifices up and down the walls of the well and instead began sliding over Léo's and Alan's bodies. She wrapped firmly around both of their thighs and bucked up violently as Alan brought himself back against her, gripping each of them tight and forcing her knot into Alan's asshole.

Alan and Léo both cried out in surprise, Alan at the sudden fullness of the knot, and Léo at having his cock squeezed intensely between Alan's flesh and Kett's bulb of flesh. Léo swore for a moment that his shaft was crushed, but soon realized that his rock-hard flesh contorted around the bulge of the knot, bending his erect member as Kett moved back and forth. Kett's tentacles continued to pry around their bodies until she pushed into Léo's wanting ass, first one, then a second, then a third thick tentacle, each twisting around each other as the forced their way into the mouse's abused hole. Finally, Kett let three of her tendrils find her own dripping pussy, sliding them in exquisitely slow and braiding them around each other inside her dripping wet passage.

Gripping the pair, Kett took control of the situation and held the two firmly in place as she pulled her knot out, and slammed it back in repeatedly. Alan and Léo cried out in helpless pleasure, unable to move and feeling the thick knot pop in and out of Alan's tight asshole. Fighting back best he could, Alan used his tendrils to probe deeper into Kett's cock, but he couldn't hold back the rough fucking Kett was determined to give. Léo dug his fingers into Alan's thighs as the violent movement of Kett's knot bent and compressed his cock inside Alan's tailhole. She grinned at their helplessness and slammed her knot in repeatedly, fucking Léo's ass and her pussy and arching her back in supreme bliss, crying out as the three of them erupted in orgasm in unison, cum filling Alan and spraying over Kett's breasts and face, pouring from the trio in thick heady spurts. Kett and Léo hilted themselves and moaned loudly, the mouse nearly blacking out from sheer pleasure.

Cum flowed from their bodies until they each collapsed, panting and delirious, into the creature's warm embrace.

Chapter 6

Hours passed, unconscious, in the depths of the well. Kett awoke first, and lowered herself into the water while her companions rested. She found a small ledge of rock just beneath the water's surface where she could sit submerged up to her shoulders, and let the cold water soak her fur. Bushy tendrils floated in the still water, waving back and forth to collect any wanted nutrients. For the first time in what felt like forever, Kett sat and relaxed, head clear of distraction.

Before long, Alan and Léo began to stir in their tentacle hammocks. The creature lowered their still-dazed bodies to the water. Finally awake and aware, the three simply looked at each other, blinking in the dim light at the bottom of the well. Alan and Léo felt the subtle voice of the creature explaining itself.

Kett broke the silence. "If either of you don't care for this, I can't keep you here."

Alan just snorted.

Léo looked around, and up, at the walls of the well. "Even if I were a slave here, it would beat being a slave for House Hykan."

The bushy tendrils slid along each of their bodies, combing through their fur. Kett chuckled, "I hope that crocodile won't be too upset that I stole you."

Léo gazed into the water, watching the creature writhe in the depths of the well. A subtle white glow could be seen near the rocky bottom, deep under the water's surface. "I guess I don't really care what Carra thinks. All I ever did was clean up after people." He ran his fingers through the wet fur on his arm, "Those parties they hold are the worst. The stains they put in the carpets are rather intense."

Kett and Alan glanced at each other. "Parties?"

Nodding, "Yeah, I guess that's a part of the whole 'high society' thing that they don't advertise to everyone else. All the great houses host these giant orgies on a regular basis. They rotate what house hosts. There's charts and everything."

Alan blinked, "I guess there's always been rumors."

Kett asked, "When's the next one supposed to be?"

"This weekend. Day after tomorrow, I guess. We're hosting this time too. So glad I won't be there."

Kett's eyes danced back and forth as she held a private conversation with the creature. "Oh, you'll be there." Smirking, Kett scooted along the ledge until she was sitting adjacent to the small mouse boy. Reaching down, she cupped a clawed hand around Léo's delicate balls, eliciting a tiny moan. "We'll all be there."

Léo swallowed as he watched Kett fondle his groin, moaning as she leaned in and wrapped her teeth around his tiny neck. The mouse's manhood stiffened in the cool water as the fox squeezed her jaw, ever so tenderly, against his flesh. Soon his cock was rock hard, and Kett slid her hand up to grip his shaft, stroking its length slowly.

The bushy tendrils in the water coiled around the mouse's calves, rubbing their suede texture against his body, rising and gripping until they could support his full weight. Soon the mouse was pulled from the rock ledge and into the water, held upright by the tentacles as they wound upwards, encircling his hips and lower torso.

Alan and Kett watched in jealous interest and scooted toward each other along the stone ledge. Kett's large shaft was already protruding from her sheath, and Alan's was growing rapidly as he touched himself. The pair only smirked at each other before Kett slid off the rock shelf and lowered herself into the water, gripping the stone wall with her feet and tentacles. Kett positioned herself between Alan's legs, fully submerged in the water, and reached forward to grip the rapidly stiffening member before her face. Not wasting a moment, Kett pulled the cock toward herself and wrapped her lips around the thick dog shaft, savoring the feel of the hot flesh pressed against her tongue.

In the middle of the water, Léo watched as a bushy tentacle wound its way around his balls and curled upwards to encircle his drooling cock, wrapping around every inch of his shaft. The coiled ooze slid forward and back, milking the mouse with long and deliberate strokes. Soon the tendril extended and doubled back on itself, the thin fuzzy tip probing to find the mouse's tiny cockhole. Léo twitched, startled at first at the still unfamiliar sensation, but quickly relaxed as the tentacle rubbed up and down over the small entrance. Panting, he watched in fascination as the tendril pushed forward just a fraction of an inch, penetrating his cock with the plush slickness.

Alan watched the show in the middle of the well as Kett's mouth slid up and down his hard shaft. He reveled in the sensation of her strong tongue wrapping around his meat, lips pursed tightly against his manhood under the surface of the water. Kett lowered her mouth even further, stretching her jaw so that she could force her mouth around the dog's thick knot as it swelled. She sucked and pressed her tongue against his flared head, drinking his pre cum greedily. Alan moaned in bliss, reaching his hands down and extending his newfound tentacles, wrapping around the fox's body, winding around her chest and hips until they found her cock, instantly grasping and squeezing her shaft in return.

Kett ground her hips against Alan's grasping cords as they gripped her body, bobbing her head rapidly over his hard meat. Pushing up against the rocky ledge, Kett brought her face up out of the water and filled her lungs with air before plunging back down and latching her jaws back around Alan's rod. The canine leaned back against the wall as Kett sucked on his member, flexing his muscles and pushing beads of thick pre into her eager mouth. The combination of Kett's warm skin and the cool water only heightened his awareness; every time the fox's tits brushed up against his legs he let out a little sigh. Noting that she would need to come up for air again soon, Alan gripped his tentacles around her torso, holding her firmly in position between his legs.

Sucking in sheer lust against the thick dog cock, Kett felt Alan coil around her body and hold fast. Her lungs began to twinge, signaling her need for air. Pushing up against the rock face, Kett attempted to bring her face up above the surface of the water, but Alan's grasp resisted her. He placed both of his hands on the top of her head and pushed down, forcing her mouth to stay latched onto his shaft as her lungs burned for air. Kett could pull herself up a few inches against Alan's grip, but failed to bring herself up far enough to break the surface, and her mouth remained filled with hot canine cock. Alan brought his feet together in the middle and found Kett's rigid shaft, pressing the bottoms of his hind paws against her hard meat, rubbing along her length as Kett struggled for air.

Kett's lungs cried out, trapped under the water with her throat stretched by Alan's manhood. The pleasure of Alan's grip on her body waned as her mind slowed, all of her focus cemented on the throbbing flesh trapped within her maw. Closing her eyes, pulsing her tongue against the shaft and losing all sensation in her body, Kett's mind knew nothing aside from Alan's thick, hard shaft. Sucking desperately, her lung's spasms pulling against Alan's flesh, swallowing hard against the head, Kett slowly faded out of consciousness, her last waking thought focused entirely on Alan's fat cock.

Alan held Kett's head down hard against his crotch as she clawed at the wall and his legs, flexing his shaft inside her mouth as she thrashed. The instant Kett's movements slowed, her arms relaxing and floating near her head, Alan pulled her body up out of the water, his shaft popping from her clenched jaws in a single motion. Kett hung from Alan's tentacles, limp and unmoving as he brought her face close to his, pressing his muzzle against hers, locking lips against her mouth as it dripped water. Alan grasped and kneaded her breasts as she began to moan ever so slightly. Kett's eyes popped open in sudden awareness, pushing back from Alan's face as she regained her thoughts, and then immediately pushed forward and locked lips with the husky.

Alan grinned and spun Kett around, lowering her onto his lap. Kett spread her legs around Alan's in anticipation, centering herself over his rod. Alan held his cock upright as it brushed up against the folds of her pussy, the tapered head parting the entrance slightly and drawing a gasp from the fox. Flexing his shaft to push out another bead of pre cum, Alan smeared the lubrication over her folds before holding himself upright and lowering Kett onto his pointed head. Kett moaned in satisfaction as Alan guided her down, parting her wet slit over his rock hard meat. She easily slid until she was resting firmly on Alan's lap, impaled fully by all but the fat knot, groaning happily as Alan reached up to squeeze her tits.

Léo watched, helpless as the tendril pushed further and further into his cumhole, the thickness of the tentacle widening ever so slightly as it traveled through his member and into his body. The underside of his cock bulged to accommodate the tentacle, distorting until he was filled with a cord of slick ooze that was nearly half the thickness of his shaft. Soft moans echoing off the walls, Léo watched as the plush slime slid forward and back through his hole, pulling out an inch before sinking back into his rod. The tiny knobs and hairs covering the tentacle compressed as they were forced into his cumslit, brushing against the smooth inside of his channel like a thousand soft bristles, pressed firmly against the slickness inside his shaft as the creature slid forward and back. Gaining speed, the tendril flowed in long smooth movements, in and out, penetrating deep into Léo's body with each thrust.

As the creature rammed the plush slime into the mouse boy's hole, the tentacle started pumping a viscous fluid into his bladder. The penetrating tendril bulged and thickened as a stream of liquid poured into Léo's body, rapidly filling his insides to bursting and stretching him even further. Léo could feel his abdomen swell, stretching outward as the fluid surged into him. Still sliding forward and back, the tendril pushed deep inside the mouse cock and squeezed more and more of the secretion into his body, and Léo cried out as his belly stretched from the strain, his cumhole filled so tight that none of the fluid could escape.

Below, deep in the water, the faint white glow grew in intensity as a sphere rose to the surface. As the glow neared, Léo noticed that the sphere was traveling along the inside of the tentacle, a brightly glowing ball about the size of his two fists put together.

Léo couldn't help but feel apprehensive as the glowing sphere traveled up along the tentacle toward his cock. The coil around his shaft loosened and expanded so that the sphere could slide toward the end, and then tightened back around him once the sphere was positioned at his cumhole. As the globe pushed forward against his entrance, Léo grimaced and panted, swallowing hard and biting his lip. The ball of light, looking much more massive now that it was positioned at his shaft's tip, pushed forward and back as the tendril stroked his rod. Each time it drew forward it gained another fraction of an inch, slowly distorting the mouse cock.

Soon the sphere was sliding in and out an inch, an inch and a half, not withdrawing fully but only driving in further. The underside of his rod bulged and swelled as the sphere filled and stretched him, pushing further and faster. Before his cock had stretched even halfway as far as it needed to, the creature gripped the mouse's hips hard and pushed, firmly and strongly, forcing the sphere forward agonizingly slowly in one long push, stretching his cumhole entrance wider and wider until at last it was wide enough to accept the full width of the sphere, at which point his cockhead squeezed tight and popped the rest of the globe into his shaft in a single rapid motion, leaving the mouse half groaning, half screaming in pleasure.

Alan and Kett watched the mouse stretch around the sphere as they ground their hips together, their lust for each other only partly distracted by the show before them. Kett clenched her pussy against Alan's cock, watching as the creature brought the mouse toward them. Léo's hips were brought up to Kett's eye level, and she reached out to run her fingers along the underside of the mouse boy's shaft, feeling his skin drawn tight against the sphere inside. The tendril slowly withdrew, pulling out of Léo's cock, leaving the sphere in place, just below his entrance. Kett reached up and wrapped her hand around his shaft head, squeezing. She was rewarded with a moan from the mouse as her closing paw slid the sphere further down his member. Grinning, Kett brought his cock vertical and slid her hand up, then back down again, pushing down against the orb, and again, each stroke pushing the sphere further into the mouse's shaft, Léo letting out a single long groan, shaking in pleasure. Soon the globe reached the base of the rod's passage, at which point Kett squeezed tight against the mouse's flesh and pushed down hard, watching the glowing ball slide back into the mouse's body, disappearing into his torso. The glow of light still visible through his skin, Léo gasped in surprise as something shifted inside him, followed by a long moan as a flood of pre cum flowed freely from his stretched cock.

Kett gripped Léo's shaft and brought it close to her mouth, opening her maw and letting the pre flow into her mouth, swallowing it greedily. The immense amount of fluid pumped into the mouse's body drained from his abused cockhole and poured into Kett's wanting maw, the sweet pre cum filling her mouth faster than she could swallow. Léo moaned as he felt movement within his pelvis, the sphere warming and shifting within him. Soon his cock began to swell, growing thicker as something bored its way up through his cumhole from within his body. Not nearly as wide as the sphere, but thick enough to stretch his shaft as it slid through his passage, pushing a surge of pre cum out into Kett's greedy mouth until a thick tendril of dark slime slid out from the mouse's cock slit. Limp and uncontrolled, the tendril drooped from his member, growing in length and width. Soon the ooze was nearly a foot and a half long, the base as thick as Kett's swollen cock, at which point it started to merge with the mouse's shaft and coalesce around it. Before long Léo's entire cock looked the same as the black slime, a thick dark tentacle protruding from the mouse's pelvis.

Léo felt a shiver as a channel ran through the ooze, nerves connecting all at once. The tentacle began oozing pre cum from the tapered tip, and Léo found that he could control the fully prehensile appendage. Kett watched in interest as Léo flexed the slick tentacle cock around, up and down, before she greedily grabbed it and sucked on the end. The steady flow of pre cum poured into her mouth and she played with the tip's hole with her tongue, prodding it playfully as she lapped up the fluid.

The mouse grinned and moaned, pulling away from Kett's face and letting the creature's tentacles lower his body. He descended until he was face to face with Kett, flexing and dragging his flexible tentacle cock across her pussy, already stuffed full with Alan's rod. Kett smiled in return as Léo pushed his tendril down, the thin tapered tip finding the place where Kett's flesh ended and Alan's began. Pushing forward, the three moaned in unison as Léo slid his slimy tendril into Kett's pussy, coiling around Alan's hard shaft several times and still having length to spare, sliding in further and further until he was pressed firmly against the fox's hips.

Wrapped tightly around Alan's member, Léo pulled back and pushed forward, bringing the trapped dog cock along with his own motions. Kett and Alan moaned, the mouse panting in pleasure as he drew his hips back and slammed back in, fucking Kett with both his own and Alan's massive shafts. Kett grabbed the mouse's body and pulled him tight against her tits, clawing at his back as the lithe rodent pumped away at her pussy, filling her to the brim.

Pistoning in and out of the dripping pussy, Léo rammed his and Alan's cocks deeper and deeper into Kett's warm embrace, slamming into her until he gripped the dog's shaft hard and arched his back, the three moaning in unison as the mouse forced Alan's knot inside Kett's pussy, cum shooting from the pair of cocks buried inside her, Kett's own cock shooting cum freely into Léo's fur, the fox clawing at the mouse's back and clenching hard against the spiraled cocks buried inside her.

Panting, Kett chuckled, "Well, that was simpler than I was expecting. I'm assuming the house kitchen has a private well?"

Léo nodded, limp in her arms.

"Apparently if we can get that seed planted in the well, we can connect this well with that one."

Not necessarily comprehending, Léo nodded again. "I can get us there."

84

Chapter 7

As the creature raised the trio up and out of the well, they noticed that they had slept through most of the day. The sun was low on the horizon, and the evening desert air was cooling rapidly. Of course, as they realized, they were also naked.

Alan peered back into the well. "Those were my clothes that ended up in there, weren't they?"

Kett paused, "Uh, yeah, I guess they were."

"I think you owe me some pants."

"I'm not sure I have anything that will fit you."

"At this point I don't think you have anything that will fit *you*."

Kett looked down at herself. "Good point. We should be able to get back to your place along the roofs."

By the time they had dressed themselves at Alan's place, the sun had set. When the three reached the servants entrance of Great House Hykan, the air carried the deep chill of night. Léo lead the way through the courtyard, threading through lesser-used hallways until they reached the kitchens, a side-building to the great hall near the center of the complex.

Léo, followed by the two others, crept up to the service door and snuck through. Inside, the kitchen was fluid with activity as the cooking staff prepared the evening meal for the estate. A dozen or so cooks filled the room, cooking and preparing some exotic meal, distracted enough that nobody noticed the three sneak around the outside of the main room to a nook between the cold storage lockers. There, a small hole in the ground marked the house's well, just barely wide enough for a small bucket to travel down.

"This is it?" Kett whispered. "Isn't that a bit small?"

Léo looked between the well and Kett, "I don't think it'll really mind, do you?"

Kett shrugged, "I guess not. I'm just surprised such a fancy place doesn't have a bigger well."

"The well isn't exactly one of the big attractions of Great House Hykan."

Just then, as the three huddled whispering in the small nook, a familiar crocodile entered the kitchen, shouting at the staff. Soon the dozen cooks scrambled to grab the food, finish the plating procedures, and carry it briskly out the far door to the dining areas. Afterwards, the crocodile walked the perimeter of the kitchen, inspecting the mess left behind, and then turned the corner and spotted the trio of intruders. "What's going on here? Who are you?" Then, as she recognized Léo and Kett, "Oh, you finally brought him back, did ya? Keeping him this late will cost you extra." The crocodile marched forward and grabbed the mouse by the wrist, "I don't know what made you think you could bring them inside the kitchens, rodent. Consider yourself lucky that you're already on this weekend's cleaning detail, so there aren't any worse jobs to assign you."

As Carra began to drag the mouse away, a slimy tentacle shot out and wrapped around the reptile's wrist, stopping her in her tracks. Kett's eyes went wide as she traced the tendril back and saw Alan, standing defiant and beginning to pull the crocodile and Léo back into the nook. The crocodile stammered, "What's the meaning of this?"

Alan pulled the croc toward himself until he could grab her arm with his paw, and pried her fingers open so that she let go of Léo. "I'm afraid Léo here no longer belongs to you. In fact, he is ours. And I feel that I must insist that you ask our permission before you touch him."

The crocodile and the husky faced each other, he still holding her wrist tight, the tendril of ooze snaking from his wrist to coil around her arm. The two glared at each other, baring their teeth. Kett watched, taken aback, as she had never seen this side of her friend before. Alan continued, "Now, are you going to ask to touch my pet?"

Carra hissed, attempting to pull her arm away but quickly found the tentacle to be too strong. As Alan watched her face, her eyes softened and glazed ever so slightly, her glare melting as the ooze slid along her rough skin. Her shoulders slumped, back slouching slowly as her mind succumbed to the delirious haze of the tendril's touch. Again, Alan repeated through his teeth, "Ask. For my. Permission."

Faintly, through limp lips, Carra croaked, "Please."

"What was that?" Alan pulled her closer, so that their faces were only inches apart.

"Please."

"Please what?"

"Please—let me touch—."

Alan released his grip from Carra's arm and she slumped to her knees, arms slack at her sides. Alan looked up at the mouse, "She's all yours."

Léo looked stunned. "I, uh, what?"

The crocodile lowered herself onto all fours, pleading quietly, "Please. Let me touch. Please." She crawled forward toward the mouse until her bowed head was at his feet. Léo looked up at Alan, and then at Kett.

Kett, mostly shocked at Alan, shrugged. "We have to get that seed out of you somehow, right?" She and Alan walked past Léo to the entrance of the nook, "We'll keep the coast clear."

Léo's little heart thumped in his chest so hard he thought it was going to kill him. He'd never been given this kind of freedom or discretion in his life. Timidly, the mouse undid the front of his trousers and pulled out the long tendril of slimy tentacle cock, and let it hang loosely in front of the Carra's face. She panted hungrily, gazing at the alien appendage, drooling from her open mouth. Léo ran his hand along the base of the tentacle, and whispered, "Suck it."

Before Léo could even prepare, the croc lunged forward and grabbed the tentacle with both hands, raising herself up onto her knees and popping the tip of the member into her massive maw. Léo gasped in surprise at the sudden sensation, the long crocodile mouth sliding forward to accommodate the length of his tentacle. Leaking thick drops of pre cum into the back of her throat, Léo could feel his shaft grow even longer, stretching outward until it curved down her throat, the thick crocodile tongue ravishing his member along every delicious inch. Léo moaned aloud as his former master slurped hungrily at his cock, driven further and further in her desire by the steady stream of pre flowing into her wanting maw.

Kett and Alan smiled as they watched the mouse enjoy himself, but then their hearts skipped a beat as the far door began to swing open. Rushing over to the door, the pair hid behind a counter as a muscular stud horse cook returned to the kitchen, carrying empty serving trays. Grumbling, the cook walked over to the sinks to drop off the trays when he heard Léo's little moans accompanied by loud slurping noises. As he crept over to investigate, Kett crept up from behind and lashed out with her tendrils, latching onto his wrists and coiling around his neck and mouth in a single flash, stifling his surprised yelp.

The horse was wearing a long white apron, loose trousers, and not much else. He struggled and thrashed wildly as Kett struggled to keep him still, coiling more of her tentacles around his ankles and knees. Kett reached her paws forward around his chest, clutching at the horse's pecks, her slimy tentacles rubbing along his skin as he watched the crocodile swallow Léo's long oozing cock. His eyes glazed over, and Kett reached down to lift the apron up and over his head, tossing it aside and smiling to see him offer no resistance. She let her tentacles slide over his taut flesh, no longer restraining him as she undid the front of his pants. Kett licked her lips as she walked around to his front, pulling down on the waist of his pants. Freeing him from the last of his clothing, Kett flexed her strong tendrils and lifted the willing horse up onto a nearby counter, positioning him on the ledge as she knelt down between his legs. The stallion's cock was already growing, sliding down between his legs, hanging limp but throbbing with his every heartbeat. Kett's tendrils coiled and slid over every inch of his muscular body as she wrapped her fingers around the thick cock, just below the flared head. She squeezed, and was rewarded with a thick drop of pre cum that she let drip onto her outstretched tongue, feeling the strong flesh flex under her grip.

Just as Alan was beginning to feel left out, the door swung open again. Still crouched behind a counter, he couldn't tell who was entering the room, but he knew it didn't really matter. He waited for the footsteps to draw closer, and then lunged out from his hiding place, tackling the intruder to the ground and wrapping several tentacles around the startled mouth before a sound could be uttered. Quickly positioning his arms and legs to pin the creature to the ground, Alan then inspected his quarry and was pleased to find himself on top of a lithe little antelope girl, probably no older than Léo. Her eyes shot open in shock and she struggled and squirmed under his body, but Alan already had the upper hand, and weighed much more than her. Her striking angular features shaking and struggling under his grip, Alan could tell that she was moving her muzzle to yell but his grip on her face and throat prevented all sound while the slime oozed over her tiny body. Soon her eyes half closed, and her breathing calmed, Alan grinning his wolf-like grin as she started subtly grinding her hips up against his body.

The antelope, like the other cook, wore only an apron and trousers. The stained white linen of her apron draped over her bare miniscule tits, erect nipples poking up against the fabric. Alan lifted the apron up and crawled underneath, letting it rest over his head and upper back as he leaned in close to her small beasts, licking hungrily at her tiny nipples. Licking and biting gently against the soft flesh, Alan ran his hands up and down the thin antelope's ribs and torso, enjoying the tiny moans his touch generated.

Léo groaned as his slimy tentacle cock continued to grow within Carra's warm maw. Lengthening slowly as the croc moved her mouth forward and back over the muscular ooze, the tendril pushed further and further down her throat with each movement. The mouse could feel his cock sliding deeper inside of her, two or three feet down her throat, flexing and sending rippling waves down the length. Carra grabbed hold of the base of the tendril and pulled back, slowly sliding the four foot long tentacle from her throat and open mouth, wrapping her tongue around the shaft, the flexible tentacle drooping between the mouse's hips and her lips. Léo flexed and a thick bead of pre dripped from his cock into her mouth. The croc grabbed the thin point of the tentacle with her other hand and opened her jaws, rubbing the slimy tip against her face, letting the pre and slime cover her skin before she popped the rubbery flesh back between her lips and sucked. She clamped both hands around the base of the tentacle and squeezed, pulling her strong paws toward herself, sliding her clenched fingers along the length and greedily sucking as a flood of thick pre cum flowed freely from the tip, letting it fill her mouth as she wrung the fluid from the shaft. Carra let the fluid submerge her tongue and leak from the corners of her mouth until her hands reached the end, at which point she tilted her head back and opened her maw, letting the flood of fluid flow from the back of her jaw and run down over her body, swallowing what she could. Immediately she clamped her mouth back down onto the tentacle and pushed forward, the tip passing back past her tongue and sliding down her throat until her nose pressed against the mouse's pelvis, sucking as hard as she could manage as Léo simply groaned aloud.

Kett stroked her hand along the thick base of the horse's cock as it grew, watching it slowly stiffen and rise in front of her face. Letting her tentacles roam his body, Kett licked in long motions along the underside of his shaft. Before long, the thick cock had reached its full length, nearly three feet of hot pulsing flesh. The horse panted with his tongue hanging out the side of his mouth as Kett held the member upright and licked from his fat balls to his swollen head, dragging her tongue over the flared head with each pass. Kett wrapped her jaws around the thick head and prodded her tongue against the tight entrance of the horse's cockhole, sucking out the sweet pre and then pushing her tongue into the hole. Slowly his flesh relaxed and accepted more of her tongue, and Kett sucked more of the shaft into her mouth as she pushed the bulk of her tongue through the tight ring at the entrance, feeling the smooth muscular flesh within.

From the corner of her eye, Kett spotted a pile of fresh carrots sitting on the counter top. She let a single tentacle reach out and grab one, pulling it back and holding it in her hand as she let the horse cock slide from her mouth. Kett bit the edge of her lip as she positioned the narrow end of the carrot at the tip of the horse's cockhead. The horse, lost in his own delirium, held his head back with his eyes closed and only moaned as

Kett pressed the rounded carrot tip against his cumhole. Kett gripped the shaft just below the flared head and pushed the carrot against the entrance, gently pressing downward and watching the flexible flesh give slightly. The ring popped open and gave way to the smooth carrot, eliciting a moan from the horse as Kett withdrew the vegetable and watched the hole close again. Pushing once more, this time with more pressure, Kett slid the carrot down, slowly, stretching the horse's cumslit with every centimeter of progress. The fox held the cock rigidly in place as she muscled the object down, stretching the hole to the full diameter of the carrot and then pushing even further until the tight flesh closed around the rounded top, trapping the vegetable within the shaft of the horse's cock except for the plume of bushy green leaves sprouting from the tip.

The horse moaned as Kett wrapped her tentacles up his back and around his head. Kett gripped the rigid horse cock with both hands and milked the entire length of the shaft, running her paws along the smooth flesh and squeezing around the trapped carrot trapped at the top. Flexing her strong tendrils, Kett slowly pulled the horse's head down toward his own erect member, his panting jaws hanging open. Soon the horse's mouth met with his own cockhead, parting just enough to let his throbbing flesh slide past his lips, and Kett continued to pull his head down until the top third of his shaft was trapped within his mouth. He closed his lips around his member without instruction, sucking himself and running his large tongue over his shaft as Kett stroked up and down over the exposed flesh, sliding her hands from the base of his cock up to his pulsing lips. The horse's tongue lapped out occasionally and slurped down the shaft as far as he could manage before sealing his lips around the flared head once again, sucking at the carrot trapped within him, feeling it move upwards against the tight entrance but unable to free it.

Kett stroked up and down along the length of his throbbing flesh, increasing in speed as the horse moaned through closed lips. Her tentacles slid up his muscular back and neck, creeping over his face and winding around his muzzle, holding his mouth closed tight over his shaft. Her entire body rose up and down as she ran her paws along the shaft, quickly building up the pace until her hands were a blur sliding over the smooth flesh, the horse tensing under the pleasure and sucking as hard as he could until Kett could feel the entire length of the cock flex rhythmically, his balls emptying in a torrent into his upright shaft, building up pressure until it shot the trapped carrot out from his cumhole with a sudden pop followed by a flood of thick hot cum jetting into the horse's mouth. Kett milked the equine's shaft as it pulsed, forcing every drop of seed into his mouth as she held his jaws clamped tight against his rod, waiting for his orgasm to subside before releasing him. With a few labored gulps the horse swallowed his immense load and the carrot all at once, the cum-soaked vegetable sliding down his throat.

Alan dug his claws into the tight flesh of the antelope, dragging across her torso as he sucked on her nipple. She arched her back and moaned, grinding her hips upward in need. Alan held her down with his pelvis, straddling her waist as her movements drove him further in his lusty sucking. The antelope floundered and struggled to pull the apron off over her head, but every time she made progress, Alan bit on her nipple and sent her into another spasm. Grinning, Alan sat up and pulled off the apron, looking down at the thin figure trapped beneath him, her eyes pleading, arms reaching out toward his chest. With a quick motion, Alan moved from his position atop her waist and grabbed her hips, flipping her over onto her stomach. Curving her back, the antelope raised her backside into the air without question, her small pants stretching tight against her tiny ass. Alan wrapped his paws around the top of the pants and extended his claws, ripping down and shredding the trousers into ribbons that fell to the ground, still whole around her calves but exposing her tender thighs and dainty buttocks. The antelope stretched forward along the ground, pressing her tits to the floor and spreading her legs slightly, giving Alan a view of her perfect pussy as he brought a paw down hard and smacked her ass.

Quickly undoing his own pants, Alan ran his hands over the wanting antelope hindquarters, rubbing and spreading the cheeks apart, sliding his hardening shaft upwards against her skin. She pushed back against him, rubbing her ass up and down against his hardening cock as Alan slid his tentacles over her torso, wrapping around her body and coiling around her tiny tits, squeezing. The antelope was already dripping wet, her tight pussy radiating heat against Alan's shaft. Grabbing his canine rod by the base, Alan pressed his tapered tip against the antelope's entrance, pulling his cockhead downward against her slit so that it pushed against her folds, running through the hot flesh but not entering her passage. Again, he pressed himself up against the top of her pussy and pulled it down, keeping pressure against her so that his cock tip popped suddenly downward, parting her lips and covering himself in her juices, but still not entering. The antelope moaned aloud and shuddered, pressing herself back against him. Finally, Alan gripped his shaft and pushed up against her entrance, pulling down again but this time pushing forward enough that his head slid down and popped into her wanting flesh, parting her lips and entering her tight channel, drawing a sharp gasp from the antelope.

Pushing forward, Alan buried his thick rod inside his prey until the fat ball of his knot pressed up against her. The husky gripped her muscular thighs and pulled himself against her backside, hilting himself in the scorching hot wetness. Pulling back and then slamming forward with all his might, Alan rammed his cock deep into the creature, causing her to flail in helpless pleasure against the ground, writhing against the tentacles coiled around her body. Looking up, Alan spotted a yellow squash sitting on the counter, a large round bulb the size of a fist at the bottom with a thinner curved stem at the top about an inch in diameter, curling out nearly ninety degrees over its six-inch length. Alan grabbed the vegetable and held it by the round base, pressing the tip of the stem against the antelope's puckered tailhole. At this new sensation, the antelope pawed at the floor and moaned, arching her back further to spread her cheeks wide.

Still rocking his hips forward and back, Alan pushed the curved tip of the gourd against her unused hole, the tight muscle giving way with surprising ease. As he pushed the squash inside her, Alan rotated it along the curve of the stem, pushing the tip of the vegetable up against the top side of her insides. The antelope cried out in pleasure as Alan pushed the squash in down to the fat bulb at the bottom, the stem curving nearly vertically inside her. Alan let go of the yellow vegetable and let the flat base rest against his pelvis, just above his cock, and grabbed the antelope's hips once more, pressing himself forward, hilting himself inside her hot flesh.

Alan pressed himself forward and back, pushing both his hard shaft and the squash into the antelope girl with each thrust, burying himself inside her greedy pussy. His swollen dog knot pushed against her entrance as the bulb of the squash stretched her tailhole with every thrust, Alan slamming himself into her harder and harder with each successive lunge. As the base of the gourd pressed against the antelope's hole, the bottom of the vegetable dug into Alan's skin, grinding against his pelvis. Each time Alan thrust forward, burying his rod inside her, the squash pressed firmer against his flesh, his skin wrapping up and around the bottom surface, sticking to it like thick ooze. Suddenly, Alan cried out as he felt his nerves snap open and his body bind with the firm gourd in an instant, a rush of blood surging from his hips as it filled the vegetable and attached itself to his mind, the curved stem deep inside the antelope's ass flexing and curling further as Alan clenched his every muscle. A warm sensation ran down through Alan's new appendage as a stream of pre cum pushed through the stem, exiting through the tip in spurts as Alan dug his claws into the antelope's hips.

Growling in intense pleasure, Alan bucked his hips forward and back roughly, fucking the thrashing antelope girl with both of his rock hard cocks deep inside her. He pulled back, drawing both of his members out nearly entirely, the curved stem of his squash cock bending straight as he pulled back, pushing upwards against her tight asshole. Then Alan slammed back in as fast as he could, forcing the stem to curve upwards inside her as stretched her pussy underneath. Alan bucked forward and back, impaling her with long strokes as he slammed both of his giant knots against her two filled holes.

Kett let her tentacles slide from the horse's head and shoulders as she let her pants fall to the floor. Her cock, already rock hard, twitched in the open air as she turned and bent over at the waist, lifting her tail for the equine still seated behind her. Not needing much encouragement, the horse stood and approached, his member already re-stiffening at the sight of the fox's bare slit. Kett coiled her tendrils around his legs and thighs, pulling him closer until his hips met with her butt, his long rod hanging down between her legs, rising slowly. Kett reached down and wrapped her fingers around the horse cock once again, sliding her paws over its surface as it twitched and stiffened, tilting her hips forward and back so that her own hard shaft slid along the topside. At full hardness the equine's shaft reached up between her tits, rubbing against her belly and chest. Kett coiled her slimy cords up around the horse's hips, sliding around to grip the base of his cock and then pulling upwards with slow, deliberate pressure, forcing the long shaft to bend as she dragged it upwards, grinding against her dripping wet pussy until the length of his shaft popped upwards and fell back onto Kett's back with a slap.

Sliding her smooth tentacles over the horse's muscular body, Kett wrapped around the base of his cock and wound around his balls. The stallion took a step back to position himself and grabbed the middle of his shaft to place the head against Kett's wanting entrance. Kett spread her legs and moaned to herself, relaxing and pushing back against the fat flare of the horse cock, pulling the servant forward with her tentacles until the broad tip popped inside her tight pussy. Both crying out in pleasure, Kett pulled the horse by the hips and forced him to take a step forward, his entire length sliding into her passage with one long, smooth movement. Kett leaned back against the horse's hips as he hilted himself inside her tight flesh, her coiled tendrils squeezing firmly against the base of his rod as they pushed up against her stretched lips.

The horse rocked forward and back, sliding his long shaft through Kett's distorted body. Coiling and tightening her tendrils in ecstasy, Kett wound the cords of ooze around both of their legs, tying their limbs together. Kett let the massive shaft bend her insides, flexing and relaxing her tight hole until it was long enough to hold the entire member, the flared head pushing forward and back within her chest. The horse fought against the grip of the tentacles in his effort to buck against her, but with every movement Kett squeezed their legs tighter together. Feeling the thick shaft flex and drool inside her, filling her entire body with hot flesh, Kett clenched down on the length and gripped the horse's hips forcefully, bearing down on his body and pressing his legs against her thighs, his hips against hers as she groaned.

Feeling the now familiar release of nerve endings, Kett sighed in pleasure as she felt her legs stick to the equine's. Clamping down harder, pulling him against her, Kett closed her eyes in bliss as their legs knit together, their skin merging and pulling together under the squeezing coils. The horse made a startled sound but there was little he could do to resist, even if he wanted to. Kett ground her hips up against the horse's pelvis, rocking up and down against him and forcing the rod inside her to grind forward and back. The warm rod inside her leaked pre cum in a steady stream, and Kett could feel the cock grow in length within her. The broad head of the horse shaft pushed forward within her chest, widening subtly as it pushed deeper into her pussy, lengthening through her body until she could feel it at the base of her neck. Her body easily shifted without conscious effort, and now the flared head of the horse cock pulsed within her throat, a flood of pre cum rushing from Kett's open mouth as the rod of flesh bore a single passage through her body.

Lapping her tongue against the stream of thick pre drooling from her open mouth, Kett reached her arms back and pulled at her ass cheeks, spreading them for the horse to see as her arms and hands melded with her torso, shoulders rapidly shrinking into her body. Kett closed her eyes and focused on the bliss within her, feeling the growing horse cock thicken and pump her body full of thick juices as it ground against her passage, clenching against the hard flesh in waves rippling from her throat down to the entrance of her pussy. Mind swimming in pleasure, Kett was vaguely aware of her face and head shifting, her mouth forced into a round pucker, her face flattening to mimic the flare of the cock within her. Kett swallowed endlessly against the steady stream of pre, the grinding of the hot muscled meat against her pussy slowing as their bodies melded together, nerves fusing together and sending a shiver down Kett's spine. Moaning aloud in her mind but only hearing blood rushing through her head, Kett reveled in the feeling of her entire body bristling with ecstatic energy. Each time the horse flexed his cock her entire torso rose and fell, pushing a fat drop of pre cum from her mouth. Kett could hear the horse's thoughts, almost clearer than her own, the confused beast wanting nothing more than to use his new massive Kett-sized cock on something, yearning for release.

Squeezing his claws into the antelope's hips, Alan watched Kett's body morph, her groans of ecstasy softening to distant moans as her flesh shifted and transformed into the body of the horse, her torso elongating into a thick hard shaft of horse cock. Alan growled in lust at the sight, sinking his dual members deeper into the antelope, pressing the fat knots of his dog shaft and appropriated squash member against her tight entrances as his flesh tingled, remembering the rapture of melding into Kett's body only one day prior. Pulling the antelope's hips back against his own, Alan rammed his knots into the tight pussy and tailhole in a single rough motion, forcing her holes wide as his flesh slid into her, baring his teeth and arching his back as the antelope cried out in bliss.

Alan reached forward and dug his sharp claws into the shoulders of the antelope, flexing his shafts as he dragged his paws back toward himself, raking against her flesh. Pushing her head down to the ground, Alan pulled back roughly, yanking his fat knots from her tunnels and then immediately ramming back inside. Again, Alan gripped her hips and sank his claws into her flesh as he popped the thick bulbs of flesh out and then pushed back in, fucking her hot pussy and ass with his fist-sized knots, the antelope's cries filling the kitchen as her holes clenched firmly around his every inch. Ramming forward harder with each thrust, slamming his hips hard against her ass, Alan clenched his teeth and pulled back on her hips as firmly as he could, drawing back and pressing forward faster and faster until he clenched his teeth and pulled himself forward with a single violent

100

thrust. His hips slammed into her backside and they slapped together, instantly melding and merging into each other, Alan's hips and torso sticking straight up from the top of her hips.

Reaching forward to sink his claws into the antelope's shoulders once again, Alan immediately noticed that he could feel everything she felt; the thick cocks knotted inside her pumping pre cum into her holes, the coolness of the kitchen floor against her cheek, his claws as they dug into her flesh and pulled back. Alan flexed his rods inside her and she moaned in semi-conscious bliss, he more aware of her pleasure than she was. His body blushed as blood surged from his legs, the antelope's calves and thighs shrinking and melting into his body. Alan felt his ball sack pull against his skin as it grew, sagging with weight. The antelope's arms shrank and withdrew into her body, and her two long pointed horns softened and drew closer to the back of her head. Alan reached forward and grabbed the horns as they came within reach, shivering as he wrapped his paw around one, stroking up over its length as it morphed into a long fleshy pointed rod. The antelope moaned incoherently, drooling onto the floor as the horns flexed and curled, small drops of pre forming at the tips as Alan stroked them.

Unable to move his hips against hers, Alan flexed his cocks repeatedly, grinding his flesh against hers in any way he could, streams of pre cum oozing into her tight holes. As Alan flexed, the antelope writhed, twitching and shaking with each motion as her head elongated into the pointed head of a giant canine cock. Pre cum flowed from the antelope's mouth as her fur drew into her body, revealing slick muscle. Alan closed his eyes in bliss as he flexed his two cocks constantly, crying out as he felt his rods dissolve into the hot flesh wrapped around them, the antelope instantly gaining all the sensitivity of his shaft. Soon the antelope was unrecognizable, Alan simply stroking the topside of the giant rod protruding from his hips, his morphed member similar to a massive dog cock aside from the two fleshy horns trailing back from the flared head.

Léo flexed his cock and filled Carra's mouth with his pre before sliding the slick tendril from her maw. She fell to the ground in desire and began licking her skin to find more of the juices as Léo walked behind her. Sensing his presence, the croc pushed her ass up into the air, shifting her massive tail to the side to expose her wanting hole. The mouse, generally unfamiliar with reptiles, held the tip of his slimy tentacle up against the single wet entrance and pushed inside, and Carra moaned as the flesh slid past her entrance with little resistance.

Exhaling slowly as he took a step forward, Léo pushed his tentacle cock into the crocodile until he had buried nearly a foot of his length, Carra crying out in mad desire as she felt him fill her. Léo quickly discovered, however, that he had pushed into the wrong hole, as a soft voice from the glowing seed within his pelvis told him that this would not do. Pausing to think, but finding only lust in his mind, Léo simply pushed further forward and curled his prehensile tentacle shaft within the croc's asshole, doubling back on himself and winding his long oozing cord around itself in a double helix until he had advanced far enough that the fleshy tip found its way back out, and then quickly doubled back again. Léo probed with the tapered tip, searching for another entrance until Carra's folds yielded, the pair moaning in unison as the mouse penetrated her warm flesh again. As Léo impaled the croc, his long tendril of slick flesh curled around itself into her ass, then curled back out, slid over her clit and then pushed up into her pussy, penetrating each hole nearly a foot in depth.

Léo buried himself in Carra's holes until his hips met with hers, grinding his supple flesh against her rigid scales, wrapping his tiny paws around her thick muscular thighs. The crocodile's head lay against the

102

floor, moaning and drooling as Léo thrust forward and back, sliding his slick tendril in and out of each of her holes simultaneously. Léo felt her clench around him from every angle as his cock slid against itself, coiling forward and back with each thrust and grinding against her flesh. He found that he could unwind the helix within her ass and press outward against her hole, stretching her wider with each thrust. Spurts of pre cum shot from the long tentacle each time Léo flexed and hilted himself within the croc's holes.

Catching his breath, Alan opened his eyes to see his new massive rod flexing and twitching before him, hanging horizontally under its own weight despite its rigidity. Panting, the husky looked over to the horse servant who was likewise entertaining himself with his morphed rod, holding his long equine shaft upright, stroking himself with his entire arms. The broad tip of the horse's cock rose above his own head by a full foot, the shaft thick enough that the horse could barely wrap his arms around the circumference. Two gigantic balls swung between his parted legs, hanging more than halfway to the ground, rivulets of pre cum dripping to the floor. Alan stood and approached the cook, his own swollen sack swinging between his legs.

Alan held his rod upright and stepped close to the horse, pressing the soft underside of his shaft against that of the giant horse cock. Rocking his hips upwards, Alan bucked his flesh against the hot horse meat, their pre cum drooling out and sliding down to cover their flesh. Alan extended his tentacles and wound them around the two massive shafts, squeezing the two together and rubbing up and down their lengths, coiling upwards and sliding his slick tendrils into each of their cumholes. Alan and the horse moaned as they ground their cocks together; Kett and the antelope's minds cried out in pleasure, deep within their hosts' bodies as their sensitive bodies rubbed against each other, pre cum flowing from their holes as Alan penetrated them.

Taking a few steps back, Alan let both of their stiff rods lower to horizontal. The broad head of the horse's shaft throbbed and drooled as the equine held it in place. Alan held his own member as he positioned his flared head at the horse's tight cockhole, withdrawing his tendrils from their entrances and winding in a firm coil down both of their lengths. Pressing his tapered tip forward against the horse's small hole, Alan pulled their cocks together with his gripping tentacles. The pointed head pushed forward slightly into the horse's tight cumslit, eliciting a moan from the servant as Kett felt the hot flesh penetrate her drooling hole.

Stepping forward, Alan slid his flared head into the slim cumhole of the horse's shaft, Kett's tight entrance stretching under the strain of the penetration. Alan pulled his coiled tentacles together and pushed forward through the slickness, filling the horse's cock. The tapered head spread the horse flesh wide, Alan pressing forward and stretching it until he pushed in past his flared tip, Kett's clenching hole squeezing and pulling Alan in further, the antelope's two fleshy prongs sliding partway in as they pressed against the topside of Alan's shaft. The canine moaned and drooled, his mouth hanging open as he felt the antelope writhe within his mind, the touch of flesh connecting his mind to the distant thoughts of Kett and the horse as well.

Taking another step forward, Alan crammed his cock into the horse's shaft, watching the two soft tendrils disappear into the servant's hole. Pushing further, stretching the cock slit to the thickness of Alan's massive rod, the husky buried himself in the horse flesh until his gigantic knot pressed up against the horse's flared head. The servant cook shook with pleasure, stumbling back a half-step and bracing himself against the counter behind him. Alan flexed and the horse gasped, feeling the dog flesh swell within his tight passage.

Kett felt the hot shaft sear through her core, filling her body and stretching her in every direction, wetness flowing freely within her from both Alan and the horse. She felt the thick bulb of flesh pressed firmly against her entrance, groaning to herself as Alan tightened the grip of his tentacles, sliding the coil of slick ooze forward and back over the transformed horse manhood, squeezing Kett from the outside and compressing her against the dog cock thrust within her body. The two tapered tendrils of Alan's rod squirmed back and forth, sliding against Kett's flesh as Alan stroked forward and back.

Alan rocked his hips forward and back as best he could, only able to thrust in and out a foot or so as the horse gripped tight to the countertop to keep from collapsing. Shifting his entire body back and forth as far as he could, drawing his oversized member out as far as his stance would allow him, Alan slammed back with ferocity, pulling himself forward by the tentacle grip he had wound around the horse's cock, impaling the equine flesh and pounding his knot against the tight entrance, pushing the chef back against the counter with each penetrating lunge. The four cried out in unheard unison, their minds melting together as flesh ground against hot flesh. Kett's body forced open by the penetrating shaft, feeling the tapered head fill her depths. The Antelope's mind an incoherent stream of ecstasy as her muscled shaft was squeezed by the horse flesh, and then compressed further by Alan's coiled tendrils.

Bucking against the scaled hindquarters of his former master, Léo gripped the croc's hips and thrust forward roughly, pulling his long fleshy tendril out from each orifice and plunging back, drawing incoherent moans from the labor master between her desperate pleadings. Carra begged for Léo's cock to fill her, yearning for his cum to spill inside her as she pressed her hips back up against him with every pounding thrust. Soon Léo could hear the distant voice within his body cry out for release as well, demanding that the mouse orgasm into the crocodile's tight pussy.

Partly driven by his own delirious lust, but also by the order of his former owner for him to fill her and the subconscious voice within his body commanding him to drive forward, Léo fucked Carra's ass and pussy simultaneously, drawing back as far as his hips could travel before plunging back in roughly, filling the croc's flesh with the thick cord of slime. Hips moving without his conscious effort, mind numb with madness and desire, Léo squeezed tight against the croc's hips and thrust again and again, his hips slapping against her thick thighs as Carra squirmed and spasmed on the floor.

Tension finally built within the mouse's body to the point of no return, and Léo pressed his hips tight against Carra's backside as cum shot into her wet pussy. Before the mouse could fully drain himself, however, Léo gasped and the seed within his pelvis shifted out of place, the thick stream of cum halting as the glowing sphere melded through the mouse's flesh and found its way into his flooded hole, stretching his passage from the inside in a rapid burning movement as Léo held his breath in surprise. Once the orb found its way into Léo's tentacle cockhole at the base of his hips, it pushed down his channel and stretched its way into Carra's entrance. Both the mouse and the croc crying out in unison, the giant sphere slid, slowly, along Léo's cock through Carra's ass, coiling deeper inside along the helixed tentacle, stretching both of their holes wide as it reached the deepest point and then doubled back and followed the coil back outward. The pair quivered and shook, powerless and at the mercy of the globe as it filled their focus, stretching their hot flesh as Léo flexed his cock again and again. Carra cried out and shook as the seed twisted around within her tight tailhole, climaxing on the bulge as it stretched her

106

from within, shaking and twitching uncontrollably. Finally winding its way down to Carra's entrance, the orb popped free from her asshole in a sudden motion that caused them both to flinch and clench, the seed then grinding over Carra's clit with intense pressure. Advancing mercilessly, the sphere pressed back into the croc's pussy, stretching her wide as it slid down the last foot of the mouse's tentacle cock, filling her hot passage as it slid, deeper and deeper, toward the tapered tip of Léo's tendril until it finally reached the end, stretching the mouse's hole wider and wider until it finally popped free of his shaft, both Carra and Léo moaning loudly as the seed bore deep into the crocs pussy followed by an intense torrent of pent-up cum flooding from the stretched tentacle, pumping deep into her flesh until she was filled past the brim and jets of mouse cum squirted back out from the croc's clenching entrance, covering them both.

Léo gasped desperately for breath, still hilted within the croc's holes as he fought to regain control of himself. Carra, however, squirmed and thrashed her body against the ground, drooling and moaning. The croc climaxed again, squeezing her pussy tight against the seed buried deep within her, feeling it shift and merge with her flesh. Slowly, with several deep breaths, Léo pulled his long tendril from the croc's holes, watching in satisfaction as she collapsed to the ground in helpless pleasure, the glowing orb performing some unseen action deep within her body.

Carra screamed and climaxed once again, cum and ooze flowing from her hole as she squirmed on the ground, pushing herself along the floor toward the entrance of the well. Driven by the silent voice inside her body, Carra found the small hole in the ground and pushed her head against the lip. Léo could see that there was no way that the croc would fit, but she was obviously determined to find a way. Once again her entire body shook and collapsed in climax, writhing on the ground and twisting in uncontrollable pleasure as black tendrils crawled out from her maw, spreading out and searching for the hole in the ground. The tips of the tentacles found the well and dragged the thrashing crocodile closer, pressing her head against the opening, latching onto the uneven stonework of the vertical shaft and pulling the croc down with force. Carra's maw and head softened like clay, melting and distorting as the slime pulled her down. Her shoulders squeezed down into the tiny hole, followed by her entire body, melding into a pliable crocodile-shaped ooze. Carra screamed in pleasure as another orgasm wracked her transformed body, echoing into the depths as her feet finally disappeared past the lip.

Pumping forward and back, grunting with each deep lunge, Alan's mouth hung open in frenzied lust as he fucked the horse cock. He and the antelope could feel the tension building within their joined pelvis, thrusting roughly as Alan's vision blurred, pulling himself forward with every available ounce of strength to fill his desire. As the burning grew, Alan pushed his hips deeper, smashing the fat bulb of flesh against the horse's stretched cumhole with every motion, pulling on his coiled tentacles with his full force until the tight ring of muscle finally yielded, Kett's entrance stretching obscenely under Alan's unrelenting thrusts, the thick swell of red dog cock forcing its way into the horse's rod in a single violent motion until the entrance slid past the widest diameter, squeezing hard against Alan's knot to pull the rest inside, trapping the entirety of the rock hard shaft within the horse's hole. The instant that Alan felt his knot pop inside the horse's cumslit, he lost all control and arched his back, grinding his hips against the flared horse cock as he climaxed, thick ropes of hot cum spraying from his tapered head deep into the horse's hole, pumping gallons of seed into the quivering stallion as he threw his head back and howled incoherently.

The horse gripped the counter as hard as he could to keep himself upright, weak and shaking in pleasure as he felt Alan pump his load into his body. He could feel the slick liquid flow into his cock with each flex and spasm, pouring into his hips and pooling in his ball sack. Kett could do nothing but cry out in her mind as she felt Alan's flesh twitch and bulge within her, emptying itself of everything and flooding it into her. The antelope, feeling as much of the orgasm as Alan, nearly blacked out from the sensation of pumping a torrent of cum deep into the horse, her flesh feeling every drop as it coursed through her body in an endless wave, tasting the heady fluid as each pulsing jet pumped from her tapered head.

Even as Alan continued to drain himself into the hose's hole, he could feel the antelope's body begin to separate from his own. Pumping pulse after pulse of cum through the oversized rod, Alan felt his own member disassociate itself from the antelope's transformed flesh, suddenly feeling the juices pumping from his rod into the servant's pussy in the midst of the orgasm. The sensation of the giant cock quickly faded to a background whisper in Alan's mind as the antelope's legs un-melded from his own. As Alan panted and shot the last of his cum into the clenching pussy, he looked down to see the now re-formed ungulate bent over at the waist, torso buried deep into the horse cock and legs hanging down to the ground, his own natural canine shaft knotted within her pussy.

Before Alan could catch his breath, Kett tugged at the antelope, rippling her smooth passage against the trapped animal to guide her further into the abused cumhole. Hungry with desire, Kett pulled at the antelope until the tension un-knotted her from Alan's member. Panting, but spent, Alan took a step back and simply watched as the horse grabbed his shaft and held it upright, flinging the servant girl's dangling legs up above his rod's hole. Slowly, the antelope slid down into the bulging horse cock, guided down by gravity and Kett's lust, until her lithe legs disappeared into the throbbing flesh. The equine wrapped his arms around his shaft and pushed down on the bulge, forcing the antelope down into the depths of his body, groaning at each sliding movement until she was deposited into his heavy ball sack, already distorted and filled by Alan's load. Finally slumping against the counter, the horse panted and attempted to remain upright, weak with desire.

Kett let herself relax, blood flowing from her transformed body back into the horse, causing the giant shaft to bend and shrink. It would be no trouble to deny the equine of the orgasm he desired, as she discovered that she could control the horse's erection with ease. Though, of course, there was nothing to stop the horse from feeling aroused for the next couple of days; in fact, she could already tell that he would most likely be driven toward the brink of insanity with lust before she let him climax at the party the evening after next.

Chapter 8

In the mental darkness of the equine's psyche, Kett lurked. Among the latent desires and half-formed thoughts, the fox hid and mingled with his mind. Kett learned that the horse's name was Marshall; the antelope was named Ell. She subconsciously guided the horse to resume his normal duties, returning to the small servant's quarters in the evening and staffing the kitchens during the day. His mind was a constant haze of arousal, his heart thumping in his chest each time his thoughts turned toward the feeling of warm flesh against his skin. Not fully aware of what was happening within his body, he stumbled onward through his responsibilities without uttering a word to his colleagues, never producing a sound aside from the occasional muffled groan or desperate whine as his body denied his every desire.

Partway through the next day, a fellow kitchen servant touched Marshall on the shoulder out of concern for his wellbeing. Unable to respond with anything intelligible, the horse simply gave a strangled smile and returned to his work, but the split second of touch, that moment of skin-on-skin sent him into a quivering stupor. His cock, forced flaccid by Kett's influence, leaked a thick drop of pre within his pants, soaking into the linen. For the rest of the day Marshall could catch subtle hints of his own heady scent, faint but undeniable, and this only drove him further into desperate lust.

That night, the equine lay in his bunk, wide awake with arousal. Kett let his shaft harden into a massive throbbing erection, but forced the horse to remain motionless. Nude, lying on his back, Marshall panted and drooled, his giant cock resting against his belly and chest, leaking a constant stream of pre cum onto his face. Arms locked to his sides, the horse could do nothing but lie motionless, swallowing in mad desire as drops of pre slid into his open mouth. In this way he spent the entire night, fully awake, until Kett once again pulled the blood from the oversized organ, denying the creature even a single moment of touch before he had to rise from bed and begin his daily duties.

Alan and Léo found that they could conceal themselves among the serving staff with relative ease. Léo knew the estate well enough, and was able to disguise Alan as a groundsman for the next day and a half without issue. Little question was given to the matter of the disappearing antelope, as servants were sold or relocated on a regular basis. Many servants were curious as to the fate of their crocodile overseer, but not enough to actually make any serious inquiries. As for Carra's superiors, a well-placed rumor or two sent the nobles searching competing great houses for a defecting slave master.

Carra's actual fate, however, went entirely unnoticed. In the depths of the well, deep below the kitchen, the creature overtook the croc's body and grew. Soon it was strong enough that it could send out burrowing tendrils, digging into the rock of the underground aquifer, emitting unheard signals. Late into the second day, these tendrils met with the seeking ooze of the creature's main body, back in the quarantine zone. In an instant, flesh met flesh and the organism became whole again, Carra subsumed into the collective consciousness along with the dozen bodies lining the shaft of the original well. Without hesitation, the creature began spreading through the rock underneath the Hykan estate.

That evening, Alan and Léo made their way to the great hall as the night's guests filtered in. Master Haxiten Hykan, a tall muscular leopard, greeted the various nobles as they arrived, accompanied on either side by Drenirya, his slender gecko wife, and Zelia, their imposing female hyena bodyguard. Alan and Léo stood by the food service table, disguised in the aprons of the kitchen staff as they watched the city's elite make friendly conversation throughout the room. The great hall itself was expansive, but warmly furnished. In the center of the room, the floor stepped down into a shallow bowl of sorts, about ten feet in diameter and filled with plush pillows. Several comfortable beds and couches lined the walls, save the side that held the food tables. At the far end of the chamber there was a raised platform, a dais that obviously served as a place for the head of the great house to sit and take audience on any other night. Currently, however, the platform held a string quartet and an unoccupied grand piano.

Within the hour the hall filled with nearly one hundred people between the noble guests, their servants, and the House Hykan staff. At first glance, the party appeared to be like any other affair, composed primarily of small circles of guests chatting politely and greeting each other before breaking off and finding someone else to talk to. As Alan watched closely, however, he noted several peculiarities. Many guests spent a good deal of time leering at other partiers, or their slaves. Most servants stood obediently by their owner's sides, many of them topless or entirely nude. It seemed customary for guests to inspect each other's servants during the course of their conversations, squeezing a breast or buttock and commenting politely on the noble's taste in companions.

Alan watched as a small group near the food tables talked politely, discussing local politics and nobleperson affairs while gazing at the hard bodies of the servants interspersed throughout the circle. One of the nobles, particularly captivated by the thin otter brought by one of his friends, requested permission from the servant's owner to inspect more closely. Upon receiving approval, he ordered the otter to give himself an erection. The servant, without so much as shifting his gaze, stood at attention with his hands clasped behind his back, his limp penis slowly lengthening and rising upright. Soon the otter's cock hardened to its full size, pulsing slightly in time with his heartbeat. The nobleman watched keenly and smiled, licking his lips slightly. Having seen what he desired to see, the noble thanked the otter's owner, at which point the servant was commanded to return to his previous state until called on again. And, indeed, within moments the servant's member was totally flaccid, and the topic of conversation returned to affairs of local gossip.

The polite discussion phase of the evening soon passed, however, once the master of the house picked the lucky guest that would help him set the party in motion. The leopard, his wife, and his bodyguard happened upon a mantis woman, an exotic treat by anyone's standards. The mantis, standing nearly eight feet tall when upright, had a proud and dignified bearing that Master Hykan found irresistible. Drenirya and Zelia watched coolly as the leopard approached the owner of the mantis, bowed politely, and received a similar bow in return.

With that single exchange, the master and his companions led the mantis to the center of the room and descended regally into the shallow pillow-lined pit. Most of the guests watched in a combination of curiosity and respect as their host removed his clothing, his half-erect manhood bobbing in the air. Haxiten bit his lower lip and walked around the mantis, inspecting the alien legs and body with growing fascination. Upon reaching the rear of the creature, Hykan stopped and looked more closely. The hindquarters of the creature were entirely dissimilar from anything he would normally be attracted to, but this itself seemed cause for arousal. The mantis remained motionless as the leopard ran his hands over her chitinous backside, drawing his face close and finding the creature's single opening, already warm and moist with anticipation. A single long lick over its surface caused the mantis to flinch and moan aloud, the entire audience smiling and chuckling in unison.

Drenirya, the slender gecko, approached the mantis from the front and confidently pressed her palms to the insect's chest, rubbing her skin over the smooth armored breasts. She leaned in close and licked, dragging her tongue slowly from the bottom of her torso up to her tits. The mantis servant remained mostly motionless, aside from the shivers and moans drawn out by the master and mistress' touch. Her chest rose and fell with her heavy breath as the leopard rubbed his hardening shaft against her backside, pressing himself against her body and grabbing at her rear legs. Soon Haxiten's cock thickened and pulsed, his seven inch shaft rubbing up and down over the mantis' entrance. Master Hykan looked sideways to his audience and smiled before grabbing himself by the hilt and positioning his barbed tip at the insect's dripping hole, pushing forward with a grunt and burying his flesh into the servant with a single lunge. The mantis cried out in a long alien groan as the cat filled her from behind, the gecko mistress grabbing and squeezing her tits roughly as the audience cheered.

Once the master of the house began pumping against the mantis in earnest, the rest of the house guests dropped all pretense of restraint. Some partiers continued to watch the leopard, touching themselves or their partners as Hykan pistoned in and out of the insect, but most nobles found whichever guest or servant they had been eyeing for the evening and laid their claims. Within minutes the entire room was naked, nearly every guest finding a servant or two to pleasure them or perform whatever deed they craved. Nobles who desired to play with other nobles did so freely, but typically with the assistance of a handful of servants as well.

Marshall stood near the food tables, eyes darting from person to person as they all touched, licked, groped and sucked each other. A few feet away, two servants from a visiting great house, small feline and lupine girls, took advantage of their master's distracted state and began groping each other's breasts. Obviously pent up from an entire day of party preparations, the pair knelt on the ground and pressed their mouths together, grinding their bare hips against each other. Kett watched the two servants through the horse's eyes, moaning to herself in desire as the cat pressed her paw against the bunny's clit, rubbing forward and back as she bit the lupine's neck. Marshall, still trapped in his denied arousal, could do nothing but stand and watch, shaking with need.

Seeing the horse servant, the cat whispered into the bunny's ear, receiving a mischievous grin in reply. Approaching the cook, the two guests ground their bodies against each other mere feet from where he stood. The bunny made a show of throwing her head back and moaning as the cat rubbed her clit. Kett felt Marshall's desperate quivering, still denying him even the ability to harden his shaft as the cat slid a single digit into the bunny's drenched pussy.

The cat could obviously see the restrained desire of the horse, and this served only to drive her further. Pushing two fingers deep into the rabbit, the cat licked her lips and looked up lustily at the equine, the bunny closing her eyes and arching her back as her playmate brought her to a quick orgasm. Legs shaking as she recovered, the rabbit girl clung to the cat and licked her neck, then whispered into her ear, smiling. The cat returned her smile, and they both looked at the horse, eyes sweeping up and down his hard body.

Kett watched in devious pleasure as the pair of slave girls crawled closer on their knees, inching forward until they were face to face with the horse's crotch. Glancing at each other once again, the pair reached up and carefully unfastened Marshall's pants, untying the laces with deliberate slowness as the servant watched helplessly. Pulling, teasing, the pair brought his pants down, revealing the giant sheath and swollen ball sack. Kett couldn't help but chuckle to herself when she saw the look on their faces: equal parts shock and desire.

The cat and rabbit drew in close and ran their paws up and down the horse's muscular legs, pressing their breasts against him as they caressed upwards, dragging their fingers closer to his sheath before moving back down again. Kett allowed Marshall to remove the apron so that he was fully nude, but could still only watch as the girls rubbed against his legs. The bunny reached out a paw and pressed her palm against one of his massive balls, squeezing gently and feeling the impossible weight. Despite the fact that his shaft was hidden inside his sheath, a thick drop of pre oozed from the opening, running slowly down his skin and sliding over his swollen sack. Both the cat and the bunny leaned in and licked at the viscous liquid, dragging their tongues against his soft skin and savoring the taste.

Feeling their tongues, Kett found herself driven to the same intense desire as her equine host, finally loosening her control and allowing his cock to slide, slowly, from its sheath. Marshall groaned aloud as his body finally obeyed his desire, the denied lust finally finding an outlet as his shaft pushed upwards, curling forward under its immense weight. The cat and bunny watched, stunned at the size of the organ, as the horse flexed his shaft and sent thick drops of pre flowing from the broad head to the floor. Quickly leaning in and grabbing the thick muscle, the pair held the flared tip at head level and let the pre cum drool into their mouths, pressing their faces side by side so that they could share. When the shaft hardened enough that they couldn't hold it down anymore, the two servants pressed their open mouths to each other's, tongues locked together as they licked at the delicious liquid.

Once the Marshall's cock had reached its full hardness, standing upright and extending up beyond the top of his head, the feline and lupine servants stood and pressed both their tits against the immense girth of his shaft. The pair rubbed up and down, moaning softly to themselves and gazing at the impossible member as they pressed their nipples against the hard flesh. Drops of pre continued to slide down the front of the shaft and the two girls raced each other for the opportunity to lick up the liquid. The bunny parted her legs and rubbed her crotch against the swollen testicles, moaning as the warm skin pressed against her mound.

Each time the girls licked up a thick drop of pre, their minds clouded further with mad lust, their pussies dripping as they were driven to desperate desire. What began as obvious impossibility melted into curious craving, and eventually wanton need. The bunny servant groaned as she pressed her body against the horse, rubbing her paws up and down the giant shaft and imagining it filling her. Soon the desire overcame reason, and the rabbit girl circled around to the food table, quickly pushing some dishes to the ground before leaning over, pressing her tits to the tablecloth and presenting her wet pussy to the horse.

At this point, Kett loosened all control she had on Marshall, as she knew that the he could only do exactly what she wanted. Spinning around to face the rabbit, the horse grabbed his throbbing member and forced it into a horizontal position, pressing the flared tip against the bunny's backside. The feline servant watched with a mix of horror, disbelief, and arousal, kneeling near the ass of her rabbit partner. Kett could see through Marshall's eyes that the girth of the shaft was easily as wide as the bunny's torso, but this only turned her on more. The thick head of the horse cock pressed firmly against the rabbit servant's hindquarters, as wide as both her ass-cheeks. Kett felt the warm moisture of the lupine pussy pressing against her transformed flesh.

The cat servant rubbed her paws across the long horse shaft, forward and back, breathing heavily as she felt the thin layer of skin slide over the rock hard muscle underneath. She clawed at the bunny's thighs as she watched the horse press forward, simply squishing the rabbit's hips between his giant cock and the table. The rabbit moaned aloud, bucking her ass up and down, rubbing her pussy against the flat head of the horse flesh. Climbing up onto the table, the cat straddled the bunny's hips, facing the horse. She reached between her legs and ran her claws against the top of the Marshall's shaft, dragging toward herself and encouraging the horse forward into her partner's body.

As Marshall leaned forward, desperately pressing against the moaning bunny girl, the flat head of his cock pinned her against the table, grinding firmly against her dripping pussy. The cat leaned down and slid her paws between the horse and the bunny, rubbing against her partner's warm entrance, feeling the surge of wetness coming from both of their bodies. She pressed her paw down against the rabbit's slit, sliding two, then three fingers inside with ease. Mouth open and panting with lust, the cat pressed more of her paw into the bunny, watching as her entire hand slid into the tight pussy with little effort. The bunny cried out and clenched down hard on the cat's wrist, arms stretched wide on the table as she moaned and twitched.

Kett's mind salivated as she watched the cat push her entire fist into the bunny and encouraged the horse to press forward yet again. Trapping the cat's arm between the flared head of his shaft and the rabbit's hindquarters, Marshall leaned in and flexed, coating the cat's wrist and forearm in slick pre cum. The feline moaned and felt the heat enveloping her arm from both sides, flexing her fist and turning it subtly within the tight grip of the bunny's hole. As the horse pulled back slightly, the cat took the opportunity to slide her other arm downwards, pointing her digits and pressing them against the place where her wrist was enveloped in the bunny's flesh. Quickly pushing her paw against her wrist, the cat positioned herself so that as Marshall drew back in, the pressure of the advancing member pressed firmly against her arms and forced the cat's second fist into the bunny's stretched entrance.

The lupine girl screamed and groaned as the cat's second fist slid into her spasming pussy, clenching as the widest part slid in and gripping so that the cat was forced further inside, enveloped up to her wrist, trapped in place by the horse flesh. Thrashing against the table, squirming and clawing, the bunny climaxed once again and squeezed down hard on the cat's fists, crying out in sheer delirious pleasure.

As Marshall leaned forward and back, pushing the cat's fists in and out of the bunny's tight hole ever so slightly, the cat began to notice a certain pliability to her partner's flesh. Positioning herself as best she could, the cat started rocking her arms and hands back and forth in time with the horse, tilting back each time he pressed the giant flat cockhead against her. As she pulled back toward herself, the cat could feel the bunny pussy stretch, widening by fractions of an inch each time she pivoted back. Soon she could pull the gushing lupine hole wide enough that she could slide in a third fist, if she had one. Each time she spread the bunny's pussy lips, the horse surged forward, pressing the throbbing cock flesh against her backside, pouring pre cum onto her ass cheeks.

The bunny, reduced to a drooling heap on the table, was lost in a mad haze as the cat stretched her wider and wider. She could feel her hips pull apart, her pulsing pussy forced open followed by the overwhelming warmth of the horse's flesh grinding against her. Eyes closed, the bunny could do nothing but clench against the cat's grip, spasming uncontrollably as her hole was pulled open. As the cat rocked forward and back she started grinding her pussy against the bunny's hindquarters with each forceful pull, breath raspy as she greedily spread her friend wide.

Kett watched hungrily as the bunny's entrance grew larger and larger, now not even having the opportunity to return to its original size between strokes. Each time Marshall shifted back, Kett could see into the gaping hole, already nearly a foot wide as the cat arched her spine and leaned back. Oblivious to the impossibilities of her actions, the cat simply pulled and pulled, each attempt growing firmer and rougher as she brought the bunny's pussy closer to her goal.

As the cat leaned back in one long extended pull, Marshall surged forward and pressed the giant flared cockhead tight against the bunny's distorted entrance. Still much narrower than the rod of flesh, the pussy refused to stretch around his shaft, but the horse and the cat locked eyes and bared their teeth, redoubling their efforts, pushing and pulling and putting their entire weight into the task. Kett could feel the flare of the cockhead bend back as the shaft pressed forward, spreading the pussy further as the broad tip crammed inside. Marshall set his legs and leaned forward as the cat pulled the rabbit wider, grunting under the strain as she felt the horse flesh push past her wrists and into her partner. Kett could feel the horse servant's mind screaming in desire, two days of denial and frustration finally finding an end, the only thing standing between him and supreme satisfaction being the tightness of the bunny's hole.

In one quick motion, the cat slid her fists out from her companion's pussy, making just enough room in the distorted flesh for Marshall to plunge forward, the flared tip popping inside in an instant followed by the rabbit and horse both screaming, the giant cock immediately sinking a full foot into the smoldering hole. The horse threw back his head and clenched every muscle in his body, pre cum pouring into the rabbit's tight pussy as he leaned forward and slid further in with excruciating slowness. Straddled above the bunny's distorted hindside, the feline partner mewled in satisfaction, rubbing her palms against the hot cock flesh as it ground past the bunny's stretched entrance. The lupine, completely debilitated with intense pleasure, scratched her claws against the table and panted, just feeling her body stretch open wider and wider, clenching desperately against the invading shaft.

Marshall could feel his body tense and spasm in ecstasy, but Kett continually kept him from reaching full climax. Each inch of flesh buried within the rabbit was squeezed by the vice-like grip of her distended muscles, her entire body shifting to accommodate the thickness. Every subtle movement would have been enough to push the horse over the edge if it weren't for Kett's influence. At each moment the fox could feel her host's body cry out in bliss, and each time she intercepted his body's intentions, reducing him to a quivering mass of yearning as he slid forward, inch by inch into the rabbit's pussy.

Grunting and panting, the horse stepped forward, diving further by a full foot, watching the bunny as her body stretched around his member. Her torso was now drawn taut against his rod, her flesh pulled thin around his rock hard cock as he pushed deeper. The cat rubbed her groin against the small of the rabbit's back, feeling the swollen horse shaft through the thin layer of bunny. As Marshall pushed deeper and deeper, the ring of flesh mid-way down his length pushed up against the bunny's entrance, pressing forward roughly until her body yielded, sending a shiver through the cat as the bulge slid underneath her, grinding against her clit as it passed.

The bunny could feel the stretching rise through her body, the warmth spreading through every inch of her core as the shaft pushed forward. Soon she could feel her upper chest and neck distend and stretch, the fat flare boring its way through her and pushing up through her throat. A flood of pre cum flowed from her mouth as the invading shaft forced her jaws open, her neck and face stretching impossibly as the horse cock pushed further and further until she could feel his warm flesh on the back of her tongue. Swallowing hard against the flesh, her entire body twitching and shaking, the bunny closed her eyes in impossible bliss as she felt the rock hard member slide through her throat, rubbing her tongue against its surface as it pushed forward through her muzzle and lips, the flare popping free of her mouth.

Unrelenting in his pressure, Marshall finally buried the entirety of his member in the bunny, grinding his hips against the stretched servant and panting. The cat leaned in close and pressed her paws to his cheeks, locking muzzles in a lusty kiss as she rubbed her hips forward and back against the bunny, stimulating the giant horse cock through her body. Kett could tell that the horse was so delirious that he was almost useless, in a state of perpetual denied orgasm, so she took more direct control of her host's body and gripped the bunny's hips. Marshall rocked his hips forward and back, desperate for the climax that Kett constantly refused.

Kett forced the horse's body into a furious rut, slamming forward and back through bunny's entire body in long strokes, pulling nearly three feet of hard flesh from her pussy before ramming back forward. The bunny could do nothing but slap her paws against the table in madness, her mind lost in a haze of pleasure as her feline partner clamped her legs around her hips, grinding her wet pussy against the small of her back and feeling the thick horse cock surge forward and back through her body. Before long the cat cried out in climax, juices spilling out onto the rabbit as she clutched at the horse for support.

Taking a moment to recover, the cat panted and touched herself as Marshall continued his desperate fucking. Looking back over her shoulder, the feline could see the flared head of the horse cock pushing forward and back, extending from the bunny's distended mouth. Licking her lips, the cat dismounted and crawled over the table, dropping down on the other side and inspecting her partner's current state. The bunny's eyes were rolled up inside her head in bliss, completely lost to the delirium as the hot horse flesh surged forward and back through her body.

The cat dropped to her knees beside the rabbit's face, pressing her palm against Marshall's member as it pushed forward and back. She looked up and met the horse's gaze, licking her lips. While he was in no state to respond to anything, Kett forced the horse to slow and then stop, hilting deep into the bunny and holding his body still. Gazing at the full length of the hard shaft, the cat could tell that her bunny companion was only occupying half of the rod's length, the other half freely exposed and protruding from her mouth.

Shifting around and kneeling before the horse cock's flared head, the cat reached up and licked in a single long drag of her rough tongue, lapping up the thick pre cum as it poured from the leaking hole. Marshall shivered as he felt her raspy tongue rub over the sensitive flesh, clenching and sending thick gobs of pre out to cover the cat's face. Licking up over the broad head, the cat moaned and swallowed greedily at the fluid, rubbing the excess into her fur and coating her fingers in its slickness as she rubbed her slit. With each lick, her jaw stretched and slackened, each drag of her tongue grinding against the horse's rod from bottom to top.

As the cat touched herself, she pressed her paw against her clit and pivoted her hips against her own touch, moaning and purring as she could feel her climax building. In a moment of mad ecstasy, she pressed down hard against herself and felt a shiver run up her spine, cumming powerfully on her fingers and simultaneously stretching her mouth open as wide as her body would allow, hooking her bottom lip onto the horse's

124

flared flesh and pushing herself upwards with her knees. Groaning aloud as she shook with pleasure, desperate to feel the horse inside her, the cat opened wider and wider until at last she could lunge forward and trap the giant flared head between her lips.

The feline's body pulsed and throbbed as her climax subsided, her mind slowly realizing what she had just done. She could feel the massive thickness of the horse's member trapped in her distorted muzzle, swallowing reflexively and lapping her tongue over the blunt head. Opening her eyes, she could see her lupine companion, a few feet away, impaled and stretched by the impossible anatomy. The bunny was moaning to herself, eyes closed and lost in bliss. Determined, the cat set her hind paws firmly to the ground and pushed forward, sliding her lips over the smooth muscle toward her companion.

Disregarding any thoughts she might have about the unfeasibility of her actions, the cat simply relaxed her mouth and leaned forward. Marshall moaned and flexed his rod as the servant advanced, the broad bulge slowly filling her throat and stretching her just as it did the rabbit. Continually grinding both of her paws against her crotch as she took a strained step forward, the feline succumbed to the intensity and warmth and came again, shaking violently and spasming, half of her body trapped around the thickness of the horse's shaft.

As the cat's body stretched, she found it harder and harder to move her legs and push forward. Kett, enjoying the sight too much to let it end, forced the horse to grab the bunny by the hips and lift his entire shaft, along with the pair of servants, up vertically into the air. The cat flung her arms out and grabbed at the massive rod for stability, attempting to balance her body. Slowly, under the force of gravity, the feline's torso slid, inch by inch, down and around the horse cock.

The rabbit opened her eyes and saw her cat friend only a foot or so away, reaching out her paws in hazy desire. Locking hands with the bunny, the cat pulled herself downwards, eyes rolling up into her head as her body swelled and stretched, the flare of the cockhead visible through her belly as it pushed through her body. Inching closer and closer, the pair of servants grabbed each other's shoulders and pulled toward each other, finally pressing their lips together at the same instant that the cockhead pushed through the cat's wet pussy, popping free into the air. Both lost in the mental haze of the horse's distortion, the cat and rabbit pressed their lips together while trapped around the thick rod of flesh.

By now, the trio had gained a significant amount of attention from their corner of the room. Even as the hall was filled with the numerous moans of ecstasy, the sight of two women impaled on a member of that size was not exactly normal. Several partiers watched the action from a distance, grinding and sucking on each other with an eye turned toward the unusual events but not curious enough to halt their activities. A handful of people, however, approached the horse with interest.

Marshall, shaking as he stood, attempted to grab the bunny and rub her up and down his shaft, but to little avail. His body betrayed his intense desire to orgasm, feeling every muscle twitch in both the cat's and rabbit's bodies, both of their heart beats pounding against his flesh, the wetness of their pussies and mouths driving him wild with uncontrolled lust. Kett guided the horse around to the end of the table and forced him to let go of his shaft, dropping the massive rod onto the bare surface, already cleared of food items by the bunny's wild thrashing.

A dozen or so party goers approached the table from either side, partly awed by the sight and partly aroused by the intensity of the scene. All of them naked and most of them already fucked at least once, the partiers looked at the insane horse and then back to each other. The horse bucked his hips against the bunny on the table but couldn't gain any traction; the pair of servants simply slid back and forth along the table. Sensing their cue to assist, the partiers reached out and grabbed the cat and rabbit in any way they could. Latching onto their arms and legs, grabbing their torsos, and straddling the servants themselves, the partiers did all they could to pull the servant's bodies and hold them in place as the horse rocked his hips.

The cat and rabbit felt their limbs stretch as they were held tight in place, every joint in their bodies made immobile between the partiers and the impaling flesh. Marshall pulled back and his cock slid through both of their bodies, his broad head stretching the cat's pussy even further as it pulled back inside her body. Taking two, then three full steps backward, the horse withdrew his shaft several feet from the pair before lunging back forward and ramming his full length through their bodies once again. The people gripping onto the servants watched the cat's body collapse back to its natural size as the rod pulled from her torso only to stretch around the shaft again as it rushed back into her. Riding astride the two servant's bodies, a handful of party goers ground against their stretched bodies as they felt the powerful muscled shaft pound forward and back.

Kett reveled in the sight of the horse fucking the cat and bunny servants, but not more than she felt the utter bliss of their taut bodies wrapped around her morphed flesh. The slave girls shook, constantly and uncontrollably, as their bodies came in a continuous chain of desperate orgasms, their moans stifled by the rock hard shaft. She gave Marshall full control of his body and cried out in his mind as he lunged forward and back, impaling himself on the pair and hilting himself with each stroke. The helpers gripped the servants and struggled to keep them still as the horse fucked rougher and rougher, desperate for climax. Finally pulling back, drawing his cock out from both their bodies and letting their torsos collapse back to their normal shapes, Marshall bared his teeth and ran forward, ramming himself back into the stretched bodies of both servants as the party-goers held them fast in place, burying his enormous shaft and slapping his hips against the bunny's ass before he arched his back in supreme bliss. Kett finally released her hold and felt the massive surge flood up from within his core, the shock of the climax coursing through the horse's body in waves before he finally twitched and clenched his every muscle. Thick jets of cum poured from the horse's flared head in a heavy torrent, spraying down the length of the table and drenching the food. Pumping gallon after gallon of seed, Marshall could do nothing but stand motionless, body locked as his balls drained.

Surge after surge of cum flowed onto the table, filling the air with its scent. As the horse emptied himself, his oversized shaft softened and shrank, each pulse of his orgasm reducing the girth and length of the impossible member. The cat and bunny felt their bodies shrink and return to their normal sizes and shapes as the cock softened, withdrawing from them inch by inch as cum continued to pour out. Once his flesh shrank closer to its normal size, Marshall pulled the rest of himself from the exhausted pair of servants, the last few pulses of his orgasm pouring from his limp cock and onto the floor.

The crowd of helpers simply stared in confused amusement at the mess of the table, slowly letting go of the bodies of the two servants before grabbing at each other. The cat and the bunny lay on the table, motionless aside from their breathing, minds lost to the bliss. Several partiers reached up to grope their bodies, licking their dripping pussies and sucking their tits, the two servants simply moaning incoherently.

At the far end of the table, the mass of cum coalesced and rippled, and a bulge formed and rose as the fluid drew together. A wet slender arm flung free from the pool as it gained shape, quickly taking the familiar

128

form of the antelope servant. Before long the bulk of the cum soaked into Ell's body, revealing her thin muscular frame. Now, however, her body bore the same markings and alterations as Kett's and Alan's. Thin lines of slick darkness coiled around her naked flesh, snaking over her body and terminating in soft nodules on her wrists and lower back. While lacking the manhood that Kett had gained, the antelope's two slender horns now took the form of a pair of thin tentacles rising up and back from the top of her head. Ell lay sprawled on the table among the cum-drenched food and drink, rubbing her hands over her skin in aroused disbelief.

Nearby, a second bulge rose and gained Kett's recognizable silhouette. While still only half-formed, Kett lunged forward onto the figure of the antelope, splashing onto her and covering her body. As the fluid drew together and hardened into a solid body, the receding cum revealed the figure of Kett as she locked lips with Ell, sitting astride her hips and pinning her arms to the table. Finally free of the horse and in her own flesh again, Kett broke the kiss and brought herself upright, licking the salty taste from her lips as she examined the room.

Chapter 9

Léo stood somewhat awkwardly by the food service tables, watching the party guests as they pulled off each other's clothes. This was not an unfamiliar sight to the servant mouse, of course. These parties were a somewhat regular occurrence, and nearly every servant of the house had a hand in either the preparations or the cleanup. But Léo hadn't ever attended one of these events while not acting as an attendant, and this new liberty left him with little clue as to how he should conduct himself. Granted, he still wore the white apron of his kitchen-worker disguise, but it was common for even the food service workers to disrobe at this point in the evening; Léo could simply discard his clothing and act as any other guest would. The problem was, he didn't know how to do that.

There was also the issue of Léo's newfound unique anatomy. He partially expected the tentacle to disappear by now, but that was far from the case. It was hard enough over the last few days to find a private corner so that he could touch himself, rubbing his soft palms along the slick tapered length, inspecting the rubbery flesh. Now he stood aimlessly and wondered how he was expected to do anything with such an alien appendage without causing a scene.

Contemplating, and fretting, Léo let himself indulge in some of the nearby food. As a servant, he wouldn't have been allowed to partake in anything without explicit permission from one of his masters, or the noble guests. But Léo allowed himself this forbidden act now that he was serving new masters, however secret his allegiances were. Grabbing an ornate goblet and filling it with an uncouth quantity of wine, the former servant watched the party guests entertain themselves throughout the room.

Master Hykan thrashed wildly at the backside of the mantis woman, to the delight of a small crowd of onlookers. On a nearby bed, twin male servant otters lay on their backs, hips together, holding their stiff rods together as a badger noblewoman lowered herself onto the pair. A woman servant, a canine brought as a gift by another great house, was tied down to a couch, bent over one of the arm rests, her ass held up in the air as a steady stream of noblemen fucked her holes, covering her backside in load after load of cum. One guest was attempting to see how many fists she could fit inside her pussy, and was currently up to three. Léo felt his tentacle flesh twinge and lengthen as he watched, swallowing hard as everyone in the room groped, sucked and ground against anyone they could get their hands on. And of course, everyone was making a terrific mess.

Léo grabbed a small pastry and took a large bite, savoring the sweetness. As the sugary treat slid down his throat, he could feel it hit his core and generate an unusual warmth. Washing it down with a couple giant gulps of wine, Léo paused to notice the sensation of heat passing through his veins, circling his body and settling in his pelvis. A drop of viscous pre formed at the tip of his stiffening tendril. Léo licked his lips and looked around, still wary of anyone approaching him. Retreating back behind the table, the mouse took another deep swig of the wine, concentrating on the sensation it brought, feeling it fill his body and then flow toward his core.

Reaching into his pants with his free hand, Léo ran his fingers along the length of his tentacle. Taking another drink, he could feel the fluid flow down toward his groin, now noticing that his ballsack felt heavier than before. Cupping himself firmly, Léo chugged the rest of his glass and shivered, reveling in the sensation of the warmth surging through his entire body and then feeling his balls swell noticeably as the pulses coalesced.

Léo wrapped his slender fingers around the base of his slick shaft and looked back up into the room. On a bed nearby, the buxom badger bounced up and down on the two otters, running her paws through her fur and grasping her breasts. Slowly it dawned on Léo that she was staring at him. When the mouse boy did a double take and met the noblewoman's gaze, she bit her lower lip and slammed herself down hard on the two thick cocks crammed into her pussy. Léo tensed, eyes trapped in her stare, his fist involuntarily squeezing the base of his shaft.

The badger ground her hips against the twin otters as she bottomed out on their rods, swiveling forward and back as the servants writhed and moaned in pleasure. Léo panted heavily, watching as the noblewoman brought one paw down between her legs, bucking her pelvis forward and back as she glared hungrily at the mouse. Heart pounding with a mix of fear and arousal, Léo slid a trembling hand down the length of his shaft, wringing a thick drop of pre from the tip as he clenched his muscles. The badger moaned aloud, watching the mouse touch himself through his pants as she ground faster against the pair buried inside her. The otters arched their backs in unison, crying out as they pumped their thick loads into the noblewoman, writhing on the bed as their climaxes concluded but the badger continued bucking against their stiff rods.

Léo watched as the badger cried out and gripped her breasts, clenching her tight pussy around the otters as she orgasmed. Thick drops of cum slid out along the servant's shafts, their loads mixing together and pouring onto their hips and dripping off their balls. The mouse stroked the length of his tentacle flesh as the trio caught their breath, the badger still locking her gaze on the servant boy. Soon the badger lifted herself from her otter toys, cum flowing out as she freed herself, licked her fingers clean. Dismounting from the bed, she took several confident strides toward the food tables, eyes fixed on Léo, daring him to move. She approached predatorily, circling around the table, grabbing the mouse by his apron and flinging him against the table.

Lowering herself toward the floor, the badger reached forward and wrapped her fingers around the waist of Léo's pants. When the mouse flinched unconsciously, the badger grinned, "If I have to ask for what I want, you'll be in trouble." Before Léo had a chance to object, she was sliding his trousers down in a single quick motion. There was a moment when the noblewoman paused at the mouse's unexpected anatomy, but a moment later she grabbed the tendril and ran her paw along its length. The pinned mouse shivered as the badger held the tip upright and slid her tongue along the soft underside of the rubbery flesh.

Grinning and wrapping both hands around the tentacle, the badger slid the end into her muzzle and massaged the flesh with her tongue, coaxing a bead of pre from the tapered tip. Léo moaned and flexed involuntarily, pushing a thick spurt of juice into her warm mouth. As the noblewoman bobbed her head forward and back along the length, the tentacle stiffened and grew. With each long, luxurious movement of the badger's mouth Léo squirmed and flexed the prehensile tip inside her embrace.

Freeing the tip from her muzzle, the badger made two long strokes over his entire length with her hands and looked over the top of the table. A quick glance at her two otter companions was all she needed to signal her desire, and soon the pair joined the badger, kneeling to either side of the noblewoman. Holding the thick tentacle flesh in both hands, the mustelid held the tapered end of Léo's cock out to one servant, watching as he sucked it into his mouth without hesitation, flexing his tongue and lips against the member before she pulled the shaft back and held it out to the other twin.

Léo gripped the table's edge with both hands, panting and twitching as he watched the trio compete over his shaft. As one otter sucked on the tip, the other licked along the base and the badger wrapped her lips around his engorged ball sack. Then the noblewoman stroked the entire length with both hands as the otters fondled his balls and ran their paws up and down his thighs. With each lick of the mouse's flesh, the three grew more aroused, their eyes glazing over and their hips gyrating unconsciously. The otters were already hard again, pre cum running in streams down their shafts and dripping off their balls onto the carpet.

The badger took the tip of Léo's tentacle into her mouth and held the mid-section still as she pushed her face forward, taking as much of the length into her throat as possible. Pulling back and pushing forward, each attempt taking another inch onto her mouth, the badger swallowed desperately at the thickness in her muzzle. Léo moaned and squirmed, feeling her clench around his flesh as she wrapped her arms around the mouse's ass and pulled forward, forcing herself to swallow every last inch of the slick tentacle. When at last her nose met with Léo's pelvis, she swallowed hard and sent shivers through the mouse's entire body.

Claws digging into the table, Léo finally cried out and exploded deep inside the badger's throat. Thick streams of cum poured from the tentacle, pouring directly into her gut as the mouse drained his balls into the wanting embrace. Flexing his muscular member inside her throat, Léo bucked his hips against her muzzle until the badger pulled herself free of the oozing cord in a single quick motion. Léo grabbed his shaft as spurt after spurt of thick white cum flooded onto the floor, pointing the tip at the pair of otters as they crowded in. Covering their faces and shooting into their open mouths, Léo poured himself out onto the desperate pair, the final drops of cum dripping from his tip as the otters and badger immediately licked the fluid from each other's faces and bodies.

Panting as he watched the three lick and claw at each other in lust and madness, Léo grabbed a glass of fruity punch from the table and finished it in a few giant gulps. Feeling the same unusual sensation run through his body, Léo could sense the liquid course through his core and then drain into his groin, filling his empty sack. Grabbing another glass, the mouse took a few smaller swallows and closed his eyes to concentrate on the warmth.

Once the otters and badger licked each other clean, they turned and grabbed at Léo's cock once again. Startled at their forwardness, Léo's eyes shot open only to see the trio stroking his length and running their paws over his chest and thighs. Immediately moaning aloud and stumbling back against the table, the mouse could only watch as the three sucked desperately, pre cum dripping from his rubbery tendril.

The badger ran her paws up the length of Léo's thighs and gripped his hips, immediately flinging the mouse up onto the table and pushing him back. Léo could hardly catch himself as he landed on a platter of food, watching helplessly as the noblewoman hopped onto the table and straddled the former servant. The otters followed suit and climbed onto the table without concern for the food and drink, grabbing Léo by the shoulders and pulling him to the middle of the table.

Pinned under the badger, Léo could only watch as the otters positioned themselves between his legs, both grabbing the tentacle and holding it upright as the noblewoman pressed her hips against the tip. As the badger lowered her round hips onto the tapered length of the tentacle cock, Léo felt the slickness of the otters' cum still buried deep inside her pussy. Filling herself with the rubbery flesh, the mustelid moaned and gyrated as she bottomed out on the thick cock with ease, raising herself upright as she straddled the helpless mouse.

As the noblewoman started to bounce up and down on Léo's squirming tentacle, the otters licked and sucked at the mouse's balls, lapping at their own juices as they dripped from the badger's entrance. Léo felt the tension rising in his groin as the noblewoman pounded against his hips, watching her ample breasts bounce and ripple with each wild movement.

In the midst of watching the badger pound on his thick member, Léo had a thought and turned his head, looking for another glass of wine or punch. A half-full goblet sat just out of arm's reach, but once the noble saw what the mouse was reaching for she grabbed the goblet and bottomed herself out on the oozing cock. Grinning as she poured the wine into Léo's open mouth from above, the badger ground her hips forward and back. Léo struggled to swallow the liquid as it splashed onto his face, gulping at what he could.

The mouse felt his balls swell and grow as he swallowed. Above him, the badger swung her hips back and forth, gyrating in wide circles and grinding her entrance against Léo's groin. She grabbed a giant glass jug of juice, biting her lip as she tipped it over. A single solid stream of burgundy liquid flowed from the rim of the jug, falling in an arc onto the mouse's face and neck. The juice splashed over the table as Léo swallowed desperately, opening his mouth wide and attempting to stifle his moans as the noblewoman bucked back and forth on his member. Léo clutched his claws into his chest fur, arching his back as his body surged and throbbed, a constant sensation of energy flowing and circling through his core and draining into his groin. His heartbeat pulsed in his ears and his chest, his hips pressing up against the badger as his prehensile tentacle dick thrashed and corkscrewed within her passage.

Between his legs, the twin otters watched as Léo's balls swelled and expanded, grasping the growing spheres and kneading them in their paws. The pair licked and sucked at the mouse's sack, one lifting the heavy globes to lick at Léo's tailhole as the other ran his tongue over the base of the tentacle cock, lapping greedily at the juices. The mouse's balls grew as he squirmed, soon swelling so large that the otters could only drag their tongues across the surface. Each testicle grew to the size of the otters' heads, and the pair of servants could only rub and lick as they touched themselves, yearning for the mouse to orgasm again.

Léo gasped for air as the badger emptied the jug onto his face and into his mouth, gulping at the remnants as the noblewoman tossed the vessel aside. She leaned forward, planting her paws to either side of the mouse's head, slamming her hips forward and back roughly as she licked Léo's face and neck clean. The pinned mouse squirmed and arched his back, bucking his hips upwards into the badger. Panting as she licked hungrily at the remnants of juice in the mouse's fur, the noblewoman put her full weight on her hands and knees, raising her hips up off the table. Léo thrust upwards into the warm embrace of the badger's pussy, his massive balls swinging up and down as he pistoned deep into her warmth.

The pair moaned and cried aloud as Léo thrashed in ecstasy, swinging his head from side to side and clutching at the table. Léo dug his hind paws into the table and slammed his hips upwards, burying himself fully in the badger and lifting her up off her knees. Thick hot cum surged from Léo's tentacle cock as he cried out in desperate bliss, eyes squeezed shut. The noble panted and groaned aloud as she felt the fluid spurt deep into her core, pulse after pulse filling her up. The mustelid came from the sensation of hot seed pouring into her, clenching around the thick tendril, crying out in bliss as she shook uncontrollably. Léo felt his balls start to shrink as he emptied himself into the badger's depths, each spurt growing more powerful and longer until the slick tendril poured cum into her tight pussy in a single unbroken stream, jetting from the tip of the tapered tentacle dick.

As the mouse cum surged deep into the badger's pussy, thick beads squirted out from her entrance. Filled to bursting by the thick tendril as it poured its warm load into her, the badger's pussy overflowed and leaked hot streams of mixed juices down and over Léo's swollen sack. The two otters lunged hungrily and licked the mouse's balls, pressing their mouths to the badger's stretched entrance as cum spurted out, grinding their tongues against the tablecloth and swallowing greedily. As they ate the mouse's load their stiff rods bobbed between their legs, rock hard and leaking pre. The twins savored the heady taste and licked at every drop as Léo jetted into the badger.

The badger's belly swelled and inflated as Léo poured gallons of cum into her body. Crying out as his mind throbbed, the mouse felt his balls shrink until his orgasm finally subsided, thick pulses of cum still pumping from his cock as he collapsed back onto the table. The noblewoman squeezed her passage against the tendril as her orgasm faded, clenching involuntarily in the mental haze. She leaned forward again on her hands and knees, and the two otters immediately reached forward to grab the base of Léo's cum-slick cock. The pair pulled the mouse's tendril free, and immediately dove forward as a surge of seed flooded from her entrance. Sucking and swallowing at the fluid as it pulsed from her pussy, the otters licked and pressed their mouths to the badger's slit and sucked greedily at Léo's tendril, licking up every last drop.

Chapter 10

As the master of the house made his move with the mantis servant, Alan strode confidently toward the center of the room. All eyes were on the hosts of the party, allowing the canine to quickly strip his apron disguise and join the group of onlookers bare-chested. Haxiten bucked against the backside of the massive insect, plunging his shaft into her flesh and slapping his hips against her entrance with every stroke. On the opposite end of the scene, his gecko wife Drenirya and hyena bodyguard Zelia groped and caressed the mantis' chest and torso as they kissed each other.

Surrounding the scene, in a crowded ring around the lowered section of the floor, a large group of partiers watched the exotic scene with curiosity and lust. While many guests fled to the hidden corners of the room to amuse themselves, these several were captivated by the rare sight of a mantis in throes of passion. Most sat on the lip of the shallow pit, some lying on their sides or backs, sitting just upright enough to watch the show. Many nobles in the crowd had a servant, sometimes two, kneeling between their legs, servicing their masters.

Unable to find a gap in the front row of the ring, Alan stood a few feet behind the closest watchers. His eye was immediately drawn to the brightly colored mistress of the house as she caressed the mantis' breasts. The gecko, already stripped naked, grabbed her bodyguard by the shoulders and slammed her against the towering upright torso of the insect woman. Drenirya latched her mouth onto the hyena's snout and grabbed her wrists, raising them up and pinning them to the mantis' chitinous chest. The bodyguard's muscular arms remained motionless, pushing playfully against the gecko's grip despite clearly having the ability to overpower her captor. The mistress drew her body in close and pressed her chest to Zelia's, raising a knee up and pressing it between her legs, grinding against the bodyguard's crotch.

Alan watched as the gecko spread her legs slightly, allowing the hyena to grind her thigh against her mistress' groin as the same was done to her. The pair moaned into each other's mouths as the gecko pressed her bodyguard against the mantis' chest. Alan could see the hyena's pseudo-penis stiffen and elongate, rising up visibly as Drenirya ground her pelvis against the soft muscle. The mistress brought one hand down and wrapped her slender fingers around the thick shaft, drawing a stifled moan from the bodyguard.

The gecko leaned in as she squeezed the rod of flesh and whispered something in the hyena's ear. Pausing and panting softly to herself, Zelia looked slowly to her left and right. She glanced briefly at Alan, paused, and whispered something back to her mistress. Drenirya, in turn, smiled and looked directly at Alan, sizing him up. She swiftly pulled away from the hyena, strode to the side of the mantis and quickly hopped up onto the horizontal back of the insect in a single motion. The bodyguard followed closely behind and boosted herself up to join Mistress Hykan as the gecko locked eyes with Alan.

The crowd of onlookers looked back at Alan and grinned. The husky felt their eyes on his body as he looked back at the mistress of the house. She only had to smile at the canine to signal her desire, and the handful of onlookers between him and the shallow pit parted to let him through. When he approached the mantis and attempted to climb up, Drenirya interrupted, "You should lose the pants, guest, or we'll think you a prude."

Alan smirked and promptly unfastened his belt, dropping his pants to the ground without hesitation. The gecko followed his movements, watching coolly from above before extending her hand to the husky. She pulled Alan upwards with surprising ease, and he soon found himself straddling the back of the mantis between the mistress and her body guard.

Facing Drenirya, Alan smirked and leaned forward for a kiss. The lizard immediately placed a single finger against Alan's muzzle and turned her head sideways, stopping him in his tracks. "Not so fast, pup. You have to get through my bodyguard first." Before Alan had the chance to react, he felt two muscular paws grab his shoulders from behind and force him flat onto his back, the hyena's face grinning directly above his head.

Alan struggled to keep his balance on the back of the moaning insect as Zelia swung around and straddled his chest, pinning him between her muscular thighs. The bodyguard smirked as her pseudo-cock flopped down onto the canine's chest, the fleshy muscle smearing clear lubricant into his fur. Glancing up into her gleaming eyes, and then back down to the unusual organ before him, Alan gripped the shaft near the base and squeezed gently. The hyena moaned softly in response, urging him to stroke his paw over the length. Her shaft was muscular and a little longer than his own cock, but instead of coming to a tip her rod had a large hole at the end, beads of pre forming and dripping out.

Zelia smiled with satisfaction as Alan stroked forward and back, the foot-long shaft pulsing in his grip. She leaned forward onto her knees just enough to push her hips forward, pressing her girl-cock against Alan's snout. The canine obediently parted his lips, squeezing the base of her shaft as he took half of her flesh into his mouth, pressing his tongue against the underside of the stiff muscle as sweet pre leaked out. He sucked gently at the smooth skin, bobbing his head forward a little as he squeezed both paws around what he couldn't fit in his mouth. Pulling back, Alan squeezed his lips around the end of the shaft and pressed his tongue against the entrance of her hole. His muscle slid effortlessly into her, the flesh quickly accepting him as he sucked her rod into his mouth and speared her with his long canine tongue. The hyena grabbed her own tits with both paws and growled with pleasure, squeezing Alan's chest between her strong legs.

Leaning back against the slope of the mantis' neck, the lady of House Hykan watched the scene in amusement. She spread her legs and cupped one of her breasts, her other hand sliding down her taut chest. Alan's legs straddled the insect, spread just before her, giving her a perfect view of his growing erection. Her nimble fingers slid to either side of her clit as the canine cock stiffened and slid from its sheath, Alan's thick red rod lying against his stomach as he pleasured her bodyguard with his tongue. The gecko slid her fingers forward and back, pressing down to either side of her hood and looked out onto the crowd of onlookers, her breath catching as she saw a dozen partiers touching themselves at the sight in the middle of the room.

Alan's head bobbed forward and back as much as he could manage from his prone position, coaxing the hyena's delicious fluids from her member. The flesh never grew stiff and rigid like a cock, instead elongating and engorging itself with blood until it was plump and thick but still flexible enough to bend as it passed through the husky's lips. Without warning, Zelia pulled her hips back and grabbed Alan's head with both paws, ramming herself forward and plunging her plump shaft into the canine's mouth, the long member curving back as it followed his throat. Alan's eyes shot open at the sudden intrusion, his hands reaching up to grab at her arms, but the hyena simply pistoned her pelvis forward and back roughly, locking eyes with him as she fucked his face with her girl-cock.

Drenirya watched as Alan struggled underneath her bodyguard, his feet digging into the mantis' back and pressing his hips upwards as he tried to throw her off. Smiling, the gecko raised one of her lithe legs and reached out toward Alan's groin, pressing the bottom of her tender foot against the base of his hard cock. Almost immediately, Alan's struggles lessened, his hips frozen in their raised position as she spread her long toes around his thick rod.

The hyena bottomed out, her hips pressed firmly against Alan's snout as she held his head firmly in place, stuffing his mouth and throat with her hot flesh. Alan struggled to breathe but could only look up pleadingly at the bodyguard, her muscular arms pressing her tits together as she grinned down at him, flexing her rod inside his throat. The canine's vision dimmed as he struggled for air, feeling the gecko's foot pressing firmly against his cock, rubbing forward and back along his shaft as she touched herself.

Alan fought to pull at Zelia's arms and hips, but couldn't beat her grip. Finally, in subconscious reflex, the canine reached out with the strong tendrils of slime and let them flow from his wrists, coiling rapidly around the bodyguard's thighs and waist. Alan flexed as hard as he could and managed to rip her hips away from his face, gasping desperately for breath as she fell back down to her knees, straddling his chest.

As he coughed and panted, Alan could tell that he won the battle of muscle mostly because he caught the hyena by surprise. Zelia grabbed at the tentacles, the slimy cords writhing around her wrists. Alan looked up and gasped for breath, locking eyes with her as he let the tendrils coil around her hips. The hyena glared, her fiery gaze daring her prey to make a move. As he stared back, a pair of tentacles slid around her waist and advanced down toward her shaft, inching out and curving around her pseudo-cock with slow, deliberate movements.

From behind the scene, the gecko could only see a handful of slick tendrils curling around the body of the hyena, but this mostly just piqued her interest. As Drenirya watched, she slid two slim fingers into her tight entrance and pressed her foot down firmly against Alan's shaft, trapping it between her heel and his belly. Slowly she pushed and coerced Alan's hips back down onto the back of the mantis, grinding forward and back playfully.

Alan relaxed only slightly as he felt the soft foot rubbing luxuriously along his throbbing shaft. He concentrated on keeping the hyena's glare as his tendrils coiled around her thick rod, holding it pointed upwards from her hips as one of the tentacles arched back and pressed against the entrance at the end of her shaft. Zelia growled softly, the tendril pushing against her moist hole, the muscular flesh of her rod parting easily as she the his oozing tentacle penetrate her. Alan felt the slick walls of her embrace clench around his tendril, the strong muscles squeezing around the sensitive end of his wet appendage.

The hyena glared at Alan with an insane look as he slid further in, her growl growing and deepening as he watched the tentacle disappear into her gaping girl-cockhole, widening and stretching as it bulged to accept the fleshy cord. Alan felt the firm muscles of her tunnel squeeze in coursing waves, constricting his tentacle like a vice. The pair groaned in unison as the Alan advanced, slowly slipping further into her stretched hole. Afraid to tear his eyes from her gaze, Alan panted softly as he pressed into the hyena's tight entrance, coiling his tendril over the outside of her length and squeezing her shaft in tight pulsing contractions.

Curiosity finally getting the better of her, the gecko mistress leaned forward to inspect the scene. Drenirya was rewarded with the sight of

Alan and the Zelia locked in an intense death-glare, a thick coil of slime sliding deliciously into her thick member. Smirking to herself, the lizard wrapped her long fingers around Alan's rigid shaft and leaned forward into the hyena's ear, whispering just loud enough for their prey to hear, "Do you need some help, pet?" The bodyguard responded with a low growl without breaking Alan's gaze, her chest heaving.

When Alan's tentacle slid down to the base of the hyena's pseudo-cock shaft the gecko repositioned herself, straddling Alan's hips. Mistress Hykan pressed her delicate tits against the hyena's back, lowering her weight onto Alan's pelvis. The husky could feel the slickness of the Drenirya's wet pussy as she rested her hips on his groin; his throbbing cock pressed firmly against his own belly, the parted lips of her entrance sliding forward and back along his length as the she ground her hips against him. Reaching up and gripping her bodyguard's breasts, the gecko rested her chin atop one of her Zelia's shoulders, gazing down onto the scene between the hyena and her prey with cool satisfaction.

Alan struggled to keep the Zelia's gaze as he felt the gecko rock her hips forward and back along his shaft. His tentacle reached the base of her girl-cock and curved upwards into her body, eliciting a slight shiver from the hyena. Drenirya grinned and squeezed her bodyguard's breasts, her strong fingers gripping the ample tits and pulling her body back into the gecko's embrace. Alan constricted his tendril along the length of her shaft, coiling tight to cover every inch of her flesh, pulling forward and back. The thick slimy tentacle buried deep in the hyena's shaft slid out several inches, the coil sliding down her length before Alan forced himself back in, at once pistoning into her stretched hole and stroking her shaft in unison. Clenching her teeth, Zelia panted and gasped between deep growls, focusing all of her energy into staring down Alan, daring him to make every move he made.

The gecko pinched the bodyguard's nipples between her fingers and whispered into her ear, "He isn't getting to you, is he, pet? I know you're not going to cum without permission." Alan was surprised to hear the subtlest hint of a whimper from the muscular hyena, and her mistress smiled as she twisted her pet's nipples. Drenirya slid her hips forward and back, pressing her wet pussy against Alan's cock and gazing back down at the canine as he let out a ragged pant of his own. The gecko smiled and reached down between her legs, raising herself up onto her knees slightly so that she could grip Alan's shaft and hold it upright, rubbing the pointed tip against her slick entrance. "I'll tell you what, pet," she whispered, "if you hold out until I make him cum, I'll let you take his throat again." The hyena's eyes narrowed in concentration as she glared at Alan. "But," the gecko continued, "if you fail, I will let him take your ass." Letting out a growl, Zelia bared her teeth at the husky.

Gripping Alan's cock and holding it firmly in position, the Drenirya slowly lowered herself onto the thick dog shaft. Her dripping wet pussy clenched tightly around his rod as she descended, easily taking his length until she rested on his swollen knot. She smirked in unhurried satisfaction as she rocked her hips forward and back, squeezing her vice-like passage against Alan's flesh. The canine pushed his tentacle forward and back into the bodyguard's shaft as the gecko moaned into her ear, panting to himself in concentration as he felt both the mistress and her bodyguard squeeze tight against his shafts buried deep within their muscular holes.

Drenirya rose up onto her knees and slid back down, rocking her hips subtly as she slowly impaled herself on Alan's cock. She moaned and whispered into her pet's ear, "I know you're going to love having this buried deep in your ass, my dear. It is quite a bit thicker than what you're used to." Alan struggled to regulate his breathing as he continued to return the hyena's glare, pulsing his tendril forward and back into the

146

pseudo-cock's stretched hole, clenching hard against the outside. The mistress grabbed at the hyena's tits and squeezed, pulling the bodyguard back slightly to use her as support. Rocking her hips forward and back, grinding her tight entrance against the top of the swollen dog knot, the gecko groaned seductively into the hyena's ear, whispering, "I may even let him knot you. Oh, it is quite large. I may even have trouble taking it myself."

Alan plunged his tendril deep into the hyena's shaft as he listened to the gecko tease her pet. Cramming himself deep into her muscular entrance, stretching her rod as he pushed down past the base and up into her body, he found where the passage continued and pistoned in as far as he could manage. Zelia finally let out a desperate whimper as Alan pulled his slick cord back rapidly, surging forward in long quick strokes while clenching the outside of the shaft with his tightly coiled grip. The gecko responded by putting her full weight on her knees and raising herself up, sliding her tight flesh along the length of his thick shaft before slamming herself down, cramming herself full of Alan's rock-hard meat and coming to rest on the top of the swollen knot. She pressed herself down, resting her weight on his knot as her pussy stretched around the thick bulb. After a moment she rose again, pulling out a few inches of his shaft before slamming back down, stretching her hole wider as she struggled to take his thickness. Squeezing at the hyena's breasts she moaned aloud, "Oh yes, this cock is going to make you scream, my pet."

Zelia and Alan panted aloud, groaning as they glared at each other. Alan reached out with one hand and extended another strong tendril, coiling around the bodyguard's neck. The hyena growled and bared her teeth as Alan squeezed her muscular throat, desperately fucking her muscular rod with his tendrils, pistoning as deep and fast as he could manage. Mistress Hykan moaned as she watched her pet struggle to breathe, raising herself up and slamming herself back down against Alan's knot, taking centimeter after centimeter as she stretched her tight pussy around his throbbing flesh. Alan's eyes glazed over as he fucked the hyena's hole, every tight rippling contraction of her muscular shaft driving him crazy with need, his balls yearning for release as the tight amphibian pussy clenched and stretched over his cock.

The gecko slammed herself down onto Alan's shaft one final time and groaned as her entrance stretched, pulling herself down while gripping the hyena's tits, mouth hanging open as her clenching hole advanced by the tiniest increment, her pussy burning with every miniscule movement until with a loud groan she passed the widest point, squeezing hard as the thick knot was suddenly thrust inside her passage, the thickness filling her pussy to bursting. Alan's eyes fluttered as he felt Drenirya's hips come to rest on his own, the entirety of his cock buried within the mistress of the house. As she clenched and wrenched herself, grinding her hips forward and back, rubbing her clit against his pelvis, Alan arched his back and forced his tentacle deep into the hyena's hole, crying out in pleasure as the gecko squeezed and pulsed on his shaft.

Fighting as hard as he could, fucking the hyena recklessly as he struggled to stay composed, Alan heard the gecko moan loudly as she gyrated on his thick rod. "Oh pet, this is just going to destroy your ass. This pup's knot will just simply end you. It's all I can do to keep it buried inside me. When he ties you, you're going to be trapped on this cock for *hours*." The hyena flexed her neck and growled, staring down the husky with ferocity and fire. Alan listened to the gecko moan into the hyena's ear, finally breaking the bodyguard's glare to throw his head back and close his eyes, clenching desperately at the hyena's throat and shaft with his tendrils as he felt the gecko's heartbeat through her pussy clenched against his cock. Finally, Alan simply opened his mouth and moaned aloud, bucking his hips up against the gecko's locked body as a wave of release flooded through his body, writhing underneath his two captors as his cock flexed and pulsed. Thick streams of hot cum poured into the house mistress, the thick knot stretching her wide and sealing her shut as Alan filled her. The husky clenched and made one final desperate effort, thrashing his tendril deep inside the hyena's shaft as he poured his seed into the lizard, but the hyena simply panted and flexed every muscle in her body, eyes filled with crazed determination.

As Alan emptied himself into Drenirya, his eyes clenched shut and ears pounding with the sound of his own blood, he could scarcely make out the sound of the surrounding crowd clapping politely. The gecko moaned as she felt Alan's powerful orgasm shoot deep into her pussy, smiling down at the canine as he writhed and moaned. "Good girl." Zelia panted and struggled to regain her breath, simply grunting in response to her mistress. Alan lay partly catatonic, offering no resistance as his mind swam. The gecko carefully unwrapped the tendrils from her pet's neck, and pulled the slick tentacle from the hyena's shaft. Alan shivered but lay mostly still, hands waving slowly but limply. Mistress Hykan slowly slid the penetrating tendril free, moaning in delight as she saw just how it stretched her pet, and far it had penetrated her. When the tendril popped free of her entrance, the gecko leaned back and whispered, "In your own time, pet."

Zelia grabbed Alan's wrists and held them together, the slick tendrils subconsciously withdrawing back into his skin. The husky lay limp and unresisting, his throbbing member still tied deep inside the gecko. Repositioning herself, savoring every motion she made, the hyena rose back onto her knees and gripped her long shaft, pushing the abused tip into Alan's panting maw without opposition. The bodyguard panted weakly and grinned, grabbing Alan's head with both paws and pushing her hips forward, sliding her slickened shaft to the back of the canine's throat.

Alan was vaguely aware of something happening, but he lacked the energy to even open his eyes. His head was pulled up by two muscular paws, and he felt the familiar intrusion of the hyena's thick shaft as it slid through his lips and across his tongue. He felt the gecko continue to clench and pulse on his knotted cock, her hips grinding forward and back as she watched her pet claim her reward. Soon the intruding member reached the back of Alan's throat, and he attempted to put up his hands and push her back, but his arms just waved weakly in front of her face. The hyena gritted her teeth as she slid herself forward, gripping Alan's head firmly in both hands and pushing forward slowly, inch by inch, savoring the feeling of her thick shaft hitting the back of the husky's throat and curving down.

Mistress Drenirya panted and watched, rubbing her clit as she rocked forward and back on Alan's knot. As the hyena pushed her hips forward, the gecko could plainly see Alan's throat bulge, an advancing bump in his neck as Zelia bottomed out and pressed her pelvis against the canine's snout. The hyena savored the feeling of Alan's throat for only a moment before rocking her hips back and pushing forward in long, deliberate motions. The gecko clutched one of her small tits and pressed hard against her clit as she admired her pet's muscular ass, pulsing and flexing as she pushed forward and back.

Alan felt the hot flesh of the hyena's member slide deep into his throat, but he couldn't turn his head to either side against the bodyguard's strength. Every movement made by the mistress sent ripples through his body, his mind in delirium as the hyena stuffed his mouth with each slow motion. His breath faltered but he was too exhausted to even choke, his body automatically adjusting to accept the long member.

Zelia grunted and set her teeth, re-affirming her grip on Alan's head as she started thrusting faster into the husky's face. Moaning aloud, the gecko thrust her hips forward and back, pressing her fingers hard against her clit as she watched her pet. The bodyguard panted, her mouth hanging open, her long tongue lolling out as she pistoned faster, slapping her hips against Alan's snout with each thrust. The canine finally found the ability to open his eyes just enough to see the hyena ferociously bucking against his face, her pseudo-cock filling his mouth and throat with every push. Just out of vision, he could see the gecko bucking rapidly against his cock, her gaze fixed squarely on Alan's face as her pet slammed into it. Their panting grew in unison, their moans matching each other's as they both used Alan's limp body together, thrusting and bucking in rhythm until they screamed and growled in unison, the gecko clenching hard on his knot as the hyena hilted herself in Alan's mouth, both spasming and shaking as they came.

The surrounding crowd clapped politely as they watched the mistress and her bodyguard shake and wrench themselves, waves of passion and flame coursing through their bodies. Several watchers groaned aloud as they timed their own orgasms to that of the mistress, clenching their bodies and pumping their seed into wanting flesh. Drenirya pushed her fingers against her clit as she came, squeezing her eyes shut and shaking furiously on Alan's impaled rod. Zelia growled through her open jaws and dug her claws into the husky's head, her thick rod pulsing and flexing in his throat as every muscle in her body flexed. After several moments of hot bliss their bodies relaxed in unison, moans quickly subsiding into ragged breaths.

Chapter 11

On the far side of the room, Kett let her mind clear itself somewhat while she examined the party. Drenched in cum and straddling the prone form of Ell, the fox licked her lips and spotted the mouse boy at the far end of the food services table. He was pinned under a delirious badger, arching his back as he dumped his seed into her. Scanning the room, Kett eventually found Alan, also pinned, in the center of the room. Marshall looked nearly unconscious, leaning up against a nearby wall, with a pair of partiers cleaning up what deliciousness they could find from his still-erect member.

The rest of the room offered plenty of interesting sights, and Kett took a moment to enjoy the atmosphere of the evening. Several beds in various corners of the room hosted piles of writhing bodies, half a dozen men and women sucking and clawing at each other in a mass of moaning pleasure. A noblewoman feline was on her knees in the middle of the floor, surrounded by several male servants. The owners of the servants stood nearby, touching themselves as they goaded the cat on, apparently speaking of some record to be beat. One corner offered the sight of two thin girl bunnies suspended from the ceiling, tied together chest to chest, legs spread horizontal, hands bound together above their heads. As they hung from a harness of ropes embracing their nude bodies, a small group of guests circled around and used the unresisting servants, filling whichever hole they desired and watching the two lagomorphs kiss and moan helplessly into each other's mouths.

And of course, there was Ell, still dazed from her recent transformation, lying on her back between Kett's legs. The antelope licked

152

her arm in hazy disbelief, but couldn't help but find the whole experience pleasurable. As Kett examined the room, Ell looked up and admired the fox, reaching out and gripping Kett's stiff cock while she was distracted. The fox glanced sidelong at the antelope and smirked, giving a quick shiver of pleasure while Ell drew her grip up along Kett's shaft. With a quick look of seriousness, Kett asked, "I take it you don't find this disagreeable?"

Ell stared at Kett's thick cock while slowly stroking her grip up and down its full length before smiling back up at the fox, "What's there to disagree with?"

Kett glanced back around the room before leaning down to share a wet cum-covered kiss with the antelope, moaning softly into her mouth as Ell gripped her rod. "Then I have a task for you."

The antelope squeezed a drop of pre from Kett's tip and kissed back, "Anything."

"I am the new master of this house. Make sure the old master understands."

Ell considered this for a moment, and then smiled. "Of course, Mistress." Kett smiled back and leaned down to bite playfully at the antelope's neck, moaning as Elle gasped and stroked her length.

In the center of the room, Alan lay on his back, slowly regaining awareness of his surroundings. The hyena slowly pulled her member from the husky's throat, panting roughly but smiling with satisfaction as she dropped down off the backside of the mantis. The gecko trembled, still knotted on Alan's thick cock, recovering from her own intense orgasm. Leaning back, the mistress moaned and shook as she forced herself pull from the bulge, crying aloud as it popped free, releasing a flood of seed onto Alan's legs.

Drenirya leaned back against the slope of the mantis woman's neck, sighing and smiling to herself as she looked down onto Alan's limp form. The husky stared at the ceiling as the blood returned to his head, concentrating on the chorus of moans and cries from every direction. The gecko played with herself lazily, smirking at Alan before extending a foot once again and pressing it against his cum-drenched cock. "She didn't break you, did she, pup?" Alan shivered at the touch, but in that instant was suddenly aware of a subtle trembling, deep underground.

Mistress Hykan glanced down toward the backside of the insect, where her husband still bucked against the massive creature. She called down as she rubbed her foot forward and back along Alan's slick rod, "How was the view from down there, dear?"

The master of the house panted and called back, "Exquisite as always."

"Would you like some help?"

The leopard smirked up at his wife, "From you, help is always welcome."

Alan felt the gecko pull her foot away and sit back upright before swinging one leg around and sliding down the side of the mantis. As she departed, Alan once again felt a trembling, but this time much closer. The mistress sauntered around to the leopard, quickly throwing her arms around his neck and kissing him deeply. She glanced down at her master's cock buried to the hilt in the exotic creature and reached down, cupping her lithe fingers around his ball sack.

With a sudden tremor the entire room shuddered. A rumble filled the air as the ground beneath the mantis heaved, deep cracks snaking across the floor toward the walls. A cry of alarm rose up from the partiers as they raised their heads. A faint purple mist crept from the cracks in the floor, hissing up from deep underground and quickly filling the room.

Alan's eyes widened as he felt the mantis panic and jolt forward, bucking the husky from her back. In a rapid instant, the master and mistress of the house took a few bewildered steps backward, out from the shaking ground in the shallow pit just as the ground split into a dozen shattered pieces and sunk downwards at a steep angle. Alan landed on the sloping floor as the mantis ran forward out of the pit. Before the insect could fully climb out, several thick slimy tentacles shot up from the cracks in the floor, lashing out around the creature's legs, quickly halting her escape.

Alan reached out for something to hold onto as the shattered floor bulged and heaved once more, erupting and blasting upwards, throwing him aside as a massive dark form surged up from the depths. A pair of gigantic eyeless crocodile jaws shot up from the center of the floor, a twenty-foot tower of slick dark flesh, maw spread wide as a mass of dozens of slimy tendrils poured from the gaping chasm of flesh and immediately lashed around the torso of the mantis, coiling around her entire body before yanking her back and pulling her into the wanting abyss, gigantic jaws snapping shut.

All eyes were fixed on the giant mutated form of Carra's head as it swallowed the mantis whole. The various party guests froze where they stood, most still buried inside or filled by other guests as their breathing shortened. Mist poured from the cracks in the floor and condensed into a thick layer of fog clinging to the ground, flowing around prone guests as it filled the room. The nobles and their servants panted in a combination of arousal and fear, their lungs filling with the new air and their eyes glazing over.

Slowly, dozens of slick tendrils crawled up from the cracks in the floor, sliding across the ground, searching. As the cords found the bodies of the party guests they wound around their legs and arms, coiling around their thighs. Once a group was found by one tentacle, several more soon crawled in from every direction, wrapping and grasping around each guest and caressing their flesh. The panic of the crowd shifted to a kind of terrified arousal as the alien slime gripped their bodies, squeezing breasts and asses, teasing mouths and pussies throughout the room.

The maw in the center of the room swallowed loudly before laying its long muzzle down across the ground. Alan examined the slick flesh of the crocodile, the back end of the jaws joining together to form a giant round tentacle that bore straight down into the earth. Several dozen tentacles crawled up from the hole surrounding the maw, reaching out and lashing around whatever body they could find. The giant mouth picked itself up and rotated around, pivoting in the middle of the room until it faced the master and mistress of the house where it rested its lower jaw on the ground and opened wide, a dozen thick tendrils surging out from the mouth toward the pair.

With a surprising amount of speed the hyena jumped in front of her masters to intercept the tentacles, immediately finding herself grabbed by half a dozen strong tendrils of slime. The maw growled deeply and coiled around the bodyguard's arms and neck, forcing her onto her knees as she struggled against its grip.

Across the room, Kett watched the scene in amazement, shivers running down her spine as she watched dozens of tentacles slide over the moaning forms of the party guests. Noting the kneeling form of the hyena, Kett leaned back down and whispered into Ell's ear, "I think that's your cue."

Ell licked her lips as she gave one final tug on the fox's swollen rod, grinning as Kett dismounted from the table and walked coolly over toward the nearest group of party guests. The antelope sat upright, her head still spinning from her recent transformation, and stood on her slender hooved legs.

156

The hyena clenched and wrenched in place as the tentacles coiled around her body, wrapping around her chest and squeezing her breasts as several more reached back and hooked around the gecko's ankles. Mistress Hykan started at the sudden touch, trying to jerk her feet away but only lost her balance, falling onto her back as the tendrils slid around her legs. The gecko's mind swam as her heart raced, dizzy as she panted and breathed in the sweet mist, skin prickling as the slick ooze crawled over her taut body. Her legs were forced wide by the firm grip of the tendrils, her muscles struggling against their strength as her body yearned, her pussy clenching in need even as it still dripped with Alan's load.

Slowly, the tentacles pulled at the gecko and hyena, dragging them across the floor toward the gaping maw. The intense warmth of the massive mouth enveloped them as they were drawn closer, lifted into the air by their legs over the row of giant teeth where they were greeted by the crocodile's gigantic broad tongue. Mistress Hykan and her bodyguard moaned as the muscle pressed up against their bodies, squeezing them against the pliable roof of the mouth as the tendrils embraced their bodies. The intense wet heat of the maw flowed over their minds and bodies, flooding their senses as the crocodile tongue sucked on the two women like a pair of delicious treats. More tentacles wrapped around their bodies and pulled them back, slowly sliding over the rough surface of the tongue until their moaning forms slipped back down into the throat of the creature.

The master of the house stood motionless as he watched their bodies disappear, his legs quivering in fear and desire as his lungs filled with the sweet mist. He took a hesitant step forward toward the gaping maw when a paw came to rest on his shoulder, the antelope whispering into his ear, "Not so fast."

Alan watched the mistress and bodyguard as they slipped down into the darkness, grinning. The husky hopped forward onto the firm tongue of the open mouth, spreading his arms wide as he let his tendrils extend, flowing from his back and wrists as the several tendrils of the creature reached out in unison, coiling around Alan's cords and locking around his arms and legs. Alan breathed deeply as the creature gently pulled him back, his cock sliding up out of his sheath as he slid down the warm throat into the darkness.

Ell experimentally let the tendrils from her wrists slide out, shivering at the new sensation as she let them wrap slowly around Master Hykan's neck. The leopard's eyes were wide, his body frozen in panic but eyes glossy with hazy arousal. His thick feline cock throbbed with his heartbeat, still wet from the mantis woman's tight pussy. Ell circled around to the cat's side, pressing her small tits against his shoulder as she wound a strong tendril around his neck, reaching down with her free hand to cup the leopard's ball sack. A slimy tendril reached out from that wrist as well, coiling upwards around the feline's member, wrapping tight and squeezing with slick firmness.

The leopard stifled a moan in his throat, eyes un-focusing. Ell smiled with satisfaction, squeezing her former master's balls, kneading them against each other as she tightened her grip around his neck just enough to cut off some blood flow. His eyes fluttered, pre cum dripping from his barbed cockhead. The antelope bit her lip as she extended the handful of tentacles from the small of her back, pressing her hips against the side of his as the thick tendrils reached forward and gripping the cat's pelvis. She reveled in the alien feeling and let the slimy flesh rub up and down, forward and back over the leopard's muscled body.

Ell squeezed her former master's sack with one hand as she caressed his cheek with the other, playfully pulsing the tentacles coiled around his neck, squeezing in waves and then relaxing. The antelope enjoyed watching his face as she toyed with him, alternating between clenching around his neck and squeezing his stiff rod. Master Hykan's face betrayed his desire, his eyes fluttering and pulse racing as the slick tendrils embraced his hips and chest.

Her body already desperate in desire, Ell slid one of her tendrils down the leopard's backside, coiling around his taut abs, around his firm hips and finding his toned ass. The feline flinched in surprise as the tendril snaked over his cheeks, sliding down and coiling fully around the inside of his thigh, snuggly clinging where his leg met his pelvis. Ell exhaled into the leopard's ear as the tentacle slid upwards, the slick cord finding the groove between his ass cheeks, wetly dragging up and over the leopard's tight tailhole.

The leopard let a small moan escape, clenching his cheeks as Ell kneaded his balls. The antelope simply moaned gently into the feline's ear, parting her lips and sighing just loud enough for him to hear. His shoulders sagged as his eyes closed, the warmth of the tentacle rubbing against his asshole melting his mind. Ell drew the tendril back down and pressed the tip against his tight entrance, letting the slimy appendage slip up and down until his hole was soaked with her slime.

Masker Hykan whimpered to himself as the tentacle pushed at his hole, the thick ooze pressing into his entrance with an unyielding firmness. Ell pulsed the tendril in short waves of strength, pushing against his clenched tailhole as she moaned hotly into his ear, groaning in desire as she rubbed her tendrils over his body, squeezing against his neck until his eyes rolled upwards. Push by push, the leopard's hole spread and yielded, forced open a fraction of an inch each time until Ell clutched his balls and pressed hard against his entrance, finally forcing him open and plunging the slick appendage deep into his tailhole in a single surging motion. The pair cried out in unison as she buried her tendril in his ass, the searing tightness squeezing around her sensitive tentacle.

The feline quivered as a thick drop of pre cum drooled from his throbbing cock. Ell moaned and pushed deeper into the cat's ass, pistoning in and out roughly as she savored the alien sensation. The antelope leaned forward and bit the leopard's ear, squeezing his neck as she fucked his ass with long, powerful strokes. She released the coiled tendril from around his cock and drew her paw up, gripping his barbed head and covering her palm in his pre before quickly stroking down the length of his shaft. The leopard's eyes fluttered as he stood helplessly, the thick ooze plunging into his tight hole as her grip slid over his entire length.

Ell moaned loudly and ground her hips against the leopard's. In a single rapid motion, the antelope shoved the feline's chest and knocked him off his balance. The cat fell backward but was stopped from hitting the ground as Ell gripped his throat with her strong tendril before he struck the floor. Ell let him drop the last few inches before jumping forward, onto her knees, straddling her former master's hips. Without missing a single delicious stroke, the antelope plunged her tentacle deep into the leopard's ass, filling him and forcing him to arch his back in pleasure. She put her full weight on her knees, hovering several inches over his throbbing cock as she rocked the cord of slime forward and back into his tight hole. Ell coiled a tendril around the base of the leopard's stiff rod and held it upright, its dripping tip held a few inches from her wet slit.

As Ell plunged her slick ooze deep into the warmth of the leopard's ass, her former master looked up at her pleadingly and raised his hips, trying desperately to get his cockhead to her wet pussy lips. The antelope squeezed harder on the leopard's neck and rose up on her knees, keeping her tight entrance always a short distance from his rod, lowering herself back down as he lowered his hips, dropping herself teasingly close before raising herself back up. Master Hykan reached out with his paws and put them on her thighs, attempting to use them as leverage as he pushed his hips upwards, but the antelope immediately lashed out with a pair of tentacles and gripped his wrists, easily prying them from her legs and pinning them to the ground above his head. Ell forced herself deeper into his ass with each surging stroke, already fucking his tight hole with several feet of slick ooze as he panted and bucked his hips upwards desperately.

The antelope breathed heavily and raised her hips up with each of his thrusts, letting him get closer each time. As they both dropped back downwards she let the very tip of his head brush against her wet lips for just an instant before rising back up. The leopard's eyes squeezed shut as Ell fucked his ass, moaning in between short ragged breaths.

Ell felt her former master's heart pulse and pound as she squeezed his neck, his delirium overpowered by his lust. She clenched her tendrils tight around his neck, pressing tight against his artery as she plunged her thick tendril into his ass, body shivering in delight with the feeling of his tight tailhole clenched like a vice around her sensitive appendage. Ell closed her eyes and threw her head back, flexing every muscle in her body as she fucked his ass harder, a desperate fervor driving her to fiercer and fiercer thrusts. Panting and moaning with every plunge, Ell clenched as hard as she could around the leopard's neck, waves of orgasm pulsing through her entire body as she speared his hole. Her pussy spasmed and her body shook as she pushed her tentacle as deep as she could into his tight hole, her skin on fire as she screamed in pleasure. The leopard's eyes rolled up into his head as Ell squeezed against his throat, his vision fading until his head thumped back onto the floor, his entire body limp and unmoving. With a single abrupt motion Ell plunged herself downwards, impaling herself on the leopard's thick rod in the middle of her orgasm, shaking uncontrollably as she bottomed out in an instant, clenching her knees and thighs against his hips and torso. The antelope came and shook and leaned forward, placing her hands on the leopard's chest and putting her weight down on him. She rocked her hips forward and back, squeezing her eyes shut as her tight pussy flexed, every movement sending pulsing waves through her entire body, her orgasm continuing as long as she kept bucking against his unconscious body.

As the antelope quivered and panted, she saw the leopard stir and tilt his head to one side. He squirmed under her, unknowing of his own situation. When Master Hykan finally looked up and saw Ell, he inhaled deeply and felt the rush of pleasure surge from his groin through his entire body. Ell abruptly rose up and pulled herself off the leopard's stiff cock just as he began to shoot his load, cum pulsing in thick ropes up and across his chest, flying up to land on his face and shoulders as he squirmed under her grip, bucking his hips desperately toward Ell's tight entrance.

The leopard whimpered and shook as his orgasm subsided, Ell still hovering over him and panting, grinning. She pulled her tentacle slowly out, an inch at a time for what felt like ages until at last the tip popped free and drew a long groan from the feline. Ell bent down and licked the cum from his face, savoring the seed before kissing the leopard deeply, making sure he got a taste of himself.

Ell let her heart calm somewhat, feeling the blood rush through her ears as she leaned over her prone captive. The leopard whimpered and groaned, his cock still stiff with desire. Ell released her grip on the cat's wrists and stood abruptly, looking down on the dazed form of her former master. The leopard breathed deeply, his head filled with the sweet scent of the mist and the taste of his own cum. Ell considered for only a

162

moment, and glanced over to the still gaping maw a few feet away. "On your knees, pet."

The leopard's eyes shot open, the command piercing through the mental fog. Timidly, the feline rose onto his shaking knees before looking up at the antelope. Ell sauntered toward the crocodile's mouth, shaking her ass as she stepped over the row of oversized teeth and onto the giant tongue. Turing back to face Haxiten, Ell simply pointed an index finger to the portion of tongue beside her feet. Blinking, the leopard began to stand when Ell growled, "Crawl."

The former master of the house lowered himself back down onto his paws and knees, slowly crawling toward the waiting jaws. As he pulled himself carefully over the teeth, a blast of wet heat hit him like a wall. Ell lowered herself onto the surface of the tongue, sitting upright with her legs spread wide as her new pet approached her. Several tentacles slid from the back of the crocodile's throat, reaching forward to embrace Ell as she reclined back slightly into their grip. Tendrils coiled tenderly around her small breasts and body, winding around her legs before reaching out toward the leopard as he crawled closer.

Ell spread her legs wide as the former master reached her, letting him admire her tight pussy and lithe legs. The antelope spread her arms outward in the grip of the creature's tentacles as it squirmed over her body. The leopard looked up at her as she lounged seductively before him, swallowing as his hard rod quivered with desire. Ell drew her knees up slightly, emphasizing her spread legs as she commanded, "Make yourself useful, boy."

The feline's heart raced as he found himself crawling closer to her body, approaching on his hands and knees over the firm muscle of Carra's tongue. As he positioned himself between her legs, one of the thick slimy tendrils from the creature's maw reached out and coiled over the leopard's shoulders and neck, pulling him down until his face was mere inches from the antelope's tight slit.

Ell smiled in satisfaction as she watched her former master's face timidly approach her wet pussy. She spread her legs wide and leaned back, reclining into the warmth of the creature's embrace and the wet heat of the giant mouth, a shiver running down her spine as Haxiten's tongue reached out toward her clit. Ell sighed to herself as the leopard drew his tongue up over her slick entrance, pressing his broad tongue against her sensitive clit before wrapping his lips around the small button and sucking gently. The leopard pulsed his tongue in gentle waves within his mouth, forward and back as he sucked, pressing his snout into her warmth and breathing deeply as he caught her delicious scent.

The creature wrapped itself around Ell's entire body, her face and chest nearly disappearing inside a thick web of slick tendrils. Several cords of slime reached down to crawl over the leopard, coiling around his chest and thighs. Ell could hear the creature's desires as it embraced her, distant urges and cravings filling her mind. She could vaguely feel what the creature felt, a shadow of a sensation as the creature's tentacles crawled over her own body, caressing the leopard's muscular thighs, and even a hint of other things further away, down underground. Ell arched her back as the sensations flooded into her mind, the leopard pressing his tongue firmly against her clit as she moaned loudly.

Panting in the wet heat of the crocodile's maw, the leopard exhaled sharply onto Ell's wet slit, gasping for breath as he sucked desperately at her button. His mind lost to the haze of pleasure, the former master of the house could only think of pleasuring the antelope, only dimly aware of the numerous tentacles crawling over his body. A set of tendrils wrapped around his muscular stomach and coiled around the base of his throbbing cock, squeezing gently to press a thick drop of pre cum from the barbed

164

end. A pencil-thin tendril wound its way along the length of his shaft before doubling back on itself and finding the leopard's dripping wet cockhole. Sliding forward, the thin rod of ooze pressed its blunt end against the tight entrance to the leopard's flesh, pushing with firm pressure until it popped forward through the thin ring of muscle. The leopard groaned into Ell's pussy as he felt the intruding tentacle surge deeper into his cock, pushing easily to the base of his throbbing member.

Ell groaned as the leopard pressed his tongue forward into her entrance, his long muscular muscle curling upwards inside her passage as he groaned and sent vibrations into her flesh. Haxiten's nose pressed against her clit as he buried his tongue inside her, the pair panting in pleasure. Ell pulled her hands from their spread position among the tentacles and reached down, grabbing the back of the leopard's head and pulling, pressing his muzzle against her pussy as his tongue squirmed and flexed inside her. The antelope groaned loudly as her body clenched, her thighs squeezing the leopard's head as she came on his face. She clutched at his head as her body spasmed in the creature's embrace, pulling him tight against her screaming clit until the waves of pleasure subsided.

The leopard withdrew his tongue from her pussy, panting for breath as the creature's tentacles held him steadfast on his hands and knees between Ell's legs. The antelope leaned her head back among the slick tentacles as she enjoyed the leopard's hot breath against her pussy, the suppressing heat of the crocodile's mouth wrapping around her body. As her heart pounded in her ears, the creature coiled tightly around Ell's legs and ankles, squeezing firmly and spreading them wider. Ell could hear the faintest of callings from the creature, her mind swimming in pleasure as she understood. The antelope dug her fingers into the fur at the back of the leopard's head, squeezing and pulling him back to her aching pussy.

Former master Hykan panted hazily as he was forced back down, happily lolling his tongue out and dragging it against the dripping slit. Ell groaned aloud as the rough flesh ground against her clit, her fingers digging into the back of his head and pulling him tight against her entrance. The leopard groaned, sending shivers through Ell's body as she leaned further back, arching her spine.

Ell pulled roughly at the leopard's head, grinding her pussy against his snout and tongue, moaning loudly. She bucked her hips forward and back against his face, holding him in place as she used him. With a scream of pleasure Ell pulled roughly, forcing the leopard's snout into her tight pussy, his mouth forced closed by the tightness of her passage as she pulled desperately and drug him forward. The creature gripped her thighs tight and spread Ell wide as she pulled the cat's face against her entrance, feeling her pelvis bend and shift as she rocked her hips forward and back. Ell threw her head back and inhaled deeply as she pulled at the cat's head with all of her strength, the creature's tentacles gripping the leopard and pushing him against her slit until the antelope's pussy stretched an aching inch at a time as her former master's head spread her wide, muscle and flesh finally succumbing to the pressure as the leopard's head slid slowly into her throbbing passage.

The antelope's grip weakened as she felt her body stretch and bend, her arms failing to pull as she shook; the creature redoubled its grip on the leopard's neck, pushing with unyielding strength. Ell's mouth opened in a silent scream as her muscular entrance was stretched wider and wider. The cat's face sank into her until he was finally in past the top of his head and the antelope's pussy clenched down hard on the intruder, forcing the feline in up to his neck in a single rapid motion. Shaking, eyes clenched shut as she dared not even to breathe, Ell felt Master Hykan's head filling her pussy and stretching her obscenely, pressing out on every centimeter of her tight flesh with an overwhelming pressure. Ell's body shook as she came again, clenching on the leopard's head with waves of pleasure that barely overcame the sensation of the incredible pressure she felt within her.

Master Hykan's mind was a blur as he felt his head forced into the suppressing heat of the antelope's passage, panting desperately in the absolute darkness as he felt the strong tentacles wrapped around his neck and shoulders. The thin tendril buried deep within his cockhole squirmed inside his rod, pulsing in and out as it coiled around the outside of his shaft. He felt the pressure of Ell's pussy clenching around his head as she came, her smell and warmth filling his world.

Ell's heart calmed slightly while her body trembled. She looked down and moaned as she saw how wide her entrance stretched, clenched tight against the leopard's neck and throat. Her tight stomach already bulged slightly, her skin drawn taut against the back of the feline's head. She could feel her former master as he breathed heavily inside her, his head rocking back and forth as he moved deliriously. Before Ell could fully catch her breath, the creature wrapped itself around the leopard's chest, coiling tightly, binding his arms and paws down to his sides. The antelope moaned in hesitant anticipation as the creature pressed the leopard forward, quickly bringing his muscular shoulders up against her clenched entrance.

The creature lashed out with several more thick tendrils, latching around the leopard's thighs and hips. A large hollow tentacle reached out and pressed itself against the leopard's cockhead, quickly enveloping his hard rod down to the base as the thinner tendril worked its way in and out of his tight cumhole. In a single motion, the creature clenched tight around both Ell and the leopard, holding the antelope firmly in place as it pulled with impossible strength against the feline's shoulders, chest, hips and thighs simultaneously. Ell watched captivated as the leopard's shoulders bore down on her overfilled pussy, the tentacles driving him forward by a fraction of an inch each with each passing breath, clenching them both tighter as Ell's entrance spread wider, the creature's slow progress as constant and inevitable as gravity. Every heart beat pounded in Ell's ear as the creature clamped onto her thighs and pulled them wide, spreading her hips and stretching her apart with an aching slowness while the leopard's shoulders ground against her opening.

Ell's eyes were transfixed on the scene as she held her breath subconsciously, clenching her teeth as the creature pulled her legs apart, wider and wider, her pussy spreading with every shift of muscle until it was nearly wide enough to accept the feline's shoulders. The antelope groaned, lost to the pleasure as the creature rammed the leopard forward, slamming his shoulders against her and stretching her entrance with a single rapid surge of strength, her mind screaming out from the intensity of pleasure as the cat's shoulders were crammed into her passage, the creature plunging his body forward roughly until the leopard was buried up to his pecks in a single instant. Ell's eyes fluttered as her head lolled back into the creature's embrace, her body convulsing uncontrollably as she came, her pussy stretched wider than her own hips, trying to clench fruitlessly as she orgasmed.

The creature stroked its slick tentacle rapidly over the leopard's barbed cock, coaxing a steady stream of pre cum from his flesh. The feline moaned helplessly, unable to move a single muscle between the impossible grip of the tentacles and the tight squeeze around his head and upper body. Panting, the cat groaned in lust and pleasure, sending vibrations deep into the antelope's body.

Her stomach bulging out, her hips pulled wide, her pussy stretched out past the width of her chest, Ell swallowed hard and tried desperately to breathe. The creature squirmed over Ell's breasts and chest, enveloping her in a thick web of tendrils as it pulled ceaselessly on the leopard's hips and thighs, dragging him forward inch by unyielding inch even as Ell fought frantically to catch her breath. Her vision unfocused and her jaw slackened, her body going limp in stupor from the sheer pleasure as the leopard was shoved deeper and deeper into her hot flesh. When Ell finally looked down a moment later, she watched helplessly as the small of the leopard's back disappeared into her stretched pussy, her belly stretched out in a massive bulge as her former master's body began to curl inside her.

As Haxiten felt his body advance forward slowly, he found his entire torso and arms buried inside the antelope's warmth. Immediately the cat brought his paws up and began touching his chest and face in delirium as the creature continued stroking his stiff cock just outside the antelope's entrance. His breath stifled by the suppressing heat and pressure of Ell's flesh, the leopard closed his eyes and succumbed helplessly to the haze in his mind.

Ell felt her former master moving within her stretched belly as the creature stroked his rigid shaft. As the leopard's body was buried deeper, the cat's dripping rod was brought up close to her entrance. The creature pulled its hollow tendril off of his shaft, leaving the thin strand of goo penetrating his hole as the leopard was pushed forward, his cock hanging away from his body under its own weight. Ell groaned, helpless to the creature's desires as she felt her body slide down slightly, the leopard's rod lining up with her tight tailhole even as his entire body was crammed into her pussy. The creature pushed the leopard forward, lining up its captive pair as the cat's cockhead pressed against the antelope's pucker.

The creature gripped the pair with every bit of tendril as it pushed the leopard forward, inching his hips deeper into the antelope's stretched pussy while simultaneously pressing the barbed cockhead against her ass, stretching the unused hole slowly until the rod forced her open. Ell cried out as the creature slammed the leopard forward, burying the cat's rod deep into her ass while pushing his body further into her abused slit. The antelope shook limply, staring up blankly as the creature rammed the entire leopard's body forward and back, surging back several inches before plowing back forward, fucking Ell's ass with the barbed cock while cramming her pussy impossibly full with the leopard's taut muscular body.

Haxiten moaned and drooled inside Ell's body as he felt his shaft squeezed by the antelope's tight asshole, his rod clenched tight against his belly through the thin wall of flesh separating her passages. The coil of ooze surged forward and back through his cumslit, pounding forward and back in sync with his body as he was rammed into the antelope's stretched holes. The uncontrollable tension built within his body even as his mind struggled to grasp what was happening, his cock flexing and clenching reflexively as his body squirmed and thrashed in pleasure.

Ell arched her back as she felt the leopard fill her holes, bucking her hips desperately against the cat's barbed rod as it stuffed her ass, bottoming herself out on his thick shaft as the creature shoved his entire body forward into her again and again. She felt the leopard moan within her bulging belly, groaning loudly as his body clenched and shook, his cock throbbing in her tight ass as he came, pulses of thick cum pouring from his shaft and filling the thin tendril buried deep within his hole. Ell shook and came as the leopard squirmed within her filled pussy, her muscles weak and limp as she succumbed to her body.

Even as the leopard continued to orgasm, thick surges of cum pouring from his cock and into the thin tendril, the creature pulled the feline back suddenly until his rod came free of her hole before slamming him forward roughly, cramming him deeper until his stiff shaft bent back

170

between his legs and his hips disappeared into Ell's passage. The antelope's eyes rolled up into the back of her head as the creature shoved the leopard's legs into her pussy in one unyielding movement, his body curving around inside her belly as it swelled and stretched, finally stuffing his feet into her aching entrance before withdrawing its grip from the cat, dragging several tentacles back out from Ell's pussy as she clenched herself shut, trembling ferociously as another orgasm rocked her entire body.

Ell shook and involuntarily fought against the tight grip of the tendrils wrapped around her arms and legs as she came, the immense fullness of her body sending her over the edge. The antelope felt the creature pull her backward, sliding her back across the giant tongue as she convulsed with pleasure, squeezing her fists and clenching her teeth. Warmth embraced her entire body as the web of tendrils pulled her back toward the throat of the creature, the closing wetness squeezing around her. Ell moaned and panted in a daze of lust and madness as the creature slid her gently into the back of the giant maw, pulling her body down into the warmth of the throat and into the pit below.

Chapter 12

Léo lay flat on his back, panting heavily as the two otters and badger licked his cum-soaked tentacle cock. The mouse boy looked up as his vision cleared, greeted by the sight of the badger taking half his length into her mouth, the otters to either side holding the base of his long shaft. Léo sat upright and reached out to put a hand on the side of the badger's face, pulling her up and pressing his lips to hers, tasting himself on her tongue. Breaking the kiss to lick the badger's cheek, Léo moaned as he felt the two otters fight to take his shaft into their mouths.

Licking his lips, savoring his own taste, Léo felt his stomach growl, his chest panging with desire. The mouse pushed the badger back, slowly guiding her down to the table as he licked her cheek and neck. Léo hovered over the panting badger noblewoman on his hands and knees, the otters repositioning themselves under his hips and stroking his slick length. The mouse licked at the badger's fur, tasting his own cum as he worked his way down her chest, sucking on a single nipple for a teasing instant before dragging his tongue down over her bulging cum-filled belly. The badger moaned, eyes half open, feeling the mouse's small tongue lap over wet fur.

Léo worked his way down the badger's body as the two otters took turns stroking and sucking his slick tendril cock. When his tongue found its way down between the badger's thighs, the mouse pushed her legs apart and pressed his lips against her wet folds, licking at the thick streams of his own cum as they leaked from her entrance. The noblewoman moaned, legs writhing as Léo pressed his rough tongue just below her clit, licking up in long gentle movements, savoring the taste of their mixed fluids.

The badger moaned, clenching her pussy and pushing out gushes of Léo massive load, shivering as he licked it from her entrance. Léo teased her clit and withdrew, licking down one thigh and kissing along her leg. With each movement down her legs Léo crawled backward on his hands and knees, the otters shifting and repositioning, desperate to keep their paws and tongues against his slick cock. When the mouse reached the badger's foot, he grabbed both her ankles and pulled them together, licking in one long dragging motion against her footpad. The badger moaned softly as Léo dragged his tongue over the bottom of her hind paws, pressing his lips against her sensitive flesh and pressing his tongue between her clawed digits.

Léo looked back at the otters and shook his hips playfully, smiling at them as they glanced at each other. After a wordless moment, one otter crawled out from under the mouse's hips and knelt behind him, while the other continued to stroke Léo's length and suck the tip into his mouth. The otter at his backside held his rigid length as he knelt closer, pressing his rounded cockhead against the mouse's tight pucker. Léo raised his wiry tail as the otter rubbed his rod against the mouse's warm flesh, coating the entrance with slick pre cum before pushing forward, slowly parting the mouse with his hard member. Léo groaned into the badger's feet as the otter filled his ass, flexing his cock and pushing a thick drop of pre into the other otter's mouth.

As the otter started rocking forward and back, slowly filling Léo's tailhole with long luxurious strokes, the mouse took one of the badger's toes into his mouth, wrapping his lips around the fur-covered digit. Léo pressed his tongue against the soft underside of her toe, feeling the tip of her sharp claw, sucking on her flesh. Panting as he pulled his mouth free,

Léo licked the side of her hind paw as the otter pushed his full length into his ass. Léo wrapped his long delicate tail around the chest of the otter and pushed back against his slow strokes, moaning and sucking the badger's two smaller toes into his mouth.

A deep rumbling filled Léo's core as he wrapped his lips around the badger's toes. The mouse felt his chest tighten with desire, pulses of warmth flowing through his body and up toward his head. Léo drooled as he sucked on the noblewoman's hind paws, eyelids heavy as the pulsing warmth intoxicated his mind. The mouse wrapped his lips around the badger's paw, pulling the entire front half of her foot into his mouth. With his entire body rocking forward and back as the otter filled his tailhole, Léo licked the bottom of the badger's paw as it was trapped between his lips.

Léo felt his jaw slacken even as his lips stretched to fit over the badger's wide hind paw. Warmth pulsed through his head and neck, his jaw opening wider than it should have as he pressed his head down onto the noblewoman's foot. Léo pulled his mouth back upwards, sucking on her feet and toes before pushing forward again, stretching his jaw until his lips wrapped around her ankle, her toes pressing against the back of his throat. The otter watched from behind and pumped his cock deep into Léo's ass, pushing his entire body forward with each thrust and forcing the mouse's mouth further down on the badger's foot. Léo pulled the hind paw from his mouth and pressed her ankles together, stretching his pliable lips around both paws, yawning wide as the otter pounded into him from behind, forcing his face downward until both of her feet were trapped up to their ankles in the mouse's flexible jaws.

The badger moaned softly as she looked down at her feet. Léo's lips stretched around her ankles as his tongue pressed against the bottom of her sensitive foot pads. She curled her toes, feeling the tight warmth of the mouse's throat, shivering as he moaned into her paws. With each of the otters' thrusts, Léo's mouth wrapped further around the badger's ankles, lips stretching taut with each movement before tingling warmth pulsed through his head, allowing him to stretch another fraction of an inch. Léo felt the badger's clawed digits press against the back of his throat, his flesh squeezing tight against her paws as he pushed her further into his wet mouth. The tingling spread through his jaws and throat as his lips stretched around the back of the badger's feet, a deep yearning building within the mouse's chest as he let his body slam forward with each of the otters' thrusts.

Léo's throat bulged and stretched as he slid his lips over the backs of the noblewoman's heels, the thickness of her paws filling his neck and pressing out on the pliable flesh. The mouse swallowed against the badger's paws, eyes half closed as the otter thrust against his tailhole, head tingling as the badger's muscular calves slid between his lips an inch at a time. The noblewoman watched in dazed fascination as the mouse crept up her legs, curling her toes within the wet heat of his flexible throat. Léo felt the badger's paws slide down into his upper chest, his flesh giving way as she passed into him, craving more of her body with each moment.

The otter at Léo's backside thrust hard against the mouse's tailhole, grunting in pleasure as his strokes grew faster. Léo found himself sliding forward up to the badger's knees, his lips drawn taut against her legs as the otter gripped the mouse's hips tight and bucked against him. As the mouse's lips reached the badger's bony knee caps, the otter thrust harder and faster, grunting and pushing Léo forward as hard as he could, watching his mistress slide into the mouse's hungry mouth. With a cry of pleasure the otter thrust forward, forcing the mouse's jaws around the badger's knees as he hilted himself into Léo's tight hole, cock pulsing and flexing as he shot his thick load into the mouse's ass. Léo moaned

175

helplessly, mouth locked around the badger's legs as he felt the otter pump his seed into his hole, the badger's feet pressing down into the mouse's warm belly.

Léo swallowed against the badger's legs, her thick calves trapped in his bulging throat. The otter pumped the last of his seed into the mouse and withdrew, cum leaking from his tight hole even as he clenched himself shut. The otter dropped to his hands and knees and crawled forward, making eye contact with the other otter before crawling forward toward the badger. As one otter knelt up and took position behind Léo, the other knelt down and kissed the badger deeply, rubbing his palms against her ample breasts as his partner pressed his hard cock against the mouse's cum-filled tailhole. Léo and the badger moaned together as the otters rubbed their respective bodies, one kissing and biting at the badger's neck as the other pushed his hard shaft into Léo's dripping asshole with a single swift motion.

Overwhelming warmth flooded through Léo's body as the badger's feet slid into his gut. The outline of the noblewoman's calves was plainly visible through the stretched skin of the mouse's throat. Léo crawled forward as the otter pressed into his ass, pushing him forward and cramming the badger's muscular thighs between his stretching lips. Jaws wide, the mouse let the legs pass into his mouth and throat as the otter plowed into his sloppy cum-soaked hole. The badger moaned as the other otter grabbed her breasts, squeezing her nipples and watching the mouse advance one delicious inch at a time.

Soon Léo's lips stretched around her upper thighs, her feet curling downward inside the mouse's distorted belly. The badger's swollen belly loomed before Léo's face as his mouth wrapped around the bottom of her pelvis, still bulging obscenely with the mouse's massive load. As the otter thrust hard into Léo's hole, the badger felt the mouse's tongue pressing up against her ass, even his massive flexible jaws struggling to wrap around her plump hindquarters and swollen belly.

The otter up by the badger crawled forward, spreading his legs and straddling the badger's face, turning toward Léo. Without question the noblewoman leaned forward and pressed her tongue against the otter's tight tailhole, drawing a gasp from the otter as he leaned forward. The otter pressed his ass against the badger's face, his hard cock bobbing in the air as he placed his palms flat against the badger's bulging belly. Moaning together, the otter pressed down on his mistress' stomach, a surge of mouse cum immediately flooding from the badger's pussy and pouring into Léo's hungry mouth. The mouse gulped as fast as he could, swallowing his own load mixed with the noblewoman's juices as fast as he could, gasping and panting as streams leaked from his mouth and flowed down his chin.

Again the otter pushed down, the badger crying out even as the otter pressed his ass onto her face, a torrent of salty cum flowing from her soaked entrance and pouring into the mouse's gullet. Léo swallowed hard, forcing his own load down into his belly, his chest tightening in lust and need as he filled himself with the thick cum. The mouse's belly stretched as the badger squirmed her feet within him, slick warmth filling his gut and flooding around the badger's hind paws. The badger pressed her tongue up against the otter's hole as the he put his weight on the badger's belly, pushing with long hard pressure, flooding the mouse's mouth until the thick cum overflowed his belly and splashed out against his face and onto the table, dripping from Léo's cheeks and jaws.

Léo gulped and panted as the otter leaned against the badger's plump belly, flooding the mouse with his own cum until the badger's belly was empty. The otter behind Léo pounded forward, slamming into the mouse's ass, forcing Léo's dripping lips to slide forward over the badger's hips and butt cheeks. The badger moaned as her pelvis slid through the cum-slick lips, her hips enveloped in the wet warmth of Léo's mouth. Léo felt his stomach stretch, his pliable flesh bending outward as the badger bent her knees within his gut. With each pounding thrust the otter slammed Léo forward, pushing the mouse an inch at a time, stretching his jaws wide against the badger's torso. The other otter sat firmly on the badger's face, grinding his ass against his mistress' tongue as he watched Léo advance up her body.

When Léo's mouth slid up to the bottom of the badger's large tits, the otter reached down and pressed on her breasts. The pair of otter servants worked together, one slamming the mouse forward as the other squeezed the badger's breasts down past Léo's lips, the mouse sucking her soft flesh into his hot mouth. Léo felt his belly grow heavier with each passing moment, the noblewoman's hips sinking into his stomach as her rib cage stretched his neck, his skin drawn tight against her muscles. The badger moaned into the otter's asshole as her breasts slid into Léo's mouth, pressing tight against her chest as they slid slowly into his throat.

The otter grabbed the badger's arms as Léo's mouth inched up her upper chest, holding them upwards as he pressed his ass against her mouth. Léo moaned, his eyes half open as his ass was filled again and again, each pounding stroke slamming into his hips and forcing him forward, his belly now protruding from his body in a giant round swell. The otter pulled himself from the badger's face as Léo's lips wrapped around her collarbone, holding her arms out as she squirmed. Léo reached forward and grabbed the badger's shoulders, pulling her forward in one last yearning effort, desperate to feel her inside him. The badger's legs and body twisted and turned within his throat and gut, pulling against the otter's grip and moaning to herself as Léo pulled ferociously, cramming her shoulders into his stretched mouth.

178

Holding her wrists together, the otter knelt and watched Léo wrap his hands around the top of the badger's head, pulling and moaning until the noblewoman slid past his lips, jaws shifting back to their original shape as he yanked quickly on her arms, stuffing them quickly down his throat. The otter let go of her wrists as they disappeared into Léo's mouth, the bulge of her head and arms sliding rapidly down his throat as she the mouse's body pulled her down into his belly. Léo panted and cried out as he swallowed desperately, pushing himself back against the otter buried in his ass, the tightness in his chest only growing as he felt the badger turning and curling within his gut.

The badger struggled to breathe in the hot wetness of Léo's belly. The noblewoman quickly found herself curled in the fetal position, the tightness of the mouse's stretched belly pulling in on her from every direction. Licking her lips, the badger realized that she was sitting in a pool of hot cum, the hungrily swallowed remains of the massive load the stretched her own belly moments before. The mustelid panted in the stifling hot air, her own breath scorching and wet as it filled the space around her. Grabbing one breast, squeezing her nipple, the badger slid her other hand down between her legs, finding her dripping pussy with her cum-slick paw.

Sliding her wet palm against her clit, the badger squeezed her knees together in her curled position, digging her claws into her breast. The noblewoman panted in hard deep breaths, struggling to find air in the wet darkness. Electric waves shot through her body as she pushed her fingers into her drenched pussy, mind fuzzing even as she touched herself. Pushing her sharp claws into her chest flesh, the badger felt her body give way, her skin turning pliable as she pressed against it. The walls closed in and the pool of cum surrounding her body rose, the taste of seed filling her mouth. She pressed her claw into her breast as they both dissolved, her wet flesh shrinking away and going blissfully numb. The badger's back muscles tensed before softening, dissipating into the wetness. Desperately pressing her paw against her pussy, rubbing furiously as her flesh melted and mind faded, the badger finally felt a flash of fireworks as her dissolving body came, mind convulsing in pleasure, clenching her jaw as it dripped, pressing her fingers hard against her clit as her flesh softened, her orgasm fading as her body disappeared beneath the rising pool of warm cum.

Léo pushed himself back against the otter, mouth open and drooling as he felt the badger dissolve within his belly, feeling her mind cry out in orgasm as she became a part of himself, hearing her cravings and desires in the back of his mind. The otter slammed into the mouse's ass and finally arched his back, squeezing Léo's hips as he pumped his load. Léo's cock drooled long strings of pre cum as his body pulsed with new pleasure, feeling his belly swollen with hot seed as the otter drained himself into his tailhole. The mouse moaned and squeezed his ass against the pulsing otter cock, coaxing every last drop from his shaft until the servant flexed one last time and pulled himself free of Léo's dripping hole.

The mouse boy spent several long moments with his face against the table, ass in the air, panting and listening to the badger's soft whisper's in his mind. When Léo finally looked up, he saw that the otter twins were already touching each other, stroking their paws over each other's slick cocks as they kissed. Léo looked over toward the center of the room and watched the giant maw, jaws hanging open eagerly. The mouse crawled toward the edge of the table, climbing down onto weak legs and taking a few steps forward. Léo smiled as the two otters immediately hopped off the table, following a few paces behind the mouse as he walked to the center of the room.

The creature's maw hung open hungrily as the trio approached. Léo turned around to face the otters as tentacles reached out from the open mouth, coiling around his body and legs. The two servants watched as the creature pulled the mouse toward the back of its throat. Without a second thought, eyes still half-closed in dazed pleasure, the two otters stepped forward onto the giant crocodile tongue and let the creature wrap around their bodies, sliding back through the wet heat and into the tight shaft of oozing flesh.

Chapter 13

Kett's heart fluttered as she watched the room. The sweet mist clung to the ground but the scent filled the air, immediately reminding the fox of the bottom of the well. A crowded room of hesitant party guests watched the enormous maw in the center of the room, every conscious thought of fear suppressed by the fog. Most guests simply froze where they were, bodies clung together in the midst of their activities, watching as Ell had her way with the master of the house. Slowly, Kett climbed down from the table and sauntered across the floor, weaving through the piles of partiers, looking into each of their eyes as she passed.

The fox wandered toward the pair of bunnies suspended from the ceiling. Only a handful of guests stood nearby, frozen to the ground as they watched Kett walk up to the two lagomorphs, inspecting curiously. The pair of servants hung from several long ropes anchored to the tall ceiling, their hands bound together above their heads. A criss-cross of ropes covered their bodies to form a sturdy harness, binding the pair together face to face. Each of their legs were spread out horizontal with a sturdy rope running from their ankles up to the rope just above their wrists, trapping each bunny girl in a bound triangle, their hips hovering conveniently at waist height. The duo squirmed against each other as Kett ran a paw down one of their exposed backs, their faces flushed after having been used for the pleasure of the guests all evening.

Kett circled around to behind one of the rabbits and lowered her paw down between her legs. Pressing her soft paw pads up against each of their wet pussies, Kett felt their cum-soaked entrances and rubbed forward and back against their folds. She pulled her hand away and licked

182

the juices from her palm, savoring the taste of a dozen loads mixed with the bunny's delicious wetness. The lagomorph pair moaned into each other's mouths as Kett caressed the firm ass cheeks spread wide before her at waist height. Glancing to one side, Kett spotted a muscular gray wolf standing stock-still nearby, his rock-hard member dripping thick gobs of pre as he stared back at the fox, breathing deeply in the rising mist.

Beckoning to the wolf with her eyes, Kett invited the guest closer. As the nobleman approached Kett held her cum-soaked paw up to his face, smiling to herself as he eagerly lapped at the juices of a dozen strangers. Kett lowered her paw and gripped the wolf's rigid shaft, his red cock already throbbing with helpless desire. She pulled gently on his rod and guided the wolf toward the backside of one of the bunnies, dropping to her knees as she moved him into position. Kett knelt underneath the suspended bunnies and grabbed the wolf's thick red cock, the compliant canine standing obediently as she slid her grip forward and back over the warm flesh. Carefully positioning the pointed tip of the wolf's member, Kett slipped the head into the dripping wet entrance of the bunny's tailhole. The rabbit girl moaned into the mouth of her partner as Kett slid the rod deeper, easily burying the thick wolf rod up to the flare of his bulbous knot, drips of warm cum leaking from her pussy as the wolf filled her ass.

Kett crawled out from underneath the suspended bunnies and quickly spotted a length of unused rope coiled on the floor. The fox picked up the rope and grabbed the wolf's wrists, quickly binding them above his head and fastening them in turn to the rabbit's wrists. The wolf moaned pensively as he rocked his hips forward and back, his thick rod spearing the little bunny with each slow pulse. Kett grabbed one of the wolf's ankles and pulled up, lashing his ankle to the rabbit's in a single rapid motion. Before the nobleman could think to object, Kett circled around and grabbed the wolf's other ankle, easily lifting it up and likewise binding it, the wolf now suspended in similar fashion to the bunnies, his thick cock buried into the rabbit's warm tailhole. The wolf, more than a full head taller than the small bunny girls, rested his jaw on the top of the bunny's head as the pair of lagomorph's pressed their mouths together.

As the wolf moaned, suspended helplessly above the ground and rocking his hips forward and back, Kett looked around and found a muscular Doberman standing nearby, stroking his rigid length as he watched. With a single look the canine obediently padded closer. Kett looked into his clouded eyes and lowered herself down to her knees, wrapping her paw around his thick dripping shaft. The fox pulled the hard rod down toward her mouth, parting her lips and bringing the dog's tip within a hair's width of her tongue. She could feel the canine's heart skip a beat as she gripped his cock, holding the tip of his member just out of reach of her mouth.

Teasingly, Kett leaned back, away from the canine's shaft, her mouth open, waiting for his flesh. The canine took a hesitant step forward, closing the gap just as Kett slid her knee back across the floor. Kett pulled back toward the suspended trio, one knee at a time, drawing the Doberman closer to her mouth, her breath hot and wet on his shaft but never letting his red flesh touch her lips. When Kett finally found herself directly under the rabbits she leaned forward with her mouth open, tongue curled up in anticipation, looking up at the canine's expectant expression, inching closer to his dripping tip until she drew close enough to lick a single drip of pre from his cumslit so delicately that she never let her tongue touch his flesh before immediately leaning back and shoving the dog's cockhead up into the rabbit's wet asshole. Kett plunged the thick rod up into the bunny's abused hole, cramming the canine's member

184

deep into her warmth until her tight pucker clenched against the top of the Doberman's swollen knot.

The canine and lagomorph cried out in unison as Kett crawled out from underneath. Grabbing another length of rope, the fox made quick work of binding the canine's wrists above his head, and likewise spreading his legs out and lashing him to his rabbit counterpart before running the rope around all four suspended bodies and binding them together. Kett stood back for a moment, watching as the pair of helpless canines bucked their hips against the backsides of the sandwiched bunny girls, their thick red cocks buried deep in their tight tailholes. The four moaned and squirmed against each other, grinding their bodies against the ropes bound tight against their flesh. The canines, each much taller than the rabbits, found themselves face to face directly above the heads of the girls, their muzzles finding each other's as their clouded minds rocked their shafts in and out of their respective holes. The wolf and the Doberman opened their mouths and let their tongues twist against each other's, panting breathlessly as they buried their lengths into the rabbits, pressing their swollen knots against their clenching flesh.

Kett watched as a handful of tentacles snaked across the floor, crawling from the nearest fissure in the ground toward the four bound figures. Without hesitation the tentacles reached up and coiled around each of their thighs, winding around their bodies until the blunt tips circled back down and found their parted legs. The four moaned, squirming against each other and the tentacles as the slimy appendages embraced their bodies, the oozing ends finding the canines' tailholes and rabbits' dripping pussies, the wet tips sliding against their tight holes and spreading their slickness against their clenching entrances. The wolf and Doberman rocked their hips forward and back, their thick rods pulsing in the bunny's tight holes as the tentacles pressed their rounded ends against

185

the unfilled holes, their firm pressure building until one by one their flesh yielded and accepted the slick tendrils. The bunnies cried out as the tentacles plunged into their wet slits, pulsing deep into their warm bodies, pressing tight against the thick dog cocks buried in their hindquarters. As the tentacles probed, they speared the tight puckers of the canine's tailholes, pressing their slickness deep into the pair as they moaned into each other's parted muzzles. The four bound figures squirmed and fought against the grip of the ropes as the tentacles pulsed in and out of their holes, the two dog cocks ramming forward and back as their owners bucked against the invading appendages.

The pair of canines arched their backs in pleasure, twisting their bodies against their restraints as the tentacles slammed into their bodies. With each coursing plunge of tentacle the canines bucked their hips, thrusting forward and back in jagged strokes. The the bunnies moaned helplessly as they were filled by the thick tendrils and cocks, the relentless pressure stretching their holes, waves of pleasure coursing through their bodies. The canines bucked against the rabbits in a frenzy, the thick tendrils filling their tailholes with slick warmth, pressing their swollen knots against the bunny's tight holes, stretching their entrances with each rough thrust.

As the pairs pressed their faces together, twisting their tongues between each other's lips in helpless pleasure, succumbing to the intoxicating pleasure of the tendril's touch, the four figures simply thrashed their hips against each other, eyes closed in bliss. The tentacles pumped forward and back, filling their holes in alternating thrusts, plunging deep and driving their own thrusts against each other more desperate. The bound partiers felt the pressure build within their bodies in unison, their cries mounting as half of the room watched their rapturous pleasure. The canines groaned aloud, their tongues lolling from their

186

muzzles as they pressed their lips together, thrusting their hips upwards in a long hard stroke, pressing their knots against the rabbit's holes. The bunnies pressed their asses back against the dogs, feeling their flesh stretch and spread as the giant knots filled their thoughts, their breath faltering as their minds clouded. The pair of thick knots plunged forward in unison, the four crying out as the hot flesh buried itself in the clenching holes, waves of pleasure surging through their bodies as they orgasmed simultaneously. Thick ropes of cum flooded deep into the bunnies' depths as they clenched down hard on the shafts buried in their bodies. The four shook and trembled violently against each other and their bindings, the hanging mass of bodies swaying and thrashing as it hung above the ground, drips of their juices flooding from their holes onto the floor.

Kett watched the four bound figures shake as their orgasms subsided, only for the tentacles to pick up once again, pulsing forward and back, drawing helpless moans from the four as they succumbed to the creature's will. The fox turned back around and watched the rest of the room. Several nearby guests had resumed their activities, a combination of the fog filling the room and the sights put on by Kett forcing their desire to overcome their fear.

Not too far away, Kett found a nobleman grizzly bear bent over on all fours, face laid against the floor in a daze as a young male deer servant stood behind him, his shaft buried deep in the bear's tailhole. Kett approached the pair, smiling at the buck as he stared back at her, eyes half-closed in a daze.

The fox circled around the guests, resting a hand gently on the deer's muscular bicep, sliding her paw across his shoulder blades before stopping at the buck's side. Kett looked down at his shaft buried to the hilt in the bear's ass and reached forward, cupping her palm around his heavy sack. The servant shivered and closed his eyes, his hips moving unconsciously. Kett brought her paw up against his hip as she circled back around behind him, placing her other paw against the opposite hip, pulling herself forward and pressing her throbbing cock against the buck's muscular ass cheeks.

Kett dug her claws into the deer's pelvis playfully, scratching against his flesh as she pushed her hips forward. Using a foot to encourage the buck to spread his legs, Kett bent her knees slightly and let her thick shaft fall forward between his cheeks. The fox pressed her hips upwards, teasing as she brought her tapered cockhead up against the buck's tailhole and let it slide over his entrance, back up between his cheeks. Again Kett lowered herself and dragged her member over his tight pucker, drawing a moan from the servant as he pressed his ass back against her.

Gripping his hips, extending her claws ever so slightly, Kett knelt once more and brought her hips upward, leaning back and pressing the pointed tip of her red flesh against the buck's clenching hole. Nestling the tip just within the divot of his entrance Kett pressed her claws against his fur, forcing him to clench every muscle in his body as she raised her knees and pushed firmly upwards, holding his hips perfectly still with her grip as her rock-hard cock pressed against his entrance. Slowly, with a surprised gasp from the buck, the flesh gave way and Kett slid her throbbing shaft upward, sighing to herself as she felt the tight ring of muscle clench around her rod in waves, tightening as she filled his hole.

The deer responded with a low moan, eyes fluttering as he clenched involuntarily against the intruding member. Kett gripped the buck's hips firmly and hilted herself, bringing her knot up against the tight hole with a gasp of pleasure. Holding tight to the buck's hips Kett drew back, bringing the buck's hips back with her. The grizzly stirred from his semi-conscious state as the servant's cock withdrew from his ass, rolling his

188

head to the side and shifting his knees in a daze. Kett pressed forward against the buck's tight hole, forcing his shaft back deeper into the bear.

With a low grumble of satisfaction, the grizzly pressed his round ass back against the deer, meeting his forward movement and hilting himself on the hard rod. The bear's own cock twitched and grew as Kett gripped the buck and pulled him back, her shaft buried deep inside his hole as she plunged him back into the grizzly's warm hole. Kett exhaled sharply and scraped her claws against the servant's muscular hips, pulling him forward and back with building momentum. The buck gazed down at his rod as Kett forced him in and out of the bear's tailhole, watching in dazed arousal as his thick member was buried again and again, the fox's claws wrapped tight against his hips and sending sharp pulses of adrenaline through his body with every movement.

Kett pressed herself harder against the buck's hole, flexing herself within his tight embrace as she plunged him forward. With each movement the fox pressed harder, bringing their hips back faster and slamming back deep into the bear, drawing moans from the pair. Kett set her feet back and leaned into the buck, clutching at his hips as she forced him forward and back, bottoming him out inside the bear with each powerful stroke and pressing her knot firmly against the his tight hole. The bear moaned as his ass was filled again and again, drooling on the floor with his tongue hanging from his open jaws as the buck's balls slapped against his own. Kett pressed hard against the deer's hole, burying him deep into the bear as she leaned in against his tight hole, stretching him wider with her knot. The grizzly pressed back against the buck, grinding his ass against his hips as Kett forced herself against his backside, clutching his hips and pulling roughly against his clenching hole until it spread wide enough for her swollen knot to plunge quickly into his warm depths.

The buck tilted his head back and moaned in delirious pleasure as Kett knotted his ass, her claws pricking against his flesh, surges of warmth spreading through his core. Kett repositioned her stance and slid her paws up the buck's chest, pressing her arms against his front side and clutching at his muscular pecks, drawing her chest up against his back. Firmly knotted inside his tight hole, Kett pulled her hips back and brought the buck's trapped hips with her, slamming them both back forward, using the tied buck to fill the nobleman's ass. The fox dug her claws into the deer's chest, using his hips as her own to fuck the grizzly, pistoning deep and hard against the bear's round ass. Kett dragged her claws down along the servant's chest as she slammed her hips forward and back, feeling him clench against her swollen knot with every movement. The buck panted and moaned, Kett dragging his hard shaft in and out of the nobleman, drawing nearly his full length from the hot ass before plunging back deep inside.

Kett slammed forward harder as the buck panted, dragging her claws against his front side as the tension grew within his groin. With a grunt the buck flexed every muscle in his body, letting Kett press his cock deep into the bear as he twitched and shook, hot spurts of cum spraying into the grizzly's ass as the fox left deep red claw marks in his flesh. The buck quivered as his balls emptied into the bear, feeling his warmth fill the tight passage and surge around his buried member. The bear's eyes closed in bliss as drool flowed freely from his mouth, long drips of pre falling from his rock-hard cock.

Quivering, the buck moaned, spurt after spurt of hot cum flooding from his cock, pulsing deep into the bear as the orgasm shook his body. The warmth of his own seed filled the tight ass, flowing around his shaft. In a rapid snap of senses, the buck shivered as he felt his nerves splice with the grizzly, every hair standing on end as he felt every inch of the bear through his buried cock. Kett grabbed the buck by the hips slammed forward, pressing his hips tight against the bear's ass and forcing his thighs to fuse with the bear's in an instant. The bear panted as his vision dimmed, his legs going numb.

The nobleman's plump body softened as the buck squirmed, cock still flexing in orgasm even as his balls were drained dry. The servant could feel rushing warmth flooding into his body from his hips, a river flowing through his flesh and into his balls, a swelling sensation filling his mind. The body of the bear thinned and shrank even as the buck watched, his thick flanks shedding away as the heat plummeted into his body, his sack growing heavier with every instant. The bear's arms shrank and pulled into his body even as he tried to put his weight on his hands, his head drawing up against his shoulders and face softening. Kett flexed her cock as she felt the surging waves of pleasure through the buck's and bear's fused bodies, the clenching warmth against her tied cock nearly sending her over the edge.

As the buck's heavy sack grew and swelled between his legs, the body of the bear rose slightly into the air, head coming up off the ground. The noble's fur thinned and receded, leaving smooth pink skin. Clenching his ass around the fox's cock, the servant watched as the bear's body rose further into the air in reaction, clear fluid pouring from the bear's mouth in a thick stream. The warmth flooded relentlessly through his every vein as his balls grew to giant globes more than a foot across each. The grizzly's body shrank in diameter until he was nothing more than a sleek shaft of flesh, his head softening and eyes closing, mouth drawing shut except for a small hole. The buck could hear the bear inside his mind, the desperate lust calling to him from his very depths as the buck clenched every muscle in his body, the flood of warmth subsiding.

Kett grabbed the buck's hips and pulled herself back roughly, pulling her swollen knot from his tight hole in a single violent motion. The buck trembled on weak knees, body crying out as Kett slammed herself back forward, cramming her bulbous knot back into his flesh. The fox set her teeth and panted, digging her claws into the buck's hips as she ripped her knot from the buck once again, drawing nearly her full length from his hole before slamming forward and knotting herself once again. The buck trembled as the tension built again, surging rapidly from his core as the fox pulled herself free and plunged back in, repeatedly stretching his asshole wide with powerful strokes. Kett slammed forward and back, slapping her hips against the buck's ass repeatedly and re-knotted his tight hole again and again, growling as she arched her back and hilted herself within the servant's hot flesh, finally releasing her seed into his warmth with a deep moan.

The buck felt powerful jets of cum spray from Kett's thick cock, waves of shivers flooding every square inch of his body. As the pleasure ripped through his body, he felt his swollen balls tense, his massive rod crying out in desperation. But even as his body clenched, the first spurt of orgasm only an instant away, Kett reached up with one clawed paw and gripped the front of the deer's throat, growling raggedly through her teeth as she sprayed her load into his ass, "You don't have my permission to cum yet." The buck's body instantly faltered, his body falling off a cliff of pleasure as he clenched his cock, the waves draining from his core with a sudden wash of aching, pulsing his shaft in anticipation of the halted orgasm. The servant, along with the bear within his mind, groaned and panted, the arousal still present but the flood of pleasure locked behind a door.

Kett flexed her shaft within the buck's ass until her pleasure subsided, draining her balls into the warm flesh. With a hard yank she pulled her knot free, globs of cum pouring from the buck's tailhole even as he clenched himself shut. Kett palmed her own stiff cock and pulled the sticky seed from her shaft, coaxing the last few drops from her tip before licking her paw clean. The fox smiled up at the deer as he turned around to face her, his enormous member bobbing out from his hips, hanging horizontal to the ground, thick drips of pre hanging from the tip. "Follow me."

The fox licked her lips and looked around the room, quickly finding what she was looking for. Not too far away, a noblewoman feline knelt on her knees, surrounded by a ring of male servants. In the rising mist, the cat's head bobbed forward and back on a servant's stiff rod, her paws working two more cocks to either side. Surrounding the ring of four servants was another small crowd of four noblemen, each stroking their hard shafts as they watched the cat. As Kett approached she turned back to the buck, "Stay here until you are called upon." The servant stood, eyes heavy with stupefying bliss as he watched Kett walk to the circle.

The noblewoman already wore several sticky loads of cum on her face and chest, slick white fluid dripping off her cheeks and mouth. Her eyes were closed as she pressed her face against the hips of a male otter servant, burying his entire length within her mouth and throat. Kett inserted herself into the ring without protest, the cat's paw quickly finding her stiff member and stroking along the hot length. The fox watched in satisfaction as the cat pawed her cock along with another servant's, holding the otter in her mouth. Before long the otter groaned, the cat pulling the shaft from her mouth and pointing the tip at herself, closing her eyes in bliss as the servant blasted her mouth and face with several pulses of hot sticky cum.

Kett watched the otter drain himself onto the cat's face, panting as his orgasm concluded. "Oh, you're going to have to do better than that."

The fox let her tentacles flow from her back and wrists, quickly snaking out across the floor, each tendril finding one of the servants in the circle, coiling around one of their legs. Kett glanced over her shoulder to the ring of noblemen, biting her lip as she called them closer, "Don't be shy. She's going to need all she can get." The noblemen stepped forward timidly, crowding around the feline as she took another servant into her hungry mouth. Letting her tendrils snake up the legs of the servants and their masters, Kett quickly found each of their tight tailholes and slid her slick tips against their entrances. Without hesitation, Kett jammed her oozing tendrils into each of their asses, drawing winces and gasps from several of the servants and masters.

The cat stroked Kett's stiff cock as she went to work on an adjacent canine nobleman with her mouth. The fox worked her tentacles forward and back through each of their asses, surging deep into their bodies to fill them with intoxicating warmth. Kett stood close to the nobleman next to her, pressing her rod closer to the cat's mouth. Without hesitation, the feline took both Kett's and the nobleman's members into her mouth, pressing their cockheads together as she ran her tongue over each of their heads. She stroked them both, gripping the bases of their rods and rubbing their tips against each other, circling them over each other and coating each shaft in the other's pre cum.

Kett crammed her tentacle into the canine's ass, probing deep and pulsing against his prostrate as the cat took his cock into her mouth. Flexing her tongue against his shaft, the cat coaxed him further, moaning on his rod as Kett pumped into his tailhole. The cat moaned as the nobleman tensed, his ass clenching against Kett's tentacle as a thick rope of cum flew from his cock, shooting into the cat's throat. The cat started to pull the rod from her mouth and point the tip at her face, but Kett reached forward and quickly pulled the cat's mouth back down onto the nobleman's shaft, holding her jaws shut against his rod and forcing her nose down to his pelvis. Her eyes shot open wide as the rigid member was crammed down her throat, the pulsing flesh shooting hot jets of cum into her belly. The cat coughed on the thick rod as Kett worked her tentacle forward and back into the nobleman's ass, plunging deep and pressing hard against his prostate. The canine threw his head back as he poured his seed down the cat's throat, stream after stream flooding from his hard member.

The feline swallowed hard, finally pulling herself off the nobleman's cock as Kett released her grip. Kett pumped her slimy tendrils in and out of the handful of tight assholes, exhaling hotly as she felt their holes squeezing against her penetrating appendages. The cat quickly turned and grabbed Kett's hard shaft, wrapping her lips around the pointed tip and taking as much as she could into her mouth. The fox put one hand on the cat's head and grabbed a nearby mouse servant's shaft with the other, stroking her paw over his slick shaft. The cat pushed her head forward, cramming Kett's long cock down her throat as she grabbed two more rods with her paws, stroking wildly as thick tendrils pulsed and coiled in their tailholes.

The mouse servant moaned as Kett pummeled his ass, stroking his cock in long quick pumps. Kett pulled the mouse close and pointed his rod at the cat's face, squeezing his shaft as she crammed her tendril deep into his tailhole. The mouse tensed as a powerful spurt of cum sprayed from his cock, his shaft flexing in waves and pumping his seed onto the cat's face. As the cat continued to thrust her face forward and back on Kett's rod, squeezing her paws against any other nearby shaft she could grab, Kett pointed the mouse's cock at the cat's mouth. Thick gobs of cum sprayed onto Kett's cock as the cat pulled her mouth back, disappearing as she sucked the fox's length into her throat.

Mouse cum dripping from the fox's balls, Kett squeezed the last drops of seed from the rodent before reaching to the other side and grabbing a fresh cock. The circle of servants and their masters drew closer as Kett pulsed her tentacles in their holes, the crowd moaning in unison as they stroked themselves. The fox pawed one rod to her side as the cat moved back and forth between her cock and two others, stroking and sucking desperately. The feline sucked on a long horse shaft, pulling him into her throat as he groaned, his balls tensing and draining their load into her maw. Another servant moaned, stroking himself and clenching his tight tailhole against Kett's tendril as he brought himself to orgasm, his thick seed pouring from his cumslit and covering the cat's face even as she swallowed the equine's load.

As soon as the horse pumped the last of his massive load into the cat's throat, she pulled herself from his shaft and grabbed two more. Kett let the cat let go of her cock and walked behind the kneeling feline, still pumping her tendrils in and out of each member of the small crowd, relentlessly pounding them even after they spent themselves on the noblewoman's face. Grabbing two thick shafts and pulling their owners side by side, the cat pressed the two rods together, side by side and wrapped her lips around the pair, opening her jaws wide. Kett stood behind the cat and watched, stroking two others as the cat struggled to take the two thick cocks. Cramming their shafts into her mouth, the cat pushed her head forward and back, wrapping her lips around their hot flesh and dragging her tongue against their sensitive undersides.

Kett coiled her tendrils within the asses of each of the circle's participants, stretching their holes wide and pressing against their insides. The cat moaned on the two cocks pressed against each other in her mouth, pre cum covering her tongue as the party guests moaned. The fox squeezed her paws around the rods of the two masters at her sides,

196

burying as much of her tendrils inside them as she could and dragging them to either side of the cat's face. The pair moaned in unison, hot streams of cum flying into the air as they arched their backs. Kett pulsed her tendrils within their tailholes, pumping the seed from their bodies. The noblewoman sucked hard on the two cocks in her mouth as cum landed on her face, her eyes closed in bliss, feeling the warm seed splash against her. Kett pulled on the two noblemen's rods, guiding them closer to the cat. Their seed flew from their thick rods in powerful jets, flying over the cat's head and covering each other's shafts and hips with their sticky loads.

The cat crammed the pair of cocks deeper into her mouth as the two servants panted, rocked by the slick tendrils pumping their tailholes. Kett reached down and grabbed the cat's face, hooking two fingers into either side of the feline's mouth and pulling her head back. The noblewoman reached up and grabbed the two shafts, pressing them tight together as the first jets of cum sprayed from their tips in unison, flying into her mouth as Kett held it open. Hot seed filled the cat's mouth, splashing onto her tongue. Kett watched the cat swallow hungrily, the two servants pumping cum into her mouth faster than she could handle, thick gobs flowing from her mouth and running down her throat. The cat gasped between hurried gulps, taking as much cum into her belly as she could manage.

Stroking the last few drops of liquid from their cocks, the cat swallowed and panted. Kett let go of her mouth and abruptly pulled her tentacles free of the small crowd's tailholes, eliciting a low groan of satisfaction from the handful of party goers. The smell of cum filled the air, warm seed dripping from the cat's face and neck as she knelt on the floor. Kett looked up and spied the buck nearby, his gigantic morphed member drooling pre cum as he watched the scene before him. The fox signaled for him to approach, placing her paw against the side of the cat's throat.

The feline's eyes grew as she saw the massive shaft, four feet of cock as thick as her torso, a pair of balls two feet across each. Kett grabbed either side of the cat's head and pushed her forward, toward the drooling cumslit. The cat opened her mouth as wide as she could, pressing her tongue against the giant hole at the tip of the sleek cockhead, savoring the intense taste of the slick pre cum.

Kett drew her tentacles up and coiled them around the full length of the buck's transformed shaft, wrapping around every muscular inch in a tight helix before lashing around the back of the cat's head, tying them together with her muscular tendrils. The fox dragged the firm coil of tentacles forward and back, stroking the thick cock and pulling thick gushes of pre from the length into the cat's mouth. Building pressure against the back of the feline's head, Kett pulled more of the buck's giant rod into the cat's mouth, stretching her jaws and lips wide, the tapered cockhead sliding slowly into her mouth.

The noblewoman moaned against the massive shaft as Kett pulsed her tendrils forward and back, pushing the cat hard against the head until her throat bulged and stretched. Kett's own cock leaked drops of pre cum as she watched the cat's mouth and neck stretch around the gigantic shaft, pulling the pair toward each other until the buck's swollen cock was buried deep in the cat's belly. The feline hung from the front of the cock, her mouth and torso stretched taut over the thick shaft, bent over at the hips, struggling to keep her feet on the ground. Kett took a step forward and grabbed the base of her hard shaft, pointing it toward the invitingly wet cat pussy.

Kett wrapped her paws around the cat's hips and pushed forward, burying her fox cock in the dripping folds. The cat moaned on the buck's

198

shaft as Kett bottomed out, pressing her fat knot against the feline's entrance. Kett stroked the exposed length of the deer's rod with slick tendrils as she pumped forward and back, pulling the buck deeper into the cat as she pushed forward. Kett's tendrils wrapped around the cat's body and squeezed, stroking the noblewoman forward and back against the servant's massive shaft. The trio moaned as Kett stroked and pumped faster, grinding her knot against the cat's pussy with every thrust.

Tightness grew in the hips of the buck as the cat was slid forward and back along his length, his heavy balls drawing up closer to his body. Kett stroked and pumped faster, pounding her thick red knot flesh against the cat's clenching entrance with every powerful motion. Finally the noble's body yielded and Kett's knot stretched her wide, pushing through her folds into her tight pussy. Kett pressed herself up tight against the cat's backside, pulling the buck deeper into the cat's body as the three came in unison. The feline's body clenched and shook, cum pouring into her belly in a torrent as the buck's cock pulsed and pumped its seed into her. Kett's shaft throbbed as it dumped its load deep into the noblewoman's pussy, her balls clenching as waves of pleasure coursed through her body.

Pulse after pulse of thick cum poured from the buck, each powerful gush of seed growing longer and stronger until there was a single unbroken stream of hot fluid pouring into the cat's body. Kett dug her claws into the cat's hips, watching her belly grow and swell from the gallons of seed flowing into her. The buck felt an overwhelming warmth sear through his mind as cum flooded from his shaft uncontrollably, his balls shrinking with each passing moment. Kett's orgasm faded as she watched the buck's cock soften and recede, pulling from the feline's body as it shrank in length. The deer's shaft finally popped free of the cat's mouth, several more spurts of sticky cum covering her face until his rod returned to its normal size and appearance.

The cat slouched forward, her legs and hips still forced upright by Kett's knotted rod. Her belly protruded from her body in a massive round swell, the buck's gigantic load stretching her cum-covered flesh. Kett grabbed the feline by the shoulders and pulled her upright, wrapping a paw around her neck and walking the two of them forward. The fox approached the giant crocodile maw, guiding the cat with small steps, her knot still tied deep inside her clenching pussy. When Kett neared the croc, the jaws opened wide and reached out with dozens of slick tentacles, quickly wrapping around the cat's chest, hips and legs. Kett guided the cat forward until they were directly in front of the morphed snout, tendrils writhing hungrily over the feline's cum-slick body.

As the maw raised its lower jaw off the floor Kett bent the semi-conscious cat forward, letting the noblewoman's upper body come to rest between a pair of giant teeth, lying against the muscular tongue. Kett let go of the feline's body as the upper maw came down slowly, wrapping its slick oozing lips around the cat's waist as the jaws closed, bringing the giant upper teeth just inches away from her skin. Darkness closed around the cat, dozens of tendrils coiling over her body as she lay in a daze, moaning into the warm crocodile maw and clenching her pussy against Kett's knot. In a rapid instant, the tendrils tightened against the noble's body, grabbing her hips and shoulders, yanking roughly. The grip of the tentacles wrenched the cat free of Kett's knot and pulled her hips and legs through the slick lips of the maw, her feet quickly disappearing into the closed mouth. Kett watched as the giant jaws opened once again, only catching a glimpse of the cat's legs as they disappeared down the wet gullet and into the creature's embrace.

Kett turned on her heels to face the room, her rod throbbing and stiff even as her cum dripped from her sack. The party goers were resuming their activities with each other, but all eyes were on her and the massive crocodile maw. Moans and gasps filled the air as the mist crawled over the floor in a thick blanket. Kett swung her arm and lashed out with a pair of tendrils, whipping the slick tips around the ankle of a nearby panther nobleman as he buried himself in a male rabbit servant. Yanking back with the alien strength of the tentacles, Kett dragged the feline across the floor toward her feet before whipping out with her other arm to grab at the bunny boy, pulling him close as well.

Without wasting a single moment, Kett pinned the rabbit servant to the ground, face up, straddled his hips and lowered herself onto his hard rod. Kett shivered as the lagomorph's cock slid into her pussy, grabbing her breasts as she bottomed herself out on his meat. Leaning forward onto her paws, Kett raised her tail and looked at the panther, still lying on the ground nearby in a daze. The fox reached out with the tentacles from the small of her back and gripped the nobleman, yanking him upright and dragging him toward her backside. The panther quickly got the hint as he was forced to his knees, the tendrils coiling around his hard cock before he had a chance to position himself. Kett flexed her tendrils and pulled the cat forward, holding his shaft out as she dragged him over the floor, leaning forward and pressing her hips upward as she guided the panther's rod into her tight tailhole, moaning into the bunny's face as she forced the muscular cat deep inside, pressing his hips against her ass.

The servant and nobleman moaned in unison as Kett rocked herself forward and back on their cocks, holding them both firmly in place with the tight grip of her tendrils as she bucked back against their throbbing shafts. Kett tightened her slick cords around the bodies of the panther and bunny, coiling around their necks and squeezing as she slammed herself back onto their stiff rods. The creature's maw opened wide, mere inches behind the back of the kneeling panther. Several thick tentacles snaked out from the crocodile mouth, reaching past the rows of sharp teeth, hanging in the air around the feline.

Kett panted, mouth hanging open as she slammed herself back on the thick shafts filling her ass and pussy. The panther let out a grunt, his body tensing as Kett pushed herself back against his hips as hard as she could, gripping his entire body and pressing him deep into her tailhole, clenching around his hot flesh as streams of cum poured into her. Kett ground her ass against the panther as he emptied himself into her, staring down at the bunny with fiery lust-filled eyes as his master came inside her. Just as the last pulses of the nobleman's orgasm faded, the creature whipped out with a dozen thick tentacles and wrapped around the feline's body. Kett immediately withdrew her grip from the cat and felt his cock slide from her cum-filled ass, and the creature pulled the panther back, lifting him up into the air and yanking him into the giant maw, jaws snapping shut just as the feline disappeared past the slime-covered lips.

The jaws opened a moment later to reveal an empty yawning chasm, tendrils snaking out once again in anticipation. Kett felt the panther's warm seed leaking from her stretched tailhole, covering the bunny's cock and balls. The lagomorph squirmed under Kett's firm grip as she scouted the room, grinding her hips forward and back against the bunny's stiff rod. Kett spotted a muscular stallion nobleman with two human women kneeling before his stiff manhood, dragging their tongues against his length. Immediately the fox reached out with her slick tendrils, lashing around all three of their bodies. Kett flung the two women into the air, pulling hard and launching them up above her head, toward the hungry croc jaws. The maw quickly snapped upright, spreading wide and catching the two humans mid-air with its tendrils, latching around their bodies and pulling them down into its hot gullet followed by a snap of its teeth. Kett dragged the stallion closer, his glossy eyes watching in a helpless daze as her tentacles clutched his chest and neck.

Kett quickly dragged the equine toward her backside, once again coiling around his long shaft and holding him steady as she pulled him closer. The bunny inhaled sharply as the flared horse cock pressed against Kett's cum-slick asshole, feeling her pussy tighten around his hilted shaft. Kett bit her lip as she pulled on the horse, forcing him forward in a single quick thrust until the broad head popped into her tailhole, dragging him forward until his full length was buried inside her. The horse and bunny panted, their bodies covered with slick tendrils, squirming against their grip in pleasure as the fox rammed herself forward and back on their lengths.

The bunny closed his eyes and moaned, feeling the fullness of the fox's ass through her pussy, the hot flesh of the horse cock pushing sloppy drips of panther cum from her stretched hole and covering the lagomorph. Kett slammed back against the pair, filling herself with their flesh until the bunny cried out, every muscle in his body tensing. The servant's cock pulsed and cum jetted into Kett's pussy, filling her warm hole with his hot seed. Cum spurted from Kett's entrance as she squeezed and clamped down on the rabbit's shaft. Kett gripped the horse and the bunny with her tendrils, grabbing the stallion's legs and yanking them forward. The horse was thrown onto his back, taking Kett and the bunny up and back with him.

With Kett now facing upwards, her head toward the creature's jaws and the bunny on top of her, Kett grabbed at the rabbit servant as he poured himself into her, moaning in satisfaction as his cum ran down onto the horse's buried shaft. The creature reached out hungrily and wrapped its appendages around the bunny, clutching at his shoulders and hips, quickly yanking him free of Kett's warm hole. One final spurt of bunny cum shot from his hard cock onto Kett's chest as the creature pulled him back toward the open jaws. An instant later the bunny slid down the creature's throat with a soft moan, the jaws opening wide once again in insatiable desire.

Kett ground her ass against the thick horse shaft, looking back around the room. Breathing heavily, she lashed out and grabbed the nearby buck and flung him into the air behind her, not even watching as the creature snapped its tendrils out and dragging him down into the yawning abyss. At the far end of the room, Kett spotted Marshall surrounded by a handful of party guests on their knees, sucking his hard length as they touched themselves. One by one, Kett snatched the partiers and dragged them closer, wrapping her slimy tendrils over their bodies, teasing their holes and hard shafts with her touch before tossing them up into the air. The creature caught each partier in turn, wrapping around their bodies and pulling them down greedily, cramming its blunt tendrils into their mouths and holes as they disappeared into the darkness. Finally Kett latched around Marshall, coiling around his long cock as she pulled him close, leaning forward just enough to give his dripping rod a long lick before the creature clutched around his chest, yanking him back into the waiting maw.

The creature opened its mouth wide once again as Kett surveyed the room, squeezing against the thick stallion rod buried inside her, cum dripping from her empty pussy. Across the room, a pair of twin wolf noblemen had their way with an otter servant girl. The two wolves, their stark white fur covering powerful frames, bucked against the otter from both directions, filling her mouth and pussy. Kett reached out with her tentacles and clamped onto all three of their bodies, pulling them free from each other and dragging them across the floor.

204

Kett leaned back against the stallion, spreading her legs wide over the legs of the immobilized horse beneath her. As the trio neared, Kett picked one wolf and brought him between her legs, reaching forward to grab his hard shaft and point it toward her cum-soaked entrance. The nobleman's pointed tip speared her lips as she gripped him with her tendrils, dragging him forward on his knees until his thick red knot pressed against her folds. Kett leaned back onto her elbows, gripping the other wolf and their otter plaything, dragging them to either side of her hips as she exposed her throbbing cock. The pair eagerly leaned forward, gripping Kett's red shaft from either side, licking the length and pressing their lips against the tapered tip.

Tentacles crawled over all four of the partiers as Kett threw her head back in bliss, snaking around to find each of their eager backsides. Probing against their tight holes, rubbing their slickness into their entrances, Kett's tentacles pushed against their flesh until they gave in with a moan, one by one. Kett gripped the wolf between her legs by the hips, coiling around his pelvis tightly and slamming him forward into her clenching pussy, bucking him against her faster than he could himself maintain. Drops of pre cum flowed from Kett's cock as the otter servant eagerly sucked at her rod, the wolf sucking one of her balls into his mouth. The stallion moaned, feeling the thick canine cock pump into Kett's pussy through the thin wall of flesh as the slick tendril probed his ass. Kett bucked her hips against the wolf and stallion with each rapid thrust, grinding up and down as the otter and other wolf stroked her length, wrapping their paws around her shaft and knot.

The stallion bucked his hips upwards, pressing himself deep into Kett's tailhole as he struggled against the tentacle's strong grip. Kett felt his long shaft tense and flex within her, pulses of warmth filling her depths as she pumped her tendril against the horse's hole. Each time she slammed her tentacle deeper into the equine flesh, a thick stream of cum poured from his cock and filled her with coursing waves of warmth. The horse's balls twitched and clenched as they emptied. Kett gripped the wolf between her legs and pushed him forward, slamming him down onto his back as the fox landed on top of him, the horse still on his back with his long cock buried in Kett's tailhole. The creature reached out instantly and grabbed the stallion by the chest and neck, yanking him back. A final spurt of cum shot out against Kett's back as the horse was pulled free, dragged into the creature's waiting embrace in a greedy instant.

Kett grabbed the other wolf and pushed him back to the ground, face-up, quickly positioning the twins with their hips together, legs intertwined and cocks pointing upwards. Rising slightly off the former's rod, Kett wound a wet tendril around the pair's shafts, pressing their undersides together and pointing both their tips at her soaking wet pussy. Cum dripped from both her stretched holes as she lowered herself onto the wolves, covering their cocks and hips with the warm seed. Kett carefully positioned the tips against her wet folds, sliding the tapered points of their red wolf shafts into her sloppy entrance. As soon as she felt them both slide past her pussy lips, Kett slammed down onto their shafts, stretching herself with the twins' thick cocks and pressing herself down against their swollen knots.

With her tendrils still buried in the wolves' tailholes, Kett rocked her hips forward and back against their shafts and pushed deeper into their tight entrances. Kett reached forward and grabbed the otter, coiling around her torso with her tendrils and spinning her around. Drawing the thin otter girl close, Kett bent her over onto her hands and knees, positioning her over one of the wolf noblemen, pulling her backside toward Kett's hips. Holding her throbbing shaft with one hand, Kett pulled the otter closer until her pointed tip pushed into the waiting pussy, drawing a moan from the girl as the fox buried her rod in a single quick motion.

Kett bucked her hips up against the otter, thrusting into the servant's tight pussy and withdrawing herself from the twin cocks buried inside her with every pumping motion. The four moaned and panted, the wolves and otter held motionless by Kett's strong grip as she pumped herself forward and back, pounding the wolves' asses with slick tendrils in time with her hips. Each stroke grew longer in length, more desperate at Kett's eyes fluttered, darkness closing in around her vision as she panted, clenching against the immense fullness of the two thick cocks filling her pussy. Kett grabbed the otter by the hips, pulling her back against her cock hard each time she came down on the wolves' knots. Each time she rose up onto her knees she slammed herself down as hard as she could manage, stretching her entrance wide against the tops of their twinned knots, burying herself in the otter.

Suddenly the creature reached out and coiled around Kett's body, squeezing her breasts and taut belly. Kett pulled the otter back as hard as she could as the creature slammed the fox down ruthlessly, a single rapid plunge pushing her down against the wolf cocks until Kett screamed and threw her head back. Her flesh stretched as her body shook uncontrollably, the creature's grip smashing her down with unyielding pressure until Kett's pussy slid slowly over the two wolf knots. The thick bulbs of hot flesh slammed into Kett's body as she pulled at the otter, her mind lost in crashing waves of ecstasy as she forced her knot into the servant girl. All four cried out, twin streams of cum pouring into Kett's pussy as she convulsed, flesh screaming in rapture. Kett came on the wolf cocks as she sprayed her load into the otter. The creature held Kett down firmly against the two wolf knots, cum dripping from her overfilled pussy in thick streams. Kett shook, her mouth hanging open and eyes squeezed shut as the darkness faded all sensation outside of pure chemical bliss.

The four hardly noticed as the creature wrapped around each of their bodies and lifted them into the air. What party guests remained watched as the four limp figures were dragged back into the waiting maw. Inside the intense heat of the crocodile mouth the creature's grip pulled each of their bodies apart. Cum poured from Kett's pussy and splattered onto the creature's tongue, each of the twin wolves sliding back down the creature's throat one at a time. Kett's eyes fluttered as the partly-conscious otter disappeared into the darkness, followed by the limp body of the fox herself.

Across the mist-filled room, the remainder of the party guests bucked against each other in a lethargic dream-like daze. The creature reached out through the fissures in the floor, extending dozens of tentacles and wrapping around each guest's body, dragging their willing bodies to the center of the room where they slid down the creature's throat, one by one.

Chapter 14

Alan shivered as the creature's firm grip pulled him into the wet heat. The back of Carra's gaping maw terminated in a slick tunnel of flesh, a tight throat that gripped the husky's legs and tugged at his body, dragging him down into the darkness. Warmth flooded over the canine, his skin tingling as the creature swallowed, his thighs and hips sliding into the muscle. Alan felt the creature unwind its tentacles from his body and the throat pulsed in a strong wave, sucking him into the clinging embrace. One swallow and he slid down to his chest, one more and his head disappeared into the depths.

Closing his eyes in the absolute darkness, Alan reveled in the clutching warmth and felt the oozing flesh squeeze every inch of his body, flowing in contracting waves over his fur. Soft whispers seeped into his mind as he descended, shadows of sensation from above and below rippling through his core. Alan's manhood slid from his sheath and throbbed, the slick walls of flesh pressing and sliding over his drooling rod, the tight muscle squeezing his entire body, sending shivers down his spine.

After several blissful moments, Alan felt his feet slide into an open space below. With a final push from the creature's throat the husky fell down into cool empty air. A flash of dim light passed over his eyes before he plunged into a pool of lukewarm water, immediately sinking a few feet below the surface. Glancing up, the canine spotted a source of orange light and swam for the surface, a couple strong paddles bringing him to a stony ledge surrounding the water.

Dull light filled the stonework chamber, a handful of neglected sconces holding sputtering torches that cast ragged shadows across the walls and floor. Pulsing cords of dark ooze clung to the masonry, covering the uneven stones with a thick web of throbbing tendrils from floor to ceiling. A fifteen-foot wide pool of clear water sat directly below the exit from the creature's throat embedded in the ceiling. The room was filled with crates and sacks, now covered in the crawling ooze.

Alan glanced back down into the water and quickly spotted several familiar figures. The gecko and hyena squirmed in the middle of the pool, several feet below the surface, held in place in the grip of several bristled tendrils. Drenirya and Zelia gyrated against the velvety appendages as they roamed over their bodies, a thick cord of slime forced deep into each of their mouths. Further down, Alan could just barely make out the form of the mantis, half-buried in the thick web of tentacles at the bottom of the pool.

Pulling himself up out of the water, Alan sat on the ledge and watched, dangling his feet over the edge. Soft tentacles drifted closer to his legs, brushing against his fur as he slid his paw over his stiff shaft, gazing into the water and smirking as the gecko and hyena squirmed. Before long, the tight ring of flesh embedded in the ceiling flexed and spat the partially-conscious antelope into the pool. The shock of water against her fur startled her back to awareness, quickly finding the surface not too far from where Alan sat. Ell panted and held onto the ledge, giving the canine an exasperated smile.

As Alan smiled back, he noticed a change in the room. Slowly, the slick ooze pulsed, thickening into puddles on the floor and crawling across the ceiling. The handful of lit torches remained untouched, but soon every inch of stone dripped and writhed with dark slime, broad tendrils rising from the surface in arcs before flailing out and recombining with the pulsing goo. Ell felt the creature slide its wet surface over her arms, enveloping her hands and pulling her from the water. The canine spied her massive bulging belly, a subtle writhing stretching Ell's skin as the slime dragged her onto the slick ground.

Ell found herself pinned to the floor, face up and spread-eagle, arms and legs fully submerged in the writhing slime and held fast in place. Her bulging belly towered above her, dark ooze crawling part-way up her stretched skin. She could feel the leopard still moving inside her, shifting his weight and rubbing his paws over his slick body. A trio of thick cords pulled from the slime between her legs, each the thickness of her forearm and several feet long. Alan watched the first dripping tentacle reach forward and slide into Ell's slit, pushing roughly and surging deep into her body with a single lunge.

The antelope arched her back against the pull of the slime, throwing her head back and shouting in sudden bliss. Plunging forward, the slick tendril bore into her body and quickly found the leopard within her belly. The half-conscious Haxiten jolted at the sudden touch, thrashing weakly against the squeeze of Ell's flesh when he felt the tentacle press against his tailhole. His entire body slick with the antelope's juices, the former master could do nothing to resist the fierce strength of the invading slime, his body immediately giving way to the tentacle and letting out a muffled cry as it pushed into his clenching hole. Alan squeezed his paw against his throbbing member and watched the thick cord of dark ooze pulse forward and back into Ell's pussy, surging in several feet at a time, rocking against her trapped body. Ell screamed in helpless bliss, squeezing her eyes shut and shaking against the firm grip of the creature, feeling the leopard thrash and squirm within her.

Then, the husky heard another splash, turning his gaze back to the water just in time to see a pair of otters fall into the pool, the familiar form of Léo already paddling to the ledge nearby. The mouse boy laboriously pulled himself from the water, his belly swollen and round, protruding in a giant hemisphere from his lithe frame. Within moments, the otter twins splashed up out of the water and landed on the slick ground to either side of Léo. The pair immediately rose to their knees before the mouse and looked up, pleadingly. Léo smirked and nodded, instantly sending the pair into a desperate frenzy. The otters dove forward and wrapped their paws around Léo's long tentacle cock, leaning close and pressing their mouths to his shaft. One servant pulled the tapered tip into his mouth as the other ran his tongue along the slick underside, both squeezing their paws against the thickness and moaning in wanton desire. Dark slime clung to the otters' knees and legs, creeping up their muscular thighs and binding them in place.

Moans echoed off the stonework walls as the thick tendril pummeled Ell's stretched slit and the otters sucked greedily at Léo's member. Alan watched as the feline noblewoman slid from the fleshy hole in the ceiling, her cum-soaked body falling into the pool below. The slick ooze beneath the water reached out and coiled around the cat's body, rubbing against her fur and pulling her back toward the ledge. Breaching the surface, a puddle of the creature lurched forward from the floor and stuck to the noblewoman, lifting her from the water. Greedy slime gripped the feline and pulled her across the floor, dark ooze seeping up over her legs and hips.

The ceiling dripped thick drops of ooze as it crawled and pulsed. A long strand of slime slid down in an unbroken cord and stuck to the feline's ankles, binding to the goo already wrapped around her legs. Slowly, the tendril thickened and strengthened, drawing taut and then pulling the feline up off the floor. The noblewoman rose into the air, hanging upside down, moaning in a daze as the creature dripped and crept down over her bulging cum-filled belly.

Alan watched the water and saw the gecko and hyena approach the surface. Several winding tentacles crawled over their bodies, pulling them up and depositing them onto the slick ground. The creature immediately lashed out with several thick cords of slime, grabbing their limp bodies and dragging them across the floor until they were directly beneath the suspended cat. Drenirya and Zelia moaned faintly, nearly unconscious but eyes half-open in dazed pleasure. Bulges of ooze pressed up underneath their bodies, winding around their torsos until they were propped up onto their knees, facing each other, breasts and faces pressed against each other's.

Ell bucked and thrashed helplessly against the strong slime that held her body against the floor, muscles flexing against the relentless pounding of the thick tentacle buried deep in her pussy. She felt the leopard moan weakly within her belly, too dazed to fight against the creature pummeling his tailhole. The slime coursed into her stretched entrance faster, slamming against her in short rapid bursts until it pulled out from the Haxiten's hole and surged deeper into Ell's body, coiling around the leopard's torso. Hot white cum flooded from the tip of the tentacle, pouring from the slime in powerful bursts. The tendril thrashed within the antelope's pussy and dumped gallons of seed into her womb, covering the leopard from head to toe. Ell screamed as the fluid plummeted into her, clenching against the slime and feeling her belly stretch further under the strain. The tentacle pulsed and then slowed, pulling quickly from the antelope's body as soon as it had deposited its seed. As the cord of slime withdrew from her pussy, the second massive tendril dove forward and plowed into her slick entrance, immediately finding the leopard's tailhole and once again thrashing against both of their defenseless bodies.

A dazed panther slid from the creature's throat, and Alan immediately lashed out and grabbed the noble with a pair of his tentacles, carrying his unresisting body back to the slime-covered ground. The creature's ooze immediately crawled up and over the feline's chest and legs, binding him to the floor. Alan approached the prone nobleman and stood with his legs to either side of his hips, gripping his shaft in anticipation. Kneeling over the helpless feline, Alan exhaled and forced himself to relax, lifting his tail and shivering as the slickness of the panther's wet tip pressed against his clenching tailhole. Wincing only slightly as the barbed flesh pressed into his entrance, Alan squeezed his cockhead until the pain subsided. The canine slowly lowered himself onto the noble, bottoming out and grinding his hips against the muscular frame, squeezing his thighs against his taut torso.

As Alan rose up onto his knees and worked himself up and down over the panther's length, the slime throbbed and crawled over the nobleman's body. The panther squirmed and writhed against the creature's grip as the ooze covered his mouth and face, struggling too late to resist its firm strength. Alan stroked his paw over his hard shaft and watched, feeling the panther's thick rod fill his ass even as the nobleman pulled in vain against the creature's grip.

Léo moaned and watched in blissful satisfaction as the otter twins fought over every inch of his long tentacle cock. The mouse's body tingled, his belly sending pulses of warmth through his flesh and over his skin. One otter pulled Léo's tip into his mouth and pressed his face forward, relaxing his throat and taking the slick shaft deep, sliding forward an inch at a time until he finally pressed his nose against the mouse's pelvis, swallowing hard. The other otter leaned over and pressed his paws to the back of his brother's head, holding his face down hard against the throbbing shaft until he choked and gasped for air. Quickly pulling

214

himself free of the long tendril, the first otter coughed while the other dove forward and likewise took as much of Léo into his mouth as he could.

Tension built within the mouse's body, a yearning calling out from his core. Léo could feel the badger woman still within him, burning for release. The two servants licked and ground themselves against the thick tendril, stroking their paws over the length and sucking at the drooling tip until Léo's mind swam and body ached. Curling his toes in the slime, tensing his entire body, Léo gasped and held his breath as the first thick rope of cum pulsed from his cock, splattering against the otter's face. Immediately both servant twins pressed their faces side-by-side, opening their mouths wide for the next powerful spurt of seed. Léo's mouth hung open, unbreathing as his body froze, mind ablaze and every inch of his flesh screaming in unison until finally another heavy pulse of cum surged from his shaft, covering the otter twins' faces.

Léo groaned aloud, flexing his body as the gallons of seed within his distended belly flowed through him, pulsing down to his cock in massive spurts of hot seed. The otters moaned in satisfaction as the hot cum blasted against their faces, feeling their minds melt in pleasure. Dripping from their panting mouths, running down their heaving chests and streaming from their thighs and balls, the liquid poured from Léo's throbbing shaft and drenched the twin servants. Their fur covered, faces soaked, the otters turned to each other and pressed their dripping mouths to each other's, clutching at their partner's body and pressing their hard cocks against each other in desperate bliss.

Pulse after pulse of hot seed poured from Léo's body, his swollen belly deflating slowly as a torrent of cum emptied onto the two servants. Panting, the mouse watched as the soaked otters appeared to shrink, their bodies thinning and shortening. Rope after rope of cum splashed against their lithe frames and the otters pulled back from each other, looking at their hands and at each other in a daze. Their outstretched paws melted from their arms, dripping from their flesh in thick drops of cum, splashing against their thighs and the ground. In unison they clutched at their cum-slick cocks, stroking in furious bliss as their bodies throbbed and liquefied. Léo pointed his surging shaft at each of their forms in turn, each spurt lessening as their bodies fell back away from each other, leaning back toward the floor. The mouse boy finally spent himself with a final thick gush, wringing himself dry and watching the shrinking otters stroke themselves desperately. Their backs against the ground, hips up in the air, the twins finally orgasmed in unison, their own cum shooting straight up into the air in powerful spurts and splashing against their melting bodies. Léo panted and gripped himself, watching the two otters melt entirely, their bodies shrinking into the pool of seed at their feet until they were nothing more than a puddle of intermingled cum.

Two human women, a bunny, and a buck slid down the creature's gullet and splashed into the pool of water, one by one. Their bodies were immediately grabbed by the soft bristled tendrils lining the walls deep under the surface, pulling them lower into the darkness. The creature throbbed in satisfaction, every inch of its slick being beating with the pulses of pleasure of each of its hosts. Several more party guests slid down and fell into the pool, and the tentacles quickly found their bodies and wrapped around their flesh, writhing over their skin and sliding into their gasping mouths. The firm tendrils pulled the partiers toward the vertical walls of the pool, attaching them to the pulsing slime. Thick cords slid into their mouths, stretching their lips wide and filling their lungs with air as the oozing tentacles clutched to their bodies, finding their cocks and pussies with questing appendages. The guests moaned against the tendrils shoved deep in their throats, rocking their hips against the embrace of the creature.

Alan stroked his throbbing cock and watched as the enveloped form of the panther squirmed against the grip of the dark ooze. Rising up and slamming back down, the canine hilted himself on the nobleman with every vicious thrust. He gripped his long shaft with both paws, timing his strokes with his hips and squeezing thick drops of pre from his cock onto the prone feline's ooze-covered body. The panther struggled and moaned, bucking his hips up against the grip of the creature as Alan crashed down and impaled himself. Finally the feline let out a stifled cry, freezing and flexing himself within Alan's clenching tailhole. Thick cum shot up into Alan's ass and he forced himself down as hard as he could manage, bottoming out on the panther's shaft and squeezing his rod. The canine moaned, feeling heavy spurts of seed fill his core, warmth pulsing through his entire body as he absorbed every drop.

Heat seared through Alan's body, pulse after pulse of cum spraying into his ass. He could hear the creature's thoughts creep into the back of his mind as the ooze gripped his knees and held him tight against the panther's body. Alan felt the noble's flesh between his legs soften and shrink, the feline's hard muscles flexing against the slick prison and then succumbing to overwhelming bliss. The nobleman's mind dulled and slowed in the clinging darkness beneath the ooze, the fire of orgasm filling his every thought and being, jets of seed exploding from his core and into the canine's depths. Alan squeezed his knees together against the panther's torso and was rewarded with a powerful surge of cum pouring into his tailhole. His balls grew heavy as warmth coursed through his body, the submerged form of the panther shrinking before his eyes, his hips lowering closer to the ground. Alan squeezed and pushed his hips downwards, relishing in the surging warmth pouring into his body, throwing his head back as he brought himself down to the floor, bottoming out against the ooze-covered stone. One final pulse of cum sprayed into his core as his tailhole clenched and closed, the panther's distant cries of pleasure singing out in Alan's mind.

As Alan knelt against the ground, stroking his hard shaft and rubbing a paw against his swollen sack, the creature's throat flexed once more and Marshal's hooved feet slid from the ceiling. The canine reached out and grabbed the horse, pulling him close even as his own knees shook and trembled weakly. Marshal's body was mostly limp in Alan's grasp, stunned into a blissful stupor. The husky took advantage of the compliant horse and laid him down on the ground, using his strong tendrils to position him on his hands and knees, hindquarters raised into the air. Marshal quickly slumped forward, face pressing against the slick ground, arms slack to either side. Gripping his thick shaft, Alan reached forward with his oozing coils and spread the horse's legs, wrapping around the equine's half-hard rod and pulling it back between his parted thighs. Alan knelt down behind the horse and held the broad cockhead in one paw, gripping his own shaft in the other, leaning forward until his tapered tip pressed against Marshal's abused cumslit. The equine exhaled roughly at Alan's touch, but the compliant servant remained motionless as the canine shaft pushed forward, spearing into his cockhole in a single slow thrust.

The cat hung from the ceiling, staring down at the gecko and hyena below. Drenirya and Zelia clung to each other weakly, kneeling on the slick floor, pressing their tongues together and digging their fingers and claws into each other's backs. A few feet above their heads, the feline moaned as the clinging ooze crept over her body, sliding over her distorted cum-filled belly and creeping over her chest. The cat watched the pair beneath her, gasping to herself when the ooze spread her legs and clung against her dripping pussy, pressing a broad bulge of ooze against her entrance until she cried out and the powerful slime flooded into her.

Ooze clung to the gecko's and hyena's legs, submerging them in the heavy goo. Drenirya reached down and gripped Zelia's pseudo-cock, stroking in mad lust. The feline watched from above, moaning as the creature pushed a thick tendril deep into her pussy, blood rushing to her head. The cat reached both paws up to her groin and pressed her fingers against her clit, moaning and swaying in the suspended grasp of the creature. Her fingers sank into the ooze covering her hips, grinding against her sensitive button as the slick substance overtook her hands and wrists, pulling her arms tight against her body. Throwing her head back in pleasure the noblewoman shook against the grip of the creature and rubbed furiously at her clit, the thick tentacle pumping fiercely into her pussy. Her head swam, scarcely comprehending anything outside her own pleasure as her arms shrank into her torso, her head pulling closer to her shoulders, spine growing weaker with every passing moment.

Zelia dug her claws into the lizard's back, jaws hanging open and panting. Wet slime slid up over their bodies, clinging to their legs and hips, pulling their chests tight together as it crept up their torsos. Drenirya stroked her hand over her bodyguard's shaft even as she fought against the slime, finally losing strength and simply squeezing her grip against the hot muscle in firm pulses. Above them, the cat's head softened and rounded, her moans quieting as her chest slimmed into a single giant rod of flesh, her swollen belly still bulging above her groin. Legs spread wide and affixed to the slick ceiling, fused paws grinding against her pussy, the cat hung helplessly and throbbed. A long stream of pre cum seeped from the noblewoman's open mouth, her eyes closing and disappearing as her head grew several fleshy barbs. The giant transformed feline cock pulsed and shook, the noblewoman's paws still grinding against her clit as the tentacle pulsed into her pussy.

Slick pre cum dripped onto the former mistress and her bodyguard as they moaned into each other's mouths. The cat's mind screamed in silent bliss, the tentacle buried in her pussy surging forward and back until her flesh tingled, a single explosive wave of orgasm pounding across her entire body. The ooze wrapped around the shaft of her body contracted, pressing with intense pressure against her distended cum-filled belly. As the noblewoman's mind lit up with incomprehensible bliss, her body convulsed and flexed, cumming from her transformed cockhead in a single unbroken flood of hot seed. A surge of warmth pulsed through her body in a single instant, gallons of cum plummeting from her morphed cumslit.

With incredible speed, the ooze embracing the gecko and hyena flexed, the cocoon of slime pulling from their bodies and spreading outward, the top opening wide. The downpour of hot cum crashed over their bodies, funneled onto their heads and in an instant the pair found themselves entirely submerged under the weight and heat of the cat's load. As soon as the last ounce of cum dripped from the feline's cockhead the slime reached up and sealed itself shut, trapping Drenirya and Zelia in an air-tight pod filled to the brim with fresh seed.

A handful of party guests descended into the underground chamber, falling into the water one by one. Two white wolves splashed into the pool, followed by an otter, and then finally by Kett, who quickly swam to the ledge and rose out of the water. Briefly surveying the dimly lit room, the fox spied Ell thrashing against the creature's grip. Kett strode over to the antelope and dropped to her hands and knees, watching as the massive tentacle buried itself deep in her stretched pussy. The fox leaned down and kissed the antelope, pressing her tongue into her mouth as she gasped and moaned uncontrollably.

Kett smiled at Ell, gripping one of her tiny breasts with a paw. "Is my new toy ready yet?" Just then, the tentacle buried in her flesh pulled from the leopard's ass and surged forward, flexing and pulsing as it poured another massive load into the antelope's womb, stretching her belly further. Ell's eyes shot open and she screamed, clenching her fists and arching her back as she came on the thick tentacle, feeling the throbbing pulses of liquid course into her depths. The slick tendril emptied itself into her and then quickly withdrew, the third tentacle immediately taking its place, plowing deep into the antelope. "Oh, he must be close."

The fox crawled forward and planted her knees to either side of Ell's face, leaning forward against the antelope's stretched belly. "Let's see if we can't help him along." Ell simply groaned in reply, her entire body trembling against the grip of the ooze. Kett rested her weight against the antelope's bulge, feeling the leopard squirm weakly through her stretched flesh. Reaching forward with a paw, Kett pressed a pair of digits against Ell's pelvis just above her filled pussy, feeling the firm tendril pulsing forward and back through her twitching muscles. The fox pushed her fingers down, letting one slide to either side of her clit. Ell groaned in reply, immobile and helpless to Kett's desires. The fox moaned happily to herself, feeling the house's former master kick and tremble beneath her chest, and raised her hips up slightly so that her stiff shaft pointed down at Ell's face.

Craning her neck, the antelope spread her jaws wide and sought Kett's member, leaning forward and curling out her tongue. The fox lowered her hips slowly, guiding her dripping cock down to Ell's wanting mouth, gasping slightly when the antelope lunged forward and wrapped her lips around the tapered tip and sucked desperately at the throbbing meat. Pressing her fingers down along either side of Ell's clit, Kett sank her rod into the former servant's warm maw, pushing until her shaft bent into the antelope's tight throat. Ell moaned on the canine's flesh, squeezing her eyes shut and clenching her fists as the massive tentacle thrashed within her body.

Kett rocked her hips forward and back, slowly fucking Ell's mouth and throat and smiling to herself, watching the thick cord of slime pulse into her dripping pussy. Sliding her fingers down either side of Ell's clit, grinding around the coursing tendril, Kett pressed her breasts against the massive bulging belly. The antelope arched her back, fighting against the clinging grip of slime as she came, gasping and screaming around Kett's thick rod. Feeling the antelope's pussy clench and spasm on the buried tentacle, the creature plunged deep into her body and bore into the leopard's ass, throbbing in several massive pulses. Ell's mind swam, haze filling her thoughts as lightning surged through her core. Cum poured into the leopard's tailhole, flooding into his body and spurting from his stretched entrance, filling him to the brim before the tentacle pulled roughly from his ass and pulsed into Ell's body. The final gushes of liquid sprayed against the former master's face, draining into Ell and stretching her belly with every powerful surge.

The antelope's belly swelled out to a massive round bulge, the leopard fully submerged in gallons of seed. Kett stroked her fingers slowly over Ell's clit as she recovered, the tentacle pulling from her clenching pussy. Cum spurted from the antelope's stretched hole when the slime freed itself, thick drops running from her slit and onto the ground. Ell shook and trembled, the body of the leopard finally motionless within her.

Alan pushed his hips forward, slowly burying his cock in Marshal's tight cumslit. The canine held the horse's rod and bucked deeper, watching his thick flesh stretch the equine muscle until his massive knot pressed against the broad tip. Marshal moaned vaguely, his mind helplessly lost, body unresponsive. The equine cock yielded to Alan, easily taking his entire length and flexing in pulsing waves against the invading shaft. Alan gripped Marshal's member with both paws and thrust forward, rocking his hips and pistoning roughly into the half-hard horse cock.

Léo stroked his long tentacle shaft and watched the puddle of seed at his feet. His mind still throbbed, but he could start to just make out subtle movement within the liquid. The surface of the thick puddle churned, small bulges rising and falling within the slick cum. Eventually, three bulges rose and drew themselves up from the surface of the puddle, pulling the warm cum closer and growing larger. Knees and heads pulled from the bulges, one by one coalescing into the figures of the badger and otter twins. The trio knelt against the ooze-covered floor, minds swimming and eyes refocusing. Léo smiled as their skin absorbed the last of the seed, revealing their new forms. The badger, her curvy frame now accented by the tight lines of slime embedded in her flesh, stared at herself in fascination. Her heavy breasts heaved as she panted, eyes drawn to her new throbbing badger cock, rigid and drooling a single bead of pre cum. The twin otters, in turn, knelt on the ground with their knees parted, pressing their paws against their firm bodies, hesitantly sliding their touch down between their legs toward their tight pussy slits. Their lithe frames lacked the slick lines of slime covering the badger's body, their chests as flat and muscular as before.

After a mere moment of unspoken glances and heavy breaths, the badger lunged and tackled one otter to the ground. In an instant of blind lust she spread the otter's legs wide and gripped her throbbing member, pausing only long enough to line her thick rod up with his tiny slit before thrusting forward, plunging deep and hilting herself in a single movement.

The pair cried out in alien bliss, eyes locked on each other as her cock throbbed in his pussy. A moment later, the other otter twin crawled forward, positioning himself on his hands and knees above his twin, face toward the badger and hips above his brother's head. Léo wasted no time in kneeling behind the second otter, gripping his slick tendril and pushing forward into the unused pussy, drawing a desperate moan from the mustelid.

Ell lay motionless, eyes closed and head throbbing. Kett pulled her shaft from the antelope's mouth and rubbed a paw gently against Ell's drenched clit, smiling in satisfaction. Thick cum leaked and dripped from Ell's pussy, flowing out onto the slick floor. The antelope's mind floated through a warm fog, heartbeat pounding in her ears as her flesh pulsed and ached. Kett sat upright, knees spread to either side of Ell's head, and pressed her paws against the giant bulge of the antelope's belly. After a moment, the fox felt a thump against the stretched skin. Ell twitched and shook her head to one side as her body throbbed, a twinge shooting down her spine.

The slime binding Ell's ankles and calves to the slick floor tightened their grip and pulled her as wide as they could, stretching her hips and causing a thick spurt of cum to leak from her slit. Kett spread her fingers against the stretched skin of Ell's belly, feeling the leopard stir within. The antelope squirmed and pulled at the creature's grip, gasping in surprise as waves of pressure shot through her veins, her head pounding into a numb stupor. Kett leaned forward slightly and put some of her weight on the antelope's belly, forcing a thick jet of hot seed to shoot from her clenching pussy. The creature pulled firmly on Ell's legs and she cried out, her core on fire as the house's former master stirred.

Kett pushed down hard on Ell's stomach, biting her lower lip and watching a thick stream of cum flow from between her stretched legs.

224

Beneath her paws, the fox felt the leopard turn and thrash within the antelope. Ell let out a low groan, a single long breath of pleasure, her entire body subsuming into bliss as the creature pulled her hips wide, her belly throbbing and clenching in waves. A white hot point of sensation speared through the fog in her mind, her thoughts fixating on the burning pressure within her hips. Kett pressed down hard on the swollen belly and Ell screamed, feeling her pussy stretch and fill from within, legs pulled taut and shifting further outward under the creature's unrelenting grip. Ell's slit gaped open and cum poured out in thick streams, pulsing as her body convulsed.

Ell thrashed as she orgasmed, body wracked by powerful waves running down her spine and through her core, mind exploding in uncomprehending pleasure. Her groin throbbed and the creature pulled at her legs, spreading her hips wide and distorting her pliable body. The antelope's pussy widened, spurts of cum seeping from her gaping hole until Kett pushed down with the bulk of her weight. Ell's mouth hung open in a silent scream, eyes clamped shut as the leopard's head slid with aching slowness through her tortured pussy. Her entrance spread wider and the creature pulled at her ankles, opening her pussy an inch at a time, distorting her lower body until her passage gaped wide enough for the former master's cum-drenched head to slide from her flesh. Ell shook helplessly and shouted before inhaling and holding her breath, white hot pressure filling her entire universe. Kett pushed down and watched as the leopard's head surged forward, finding a place to grip through Ell's stretched skin and pushing toward her pussy, forcing the feline's shoulders through Ell's helpless body in a single rough movement. The antelope trembled as her orgasm renewed itself, unending waves slamming through her entire being. Kett and the creature bore down in unison, pulling against Ell's legs and pushing on the leopard, shoving his entire torso through her distorted pussy. Ell screamed and bucked against her restraints and the world, the single point of pressure detonating into an explosion of euphoria.

The leopard floundered, half-conscious, as his hips pulled from Ell's pussy, cum flooding from the gaping hole around his thighs. Haxiten's elbows found the ground and he slid himself backward, struggling against the antelope's clenching muscles and freeing himself in a daze, removing one hindpaw and then the other before collapsing flat against the ground, breathing heavily. Ell's body quickly resumed its taut form, hips pulling back once the creature released its grip. The antelope lay motionless, eyes shut and chest heaving, echoes of intense waves of orgasm coursing through her mind. Haxiten lay motionless on his back, drenched in cum, unaware of his transformation.

Kett immediately lunged forward and grabbed the leopard's ankles. Extending her tentacles, the fox wrapped around his legs and feet, pulling the former master's hips up and wrapping his ankles down toward his head, his cum-slick ass up in the air. Haxiten's feline cock pointed down at his own face, his sack lying down along the underside of his shaft to reveal his dripping new pussy folds. Kett didn't hesitate for a moment, gripping her throbbing cock and pointing the tapered tip down at the leopard's slit, squeezing her tentacles tight against his ankles and thighs before plunging her thick shaft into the unfucked hole. The leopard's eyes shot open, the sudden alien sensation blistering through his consciousness. He clenched his pussy against Kett's rod, flexing his entire body and thrashing against her tentacles. The fox gripped her paws around Haxiten's hips and wound her slimy cords around his entire body, fixing him firmly in place and thrusting roughly. Kett bucked her hips down against the leopard's tight slit, gasping in glee as she watched his eyes bulge in confusion and pleasure, her balls slapping against his ass.

226

Marshal let out a gruff pant as Alan's shaft throbbed within his cumhole. The canine slammed his hips forward and buried himself in the horse cock, gripping both paws against the equine flesh and squeezing, putting pressure on his own rod within. Using Marshal's long member as a tight cock sleeve, Alan stroked his paws forward and back, dragging the horse's shaft along his thick length, bringing himself closer to the brink as the horse moaned helplessly. Marshal's legs quivered weakly and Alan jacked himself roughly with the horse meat, grunting and slamming the tight hole against his thick knot, pre cum dripping out and covering the canine cock. Alan grunted, mouth hanging open, panting heavily as tension grew in his swollen balls. The husky squeezed tight and yanked the horse flesh over his rod, pushing his hips forward and groaning aloud as the cumhole spread wide, sliding with aching tightness over the fat bulb of Alan's knot. Marshal's cock flesh yielded to the pressure and stretched wide, Alan's knot bulging the end of his shaft out into a swollen sphere locked around the canine rod. Immediately Alan threw his head back and howled, body erupting and spraying searing cum down into Marshal's long rod. The horse shook and drooled weakly against the ground, feeling the seed flood into his flesh, running through his veins. In a hurried instant, the creature's slime crawled up the horse's face and legs, creeping over his back and hips until he was wrapped in a tight cocoon, the last spurts of Alan's load draining into Marshal's body as the canine pulled back roughly and popped his knot from his stretched cumhole, a final rope of seed splashing against his ooze-covered ass.

Léo and the badger slammed their hips against the twin otters, the four panting in unison. Each otter pressed their faces toward their twins' new pussies, clamping their lips against their partner's clits as thick cocks filled their tight holes. Mind blurry with new sensation, the badger thrashed against her otter servant, slamming her rod into the sopping wet slit and slapping her balls against his ass. The badger leaned forward and Léo met her halfway, pressing their lips together and exhaling hotly into each others' mouths. Léo felt the otter squeeze in strong pulses against his tentacle cock, his slick member thrashing and corkscrewing within his fresh hole. The mouse and badger pressed their tongues against each other and slammed their rods into the twins, pressure building within their balls with every passing moment. Léo groaned, digging his delicate claws into the otter's thin hips, and the badger leaned forward and bit the mouse's tongue. The badger and mouse hilted themselves in unison, crying out into each other's mouths as they came, pulling their hips tight against the otters' tight holes and draining themselves. The otters cried out at once, arching their backs and pressing back against the cocks buried in their passages, clenching down as waves of orgasm surged through their minds, feeling thick spurts of cum splashing into their bodies. The four shouted and pressed tight against each other, frozen in bliss as pulses of hot seed slammed into the otters' transformed flesh.

Kett grit her teeth and slammed into Haxiten's pussy, squeezing every inch of his cum-drenched body with her strong tentacles. She wrapped a tendril around his throat and pulled his ankles down, thrusting with all her strength and bending him back on himself with every movement. The leopard's cock throbbed, hanging free in the air just above his face, dripping the creature's load onto his cheeks and into his mouth. Kett bore down and pummeled the feline's pussy, bringing her swollen knot against his quivering entrance with every ferocious thrust. Haxiten's cock inched closer to his open jaws every time the fox brought her weight down on his hips. Kett squeezed each of her tentacles and flexed every muscle in her body, growling to herself through bared teeth, fucking his clenching pussy with every ounce of her alien might. Finally Kett held her breath and bucked her hips forward, burying her thick knot in the leopard's pussy, slamming deep with a rapid pop, crying out as she unloaded herself in the former master's flesh. Haxiten shouted in surprise, eyes wide as his mind lit up, the thick swell on Kett's knot filling his focus as he orgasmed. The leopard's mouth hung open in shock and bliss, and he clenched his pussy hard on Kett's rod. The sensation of cum pouring into his fresh pussy put him over the edge, and Haxiten's cock burst and sprayed its own load onto the leopard's face, blasting into his open mouth, forcing him to swallow desperately and mindlessly at his own seed. Kett watched in cool blissful satisfaction as the leopard gulped down his cum, licking his lips without a second thought, her load still coursing into his passage in powerful surges until her body was truly drained.

Panting in the afterglow of an evening of insanity, Kett looked up and watched as several party guests slid down the slick crocodile gullet and into the pool of water in the center of the room. She could feel the leopard's heartbeat pulse against her cock as color returned to her vision, some small portion of the fog lifting from her mind. Partier after partier splashed into the water, one by one, noble and servant alike. Some figures were pulled from the water and dragged along the ground before the creature found an empty spot on the wall or ceiling, affixing them to the slime and covering their bodies, invading their flesh and drawing moans and gasps from the wanting men and women. The underground space filled with figures and sound, the dim torchlight barely illuminating the immobile guests.

Kett pulled herself from the leopard and left him to collapse on himself. The creature pulsed and throbbed in untold pleasure, the slime on the floor reaching out to caress the fox as she walked toward the water. Upon reaching the ledge of the pool, Kett spun on her heels and gazed upon Alan's dazed figure, and then Léo's. Smiling, she spread her arms wide and fell backward into the water. Floating on the surface of the pool, Kett closed her eyes and heard the creature's thoughts. Warmth penetrated her body, the creature's every sensation pouring into her mind. With a contented sigh, Kett let her mind drift to sleep, caressed by the ebb and flow of desire and lust, and simply felt.

\